The Union of Shadows

Emma Bradley

NOTHING IS AS IT SEEMS IN THE SHADOWS

DEDICATION

For those who wanted more, and for Katina, Alison and Emma
at #ukteenchat who helped put the eventual idea in my head,
thus putting me on this absolutely mad journey back into Faerie.

CHAPTER ONE
KAINEN

In Faerie, anything can happen. But for Kainen Hemlock, Lord of the Court of Illusions, waiting for his past to crash land into the present was like waiting for a cart with a runaway horse.

He stood in the main hall of his court with his foot tapping an irritated rhythm on the rocky floor. He was ready to welcome the royal family of Faerie and had spared no effort to create a welcoming atmosphere. He'd had an abundance of mood lighting installed to brighten up the under-mountain halls he called home, and even had sky-holes hewn into the ceiling of the main hall.

It wouldn't be the Oak Queen Tavania visiting either, but the entourage of the Holly Queen Demerara. After the torment she'd experienced in his halls during the war almost a year ago, he wanted to make her feel as comfortable as their past would allow. If he could show that he was overturning the old ways of his court, those of his father's time and briefly his also, she might one day forgive him.

It would be painful to see her and he guessed calling her Demi would be overstepping the mark now that she'd been crowned. He hadn't seen her since the Battle of Queens, except a few times in passing in the hallways at Arcanium, the headquarters for the FDPs that took on assignments in

Faerie. Each time he even looked at her, her king consort Taz seemed to be there glaring right back at him. Once Prince of Faerie in his own right, Taz was by all accounts the perfect choice to stand at Demi's side.

Kainen had escaped back to his court after the battle with his dignity mostly intact, glad of a chance to leave Arcanium behind and take up his role as Lord of Illusions.

But that meant it was his job to host Demerara, Taz and also Lady Blossom, Taz's sister, who was being brought along for a meet and greet as his potential future bride.

Collaboration between the courts one day, and I'm being married off to a princess who probably fought alongside the enemy the next.

His insides crushed tight at the thought of Lady Blossom, who had once been a friend of his. He slid his hand into the pocket of his black jeans to hide his clenching fist, determined not to show all the gossip-hungry fae gathered for the occasion exactly how unsettled he was.

No doubt everyone would think a union between him and Blossom was fitting considering he'd originally been on the enemy's side too. But as for Demi, he had no idea what she'd think about any of it. Even when she'd considered herself his friend and he'd hoped for much more than that, her thoughts had been a mystery to him.

Perhaps that was why he'd loved her, and why even the mere thought of her coming back to his court set his nerves on edge. Because she was a fairy without any known fae blood, and the girl who had fought and earned her role as queen so young and in such a short time. Even more unnervingly, she'd always been somewhat immune to his mind-reading and compulsion gifts.

Etiquette dictated that he summoned his court to welcome her as his guest, but their presence gave him extra excuse to put on the routine mask of indifference he usually wore. A casual smile here, a wink or a joke there, and he was who everyone knew him to be. Fears that Demi would see through him bounded around his head all the same.

The gathered crowd stood in varying stages of boredom, but he noticed there were several members who looked excited. Even for Faerie's ruthless social elite, a visit from one of the queens wasn't an everyday thing. Several members of the court had donned expensive dresses or suits, revelling in any excuse to flaunt their excess. He never insisted any of his court staff wore uniforms though, so several of them were dotted around in casual clothing. Meri, his second-in-command, had insisted that as lord of the court, he should wear charcoal-coloured jeans with a ripple of silver sheen and a matching silk shirt. He'd conceded but rolled up the sleeves and undone the top buttons the moment she left the room.

He flinched as a shiver filled the main hall and the air rippled in front of him. One moment he stood waiting, and the next he stood facing the Faerie royalty that had realm-skipped into his court.

Queen Demerara and King Consort Taz stood before him, both looking more like two people out for a day trip than rulers of the Faerie realms. Whispers began to rustle through the crowd as they took in their regent's baggy jeans and her *Demon Babies* hoodie that was definitely not a new one given the thumb holes in the cuffs. Her wild black curls were brushed back from her face, but the bright blue eyes were exactly the same as he remembered. Piercing sharp and twice as watchful.

The king consort didn't look much more formal, although his jeans were tucked into extremely polished black boots. While the queen surveyed the crowd, the king consort gave the gawking spectators a cheerful wave.

If the queen noticed the improvements, her expression didn't brighten at the sight of them. Kainen pushed the swell of disappointment deep down underneath the fluttering nerves at having to face her.

Better nervous than sad. I can do this.

Another ripple disturbed the otherwise silent air before he could approach. This time there was no mistaking who had arrived. Lady Blossom stood before him, Princess of Faerie, daughter of Queen Tavania and pain in the behind to all who'd had the misfortune to deal with her.

His intended bride.

Unlike the queen and king consort, Lady Blossom had a collection of guards and servants flanking her and fussing quietly, one even petting down an invisible stray lock of blonde hair.

Formal mode it is then.

He took a couple of necessary steps forward and dropped to one knee in front of the group.

"Welcome, my queen."

He stayed bowing until the briefest flash of her hand flickered in his line of vision, a command to rise. Next he faced the king consort. Taz looked no different, his curly honey brown hair unruly and his turquoise eyes sharp.

Kainen bowed low, the proper respect for one chosen to stand alongside a queen. He expected Taz to make some cutting remark given their past but none came. With much more practiced ease, Kainen faced Lady Blossom last.

While she was a princess, he was leader of a court and she was not, so she received a polite head bob and a roguish smile. When she returned the attention with pleasure but absolutely no warmth in her eyes, he risked kissing her hand.

After a quick glance up he stepped back, assessing the young woman that the queens apparently thought his equal. But while Lady Blossom was faeishly pretty, Queen Demerara stole the room, and he couldn't stop his gaze going back to her.

She looked absolutely ravishing. Her dark curls flickered with oil-slick shimmers of colour, her pale-skinned beauty chilly and distant like the winter holly element she now embodied, her beauty effortless.

Kainen waited for the inevitable pangs that came with seeing her, the longing and residual stab of bitterness at her not returning his attentions. He expected the tumult of fear that she'd stare at him too long and see him flayed wide open, emotions burning. His desperation to convince her somehow to be his instead would overcome him again.

He took a breath to begin welcoming them and introducing them to the court, but hesitated.

Not a single quiver. Nerves sure, but no burning insides, no desire to catch her glance, to share something secret just for them.

Have I stopped loving her already?

Realising everyone was staring at him, royals and court alike, he pasted on a smile.

"Welcome to you and yours, my queen," he began. "I hope you will find your stay here enjoyable."

He managed to refrain from adding 'this time' after what had happened to her here before. He also couldn't hope the changes would live up to her expectations, although those weren't likely to be favourable either. He might at least achieve 'passable' if she was determined to judge him.

When she frowned, he tensed. He hadn't ruled out this visit being some kind of humiliation trip for her, vengeance for the past. It wasn't her style but then how well had he really known her in the end?

"The past is done, Kainen." Even when she said his name, he no longer felt fizzles of excitement like he used to. "While we're visiting your court, call me Demi at my request." She smiled wickedly then, a flash of the girl he remembered. "Taz might still make you call him by title though."

Kainen risked a smile. Even then he expected some feeling to pass through him as a ripple of laughter travelled the crowd, anything to hint that there was still some kind of unrequited passion or yearning for this girl.

None came.

Only relief, as if his feelings had faded and now all he had was the memory of them, an imprint of shadow cast in a faraway light.

Taz gave Demi a weary look. "Taz is fine, the past is

the past."

It sounded rehearsed and Kainen held in a derisive snort with valiant effort. Demi turned again to see the room where she'd experienced so much torment before and Taz took the opportunity to give Kainen a dark look, trustless and full of warning.

"You've made some improvements," Demi said, her voice quiet.

'Improvements' was an accolade coming from her.

A throat cleared nearby and Kainen turned his attentions dutifully to Lady Blossom. One quick once over, a flashing glimpse into her mind with his gift, and he knew she was as ruthless as he remembered from fleeting days of childhood. Although she smiled prettily, her lashes were artfully lowered and her mouth curved with the kind of fake innocence that could only be manipulative. No doubt she was eying him up with every intention of eventually taking over his court. Perhaps she intended to eventually challenge either her mother or Demi for a queenship.

I can't be lumbered with her.

It wouldn't work. They'd end up killing each other and he'd had enough of torment and death.

A flash of uneasiness passed over Demi's face as she looked from Blossom to Kainen. The look suggested this wasn't her decision, which made him feel ever so slightly better.

"You two might want to organise some time to get acquainted," Demi suggested. "Or reacquainted."

Kainen barely heard her, aware that Blossom was trying to have a staring contest with him now. In her eyes he could see his whole life mapped out, dribbling away from him like it had when he was under his father's thumb.

He panicked, the sudden roar in his mind urging him to flee, even from his own court. The words tumbled out of his mouth without his brain intervening, fuelled on pure instinct.

"Apologies, but I fear that would be improper." He laid the formal wording on thick, knowing what he was about to do next would cost him dearly no matter what way he cut it. "Although there are always potential changes in the future, I'm already currently promised elsewhere."

He hoped it was enough of an attempt at word-tangling not to count as a lie. He was promised elsewhere, to his court. And if he put his court first, marrying Lady Blossom would definitely be in conflict with that considering how ruthless and self-centred she was.

Demi might ask where he was promised and then he would have to fib, something Fae only did at horrible cost to their souls.

Shock rippled through the crowd, the buzz of frantic conversation filling the air. His court knew nothing of this and they were horrified to have missed it as gossip.

Blossom's eyes narrowed. "What's this? I've been dragged away from other pursuits for nothing? Insolence! I'll have you whipped for lying to me, for leading me on!"

Nobody paid attention to the threats while she flourished the drama around, but as Demi and Taz looked at each other in confusion, Kainen frantically scanned the crowd.

He needed someone from his court to pretend, someone

who couldn't betray him or say no. Demi and Taz were only here for a couple of days so it could work. It had to be someone believable but sworn to the court so that they couldn't disobey him if he ordered them to pretend.

A few faces stood out from the crowd, all with merits and pitfalls. And every single one of them would be hoping for social or financial advancement as much as Blossom was. Every person in the room and the court would use him for their own ends if it suited them.

His gaze landed on a young woman cloaked in shadow. Her shoulder-length blonde hair was tied back with a smoky grey ribbon, but the rest of her was obscured by the darkness that played across her body, the shadows of the room rolling toward her. She was paying attention to the scene but carelessly, almost as though she knew it would make little difference to one so far out of the social loop as she was.

Reyan. Kainen forced himself not to smile. *She'd be a perfect pretend bride.*

"You're promised to someone else?" Demi clarified. "Already? Who? And why didn't anyone bother to tell me anything about this?"

Kainen kept his gaze on Reyan and let the tiniest element of his compulsion gift drift behind his desire for her to lift her head and look his way. The compulsion weaved its magic and she glanced at him. When she noticed that his gaze was fixed on her, she shook her head as realisation widened her eyes.

He would apologise later. He'd offer her anything she wanted. Even the one thing she coveted above all else, if he could.

Kainen faced Demi, a strange mix of embarrassment and mortification washing hot over his skin.

"It's rather a recent thing," he said, not a lie because technically his decision to strong-arm one of his court into pretending to be his bride was brand new. "I think you know Reyan Roseglade?"

He held out his hand in Reyan's direction without daring to look her way. Somehow, looking at Demi was now less stressful than facing Reyan, who had a sharp tongue when she needed it. She and Demi had met and dealt with each other briefly before, but they weren't friends so Demi wouldn't know her mannerisms to detect if something was unusual.

Reyan couldn't disobey him either because she was sworn to his court, bound to do his bidding. As the crowd parted to let her through, he guessed she was going to absolutely slaughter him for this. He forced himself to meet her gaze and gulped at the sheer bewildered panic burning in her shadowy hazel-grey eyes.

CHAPTER TWO
REYAN

What absolute humiliation.

When Reyan heard Kainen call her forward, she couldn't quite believe it. But it was definitely her name that tumbled past his lips and definitely her gaze he found now. Rueful apology lingered behind the schooled mask of lordly expectation on his face, but the command was there and she couldn't disobey. Literally couldn't even if she tried to.

He stood there in his fancy clothing with his dark brown hair swept back behind his ears and every essence of his being screaming that he was exactly where he was supposed to be: lording it over everyone else.

Her cheeks burned with embarrassment and she risked a glance around. The entire court seemed to have turned out to welcome the queen but they were muttering now. People she worked with every day but wasn't friends with were whispering and giving her evil looks.

I have to be obedient. She took a couple of steps forward. *I can't disobey a direct command, and I can't risk him sending me back to my father. At least here I'm only used for laundry and kitchen duty, and the odd performance.*

Her father would use her for worse if money ran dry. Being tied in service to the Court of Illusions and Kainen had its benefits, but she would one day find her escape.

Pretending to be his future bride really wasn't what I had in mind though.

As she approached the group, Lady Blossom looked her up and down, a curl on her lip and vicious intent gleaming in her eyes.

"Does she have to be announced, this future bride of yours?" Blossom asked. "Where's your mistress, girl?"

Reyan ignored the suggestion she was a servant to Kainen's intended person rather than the person herself, because technically a servant is what she was. She stood before royalty wearing ragged leggings suitable for cleaning in, an oversized sweatshirt and scuffed boots. When Queen Demerara turned toward her, Reyan felt distinctly underdressed as she dropped to one knee.

"My queen," she said.

A royal hand appeared in her line of sight and retreated again, a signal to get up.

"We're friends. Call me Demi, please."

Reyan lifted her head then and rose to her feet, a shy smile sneaking onto her face. She couldn't help it as the muttering around them intensified. That'd be doing the gossip rounds next, that perhaps Kainen was using her for influence with the queen if they were friends already. She did as she was meant to, bowing to Taz next. But a tingle of rebellion shot through her and she returned her attention to Demi instead of acknowledging Lady Blossom. Kainen could tell her off and force obedience if he had to, but she wouldn't show deference by choice.

Demi's lips twitched at the sleight, but she didn't insist

on Reyan remembering her manners and Kainen didn't either.

Perhaps he doesn't dare right now. I can't kill him because I'm sworn to his court, but I'm going to get him back for this somehow.

"This is what you've chosen to marry?" Blossom didn't take the sleight well. "She looks like someone skinned a rat and put a wig on it."

More muttering from the crowd, some of it unashamedly gleeful. Reyan held herself tall and refused to be cowed by the cruelty, but her cheeks flared with embarrassment. Demi's eyes narrowed at the insult but Taz was rolling his, clearly used to his sister's vile behaviour.

"Do you have rooms for us?" Demi asked Kainen, her tone sharp. "It would be a good idea to see the rest of the court, but we'll freshen up first. Then clearly the four of us have some catching up to do."

Kainen smiled, his dark eyes dancing. Reyan knew him well enough; he couldn't insult Lady Blossom as his guest, but he'd recognised Demi's decision to leave her out of the catching up invitation.

He nodded. "Of course, follow me. I have the new queen's quarters prepared for you both, and for Lady Blossom I thought something with a bit more space and tradition would suit."

Reyan almost scoffed out loud.

Oh, he's smooth when he wants to be.

Blossom seemed to forget the situation as he pandered to her and gave her his warmest, most disarming smile. She would of course be planning her own underhanded schemes, but no doubt playing along in sight of the crowds suited her better right now than throwing a tantrum.

"Ciel!" He clicked his fingers as he called out. "Please escort Lady Blossom to the Ardia suite."

With Lady Blossom palmed off onto Kainen's oldest friend, that left Reyan to follow him with the others. She could have melted into the shadows, but her merging gift was contained when not performing. While she could call the shadows to her still, she couldn't use them to hide in. Kainen could release her gift when he chose, but no doubt right now he'd be keeping a tight rein on any ability she had to flee.

As they climbed the sweeping stone staircase leading up to the court's accommodation wing, the main hall exploded in a burst of furious muttering.

The noise followed them as they walked a few moments down the hall and stopped outside a set of double doors.

"The queen's quarters," Kainen said.

He opened both doors with a flourish, the mahogany wood inlaid with veins painted white, red and green. Reyan peered past him and gasped, aware of Demi doing the same beside her.

The room was larger than any Reyan had seen, big enough to host a ball in. The walls had been strategically decorated with ivory to lighten the effect, the floor also. In the middle of the room, a bathing pool had been hewn into the ground. There were no other doors besides the entrance, a touch of devilry in the design that suggested privacy wasn't an option without putting your head under the bedcovers.

The rest of the room had been adorned with berry red and dark evergreen, the queen's court colours. Reyan couldn't imagine being able to relax in such extravagance, but when she glanced at Demi, she wasn't looking at the room. Her gaze was stuck on a different door on the opposite side of the hallway.

"Dem?" Taz noticed immediately, shoving both Reyan and Kainen aside to give her space.

She shook her head. "It's fine."

He opened his mouth, no doubt to argue, but Demi gave him a look.

"It's fine. At least we know where to find you when we're done."

Reyan realised then, because of course the queen's quarters were directly opposite Kainen's own rooms. Rumours had spread around the court that Demi was once destined to be Lady of it before she'd been crowned queen, but Reyan had seen more than they had, and she knew Demi shared no love for Kainen whatsoever.

Given the way he looked at her though when she arrived, he's still halfway in love with her.

Which would make the whole 'fake' part of Kainen's manipulation easier for both of them, not that she was planning to let him get away with using her lightly.

She shuffled backwards so that Demi and Taz could enter their room and shut the door behind them. Whatever conversation the queen and king consort were about to have, it would pale in comparison to the agony she was about to unleash.

"You couldn't have told them earlier and saved them

the journey?" she hissed.

Kainen grabbed her elbow and pulled her across the hall toward his bedroom door. Reyan shook him off, storming past him into the room. She had no fear of him, but he was her lord and she was sworn to his court, so kicking his extremities clean off was unfortunately out of the question.

Unlike the queen's quarters, his room was bare rock and wooden floorboards stained dark with deep green furnishings. None of the grandeur cowed her raging fury. She waited while he shut the door and faced her.

"I'm sorry." He gave her a sheepish smile as though that absolved him of everything. "I panicked."

She folded her arms, gearing up.

"There are hundreds of willing sycophants out there begging for your favour, so why pick me?!"

"Because you're not a willing sycophant and therefore my chances of being used or fallen for by you are slim."

"You've got that right." She glared at him. "So what, I'm supposed to pretend to be your future bride? We can't lie!"

Kainen moved across the room and slid onto the jewel green sofa in the centre. He lounged as though he hadn't absentmindedly screwed up the next two days of her routine without a second thought, and she had the urge to stalk over and throttle him. The winding band of shadows around her wrist, her mark of being sworn to his court and his service, wouldn't let her harm him. It might let her school him a tiny bit in manners though, for his own good of course.

Without answering her, Kainen kicked off his boots,

hooked one ankle over his knee and pulled his sock off with a forefinger. She stared in horror as he pinged it across the room.

"Sorry, is that supposed to be some kind of intimidation tactic to get me to comply?" she asked.

He raised his eyebrows. "Is it working?"

"No! I can't injure you but trust me, if I weren't sworn to this court, your ears would be ringing right now."

He had the gall to laugh.

"Reyan, it's two days. Demi will want to speak to you no doubt, but we can keep you busy with other things, a fake wedding if need be. We're planning to host the Marrowblades next month, so you can word-tangle about their event as if it's ours instead."

Reyan threw up her hands and raised her gaze to the ceiling in torment.

"I literally can't say no obviously. But you… no, I can't even tell you that you owe me for this because you own my service. Fine. But if I happen to slip, and you end up married to that smacked-face princess, it'd serve you right."

Kainen's dark eyes glittered with amusement, his fingertips drumming soft, slow beats on the back of the sofa.

"You know, I really think you mean that."

Reyan rolled her eyes, her anger calming. She needed a way out of his service and her father's debt that kept her tied to the court. Angering Kainen might keep his interest for a while, but she couldn't cross any boundaries and risk becoming a nuisance that he might then choose to sell on to someone else. He also might decide to punish her by never setting her free. Or worse, start taking more of an interest in her.

"I do mean it." She sighed. "What orders then, am I supposed to wait here for the queen to fetch me to talk about- I don't even know what these high-born people talk about. Crowns?"

Kainen started laughing then, his shoulders shaking. She hadn't seen him relax in a while now that she thought about it. Often before the war he was charm personified, but then he'd been stressed before and during. After the war, the court had taken all of his time and attention. The days where he used to drink with his noble friends and be seen enjoying himself at revels seemed a distant memory now.

"Demi isn't high-born," he reminded her. "She's a fairy who was raised by humans. Talk to her about whatever you want, but at least try to convince her you're happy here."

"What part of I can't lie don't you understand?"

The words shot out so fast and with so much vehemence on instinct that Kainen blinked, surprised. Reyan wished she could claw them back but a knock on the door broke through their silent stare-off.

Kainen didn't move an inch so Reyan huffed at him and went to answer the door. He might be a court lord and she might be sworn to his service, but she wouldn't give him an easy run either way.

She threw the door open and fixed a smile on her face. Demi blinked back at her, the hesitation lingering before both of them laughed. Taz appeared at Demi's side and peered into the room over Reyan's shoulder.

"Are you sharing a room before the wedding?" He grinned wickedly. "That is fast."

Demi elbowed him in the ribs with a good-natured grumble, but Reyan tensed as the shadows warned her of Kainen's approach. Her shadow-weaver gift allowed her not only to dissipate into the shadows and travel by them, but to use them as a sense of sorts, similar to bees having a hive mind. That was the only reason she didn't flinch when his hand landed on her shoulder and the warmth of him loomed at her back.

"Reyan is staying with me," he said.

Vague enough that the statement could mean in the room, at the court or forever.

What else should one expect from a lord of illusions, trickery and secrets?

"Against her will, or...?" Taz left the statement hanging there.

Reyan realised he was giving her a chance to answer, to confess if Kainen was forcing her. Any reluctance or refusal to answer on her part would as good as confirm it. Technically, Kainen *was* forcing her, but then it was only two days and she could more than handle him. She could make her own decision to play nice for that long, then it wouldn't exactly be by force. Besides, staying in his room or sequestered somewhere else secretive would be quieter and more comfortable than being in the dorm with everyone else.

"No, of course not," she said. "Trust me, everything I do is my own choice one way or another."

Demi grinned. "I knew I liked you. Are you bored of wedding talk already? I know I am and we're not even anywhere near that yet. Countless relatives, all his, asking when we're getting married and when the little heirs are going to be along and who will inherit my crown if I mysteriously disappear and there aren't any heirs yet."

In that easy flow of speech, Demi not only managed to dismiss her queen status, but make Reyan feel entirely at ease with her as though they were equals.

"We host weddings here sometimes for our court," she admitted, word-tangling as best she could to avoid the subject of her own supposed nuptials. "It's nice but the crowds and drama always gets a bit much for me. Is there something you want to be doing now? Conscious we're still standing in a doorway."

Demi's gaze flicked to Kainen's face even as Taz reached for her hand in preparation. Reyan would have put a large sum of money, if she had any, on Taz being charged up to the hilt with ways of protecting the girl he loved.

Sweet really. A pang of discomfort hit her gut at the thought. *I wonder how that feels, having someone who loves you enough to do anything for you.*

"A tour then," Kainen suggested. Reyan fought the urge to pull a face as he slid his fingers around hers for all to see. "You can see what changes we've made."

He held out his free hand, indicating that Demi and Taz should go ahead of them down the hall.

I can't badly harm him. Then again, she knew that he sometimes joined the court guards at sparring practice. *I could probably get away with giving him a warning to behave, a little lesson to remind him to stay on his toes.*

The moment he shut his bedroom door and turned to follow them, she gave him a look.

In no uncertain terms, it meant 'you're in so much trouble'.

As did the savage lesson she 'accidentally' landed on his shin with her foot a second later.

CHAPTER THREE
KAINEN

The tour took hours and Kainen's feet were threatening mutiny if he walked as much as another step.

Reyan had seemed to sense that he was weary and on edge when they started, because she made sure Demi and Taz saw every single inch of the court, including the dining hall, the kitchens and even up to the library. Demi took everything in her stride, even the rooms that would hold bad memories for her, as Reyan powered on with boundless energy. Attention was dutifully paid to all of the recent changes, and Kainen almost congratulated himself when Reyan spoke of the improvements as if she approved of them. But of course she was angry at him, so he didn't get a single mention.

"Oh, the court is thriving."

"The whole court has worked so hard to fix this, mend that, get better at so many things."

"The court is so glad you're queen now."

Kainen had instigated most of the work and changes himself, but no matter. If the court thrived then by extension he was happy with the result.

By time they were back outside their rooms, Kainen reclaimed control for everyone's sake.

"Do you wish to dine with the court?" he asked Demi and Taz. "If not, you can request food be brought to you in your room."

Demi gave him a weary smile. "I think we'll stay in tonight after such an in-depth tour."

Even Reyan managed a rueful blush at that and Kainen smiled to see it. It had surprised him how proud she sounded about being part of the Court of Illusions, especially after what she'd said in his room about not being happy there. She wasn't exactly sworn to the court by choice either, which was something he as the lord should have given more attention to by now.

As Demi opened the door to the queen's quarters, Reyan was already turning to go in the direction of the dorms. Panicking about their pretence, Kainen held out a hand to her departing back.

"Come with me. We can get a quiet night in as well."

It was a command and her feet stumbled to a halt. Nobody sworn to the court could disobey a command he gave them, but reluctance to use that part of his title bubbled up all the same.

Taz's face dropped into an instant frown, suspicion swimming in his eyes, and Demi's face twisted with uncertainty.

After a moment of stillness, Reyan turned with a gentle laugh and the most natural smile on her face.

"Habit," she said. "Takes a while to adjust to the idea of sleeping somewhere different."

She strode past Kainen and pushed the door to his room open as if she truly belonged there. Bewildered because the door usually only opened at his command, he made sure Demi and Taz were retreating. Once they'd shut the bedroom door behind them, he took a deep breath in preparation before following Reyan into his bedroom.

She stood in the middle of the floor with her arms folded across her chest.

"I get you're not happy about this," he said. "But I had to pick someone."

"Why not one of your many courtiers? Or friends even? Surely someone else would have been happy to play lady for a while and earn your favour?" she demanded.

He pulled a face. "None I'd trust. I doubt anyone would believe me if I said Ciel and I were an item. Friends are a luxury even for a court lord."

"That's… surprisingly sad. Surely though you could have placated Lady Blossom for a few days then found some way out of it?"

Kainen frowned. The only thing worse than her anger was her pitying him. But she had a point.

"Do you really think Demi being here is about my arranged marriage? I admit I panicked, but even if I went along with it she'll be here for a deeper reason."

"What kind of reason?"

He wanted to sit down and shrug off some of the stress he'd been carrying for far too long now. Stress of running his court, of keeping those in his court amenable, of worrying about what the impending royal visit was really for. But Reyan seemed to be dominating an awful lot of his personal space and he found his feet rooted to the floor.

"I don't know." He had a fair idea, but nothing concrete yet. "There's been a startling amount of peace though since the war. I wouldn't be surprised if she wants to get our help with something."

Reyan's hostile gaze narrowed even further.

"And you expect me to help with that somehow?"

The thought hadn't occurred to him, but her shadow-merging gift would come in handy for the odd bit of snooping.

"I could do with not having to placate the person I'm pretending to marry," he admitted. "I clearly won't have to worry about you developing any kind of expectations."

Her eyes widened. "Orbs no. Eww. It's not like I can disobey either way I suppose."

The 'eww' was definitely uncalled for, but he couldn't blame her for lashing out.

"Fine. Ground rules." She didn't even give him a chance to protest. "I am not sleeping with you, not in *any* capacity. Summon another bed or have one brought in. If you snore, you sleep elsewhere, or I will."

She waited a moment to see if he was going to rebel, but when he didn't she pressed on, her glare pinning him in place like a naughty child.

"No crass jokes and no stupid innuendos. I accept you may need to hold my hand or something like that to make it seem realistic, but no kisses or anything gross."

He raised his eyebrows at that, the natural desire to taunt and play rising.

"Kisses are gross in general or only with me?"

She looked around the room. He wondered with surprising intrigue if she was searching for something to throw at him. In all the time he'd known her while she was at his court, she'd been quiet, but with more than enough fire to stand up for herself when she had to. Now he realised he'd been seeing her in the halls and at the court occasions as a girl, but she was eighteen the same as he was, fully grown and twice as daunting now that she stood glowering at him.

"With anyone at the moment. I'm sure with the right person, they're more than enjoyable." She paused just long enough to glare at him again. "And you are not the right person."

That was him told. He held up his hands in defence, sneaking past her and dropping onto the sofa as he tried to hide his smile.

This was going to be fun.

"It's only for two days," he reasoned. "I'll abide by your rules as best I can."

It was a pointless thing to say. He didn't have to abide by anything in his own court, but he'd honour what she wanted as long as it didn't jeopardise anything. Two days and they could return to normal. There might be some fall-out if the court found out it was all a sham, and Blossom would make it her mission to pulverise him and the court if she realised she'd been snubbed. But perhaps a quiet breaking up, some sobbing on Reyan's part, or his if he really had to, and all would go back to the way it was before.

He pulled off his socks and threw them over his shoulder. The best thing about court life was he didn't have to worry about cleaning things up. He only had to worry about making sure everything ran smoothly.

"Did you just throw your socks randomly on the floor?"

Reyan apparently didn't share his ideals about cleanliness.

He shrugged. "Yes, I did. And?"

She stood with her fingers twitching. He wondered if she maybe wanted to find some way of shoving them back in his face, but all too late he realised that she would no doubt be one of the court members who had to pick up after him.

"You're a pig," she muttered.

He twisted in time to see her pick up the offending socks between forefinger and thumb with a wrinkled look of disgust on her face.

"I am ruler of this court you know," he said, amused and also mildly insulted.

She snorted. "You're a pig, your Lordship."

She clicked her fingers and the socks vanished. Kainen hadn't put much thought into how things got done around the court, but he hadn't realised his staff could vanish things at will.

"Did you just vanish my socks?"

She turned to face him, her expression incredulous, along the lines of 'oh you cannot be this dim'.

"They don't teach you vanishing and summoning at Arcanium?" She frowned. "Vanishing is basically reverse summoning, you know."

Of course he knew. He'd learned vanishing and summoning when he was about nine years old, but he never had to worry where the stuff he vanished ended up. Reyan's face said it all, she both knew that fact and thought less of him for it.

"Of course I know how, but I didn't realise my staff did." He had to ask. "Where did you vanish them to?"

"Have you ever heard of a laundry?"

He rolled his eyes. "Okay, sweetheart, I get it."

She surveyed the room, as if looking for more mess to hold against him.

"No nicknames." She added to her rule list. "No pet names. No endearments."

Kainen shook his head, leaning forward to brace his arms on his knees.

"Not agreeing to that one. Demi knows me, so if I don't at least have one nickname for you she'll think it's odd."

It wasn't exactly a lie. He had no idea whether Demi would even remember that about him, but she wasn't the kind to forget things so he could assume well enough to believe it was true.

"This keeps getting worse." Reyan huffed loudly. "Fine, 'sweetheart' I can stomach. What do we do now then? Pretend to eat dinner like a cosy couple and get into matching beds with matching pjs?"

He shrugged. Getting into bed with her would be like going to sleep with a wolverine. She couldn't harm him what with her being court-sworn, but she might find all sorts of torturous ways to torment him as payback. His shin had smarted for ages after she kicked him.

Intrigued by the mere idea of tangling with her, he gave her a wicked grin.

"If you want. I usually do paperwork and things until late, but if you want me to tuck you in and match your pjs you only have to ask."

As she stalked away toward the bathroom door, he heard the furious muttering under her breath which contained several uncomplimentary titles for him.

"So you can have nicknames for me, but I can't have any for you?" he called after her. "Unfair!"

He was rewarded by the sound of the bathroom door slamming. Settling back against the sofa, he clicked his fingers. A curl of glittering black smoke obscured his hand.

"Food for two to my room," he said. Then, remembering what Reyan had said about the whole sock thing, he added, "please."

The fact that whoever he was speaking to in the court kitchens sounded startled at the mere sound of pleasantry didn't bode well.

I'm kind to people aren't I? He knew he was at least preferable to his more traditional father, who'd seen torturing the staff as sport. *Reyan clearly doesn't think so. Is that what everyone says behind my back?*

The tide of friendlessness washed over him. He was used to having allies and acquaintances rather than friends. He'd envied Demi and Taz that, even though he'd never admit it. Wherever they went they endeared themselves to people. Demi was popular with most of the FDPs at Arcanium, and rumour had it she was a firm favourite at most of the other courts already. Taz, when he wasn't being a protective arse, could charm and joke with the best of them.

The only friend Kainen had was Ciel, and if the opportunity came for Ciel to better his own fortune or further his family's agendas, he would take it without looking back.

I know that's exactly why he stays as well, because his family wants power and influence and he's their best route in.

"I'll go to the kitchens and sort food for tonight." Reyan's voice made him jump. "I suppose not having to eat in the hall with the others is a tiny luxury all things considered."

So deep in morose thought, Kainen hadn't even heard her sneak up behind him.

"You're very light on your feet," he grumbled.

"Well, I can't use my shadow gift because you bound it, but that doesn't mean I have to stomp around like an elephant."

Kainen let that slide. His father had insisted on having her power bound, otherwise she'd probably use the first opportunity to flee. He hadn't given any thought to it since taking over the court either, but rumour was that she hoped to one day dodge the debt that her father had raised against her.

"I've ordered food already," he said.

"Presumptuous of you to assume you know what I can eat."

She was right of course. He hadn't considered she might have eating restrictions, but something told him that she was merely biting back, punishing him for making her do this.

"Do you want me to make changes?" He raised his hand, fingers ready to contact the kitchens.

"No."

Reyan hovered nearby as if afraid to take a seat beside him. Irritated, Kainen snapped his fingers and summoned an armchair for her, dark green velvet to match the sofa. He half-expected a grateful look, but she had all the grace of a lady as she walked across to it without so much as a smile or a glance in his direction.

He summoned a second bed next, placing it a respectful distance from his own. The use of his gifts in the safety of his court calmed him and allowed some of the restless energy to settle.

"You can go get on with whatever you need to do," Reyan suggested after an excruciating pause. "I'll stay right here until the food arrives."

Kainen raised his eyebrows. "And what will you do right there?"

"Does that matter? You go into your study and do whatever."

It did matter but he couldn't work out why. Sullen at how hostile she was being, and the fact she was essentially trying to dismiss him from his own room, he drummed his fingertips on the arm of the sofa.

"I'll wait here."

She rolled her eyes in annoyance. "Why?"

Because it's my room? Because it's my court to do with as I see fit? Because you ordering me around like you're my girlfriend or my equal is infuriating, and the only thing it makes me want to do is the opposite?

A knock came at the door then, saving him from descending into childish baiting.

"That's why," he said, his voice a note too triumphant.

He strode to the door and threw it open, but it wasn't the food he was expecting on the other side.

"Oh." Demi took a step back. "Reyan said she hadn't read any *Carrie's Castle* yet so I brought her the first one to borrow."

She held out a book, the edges buffed and the pages yellowing. Kainen took it.

"Thanks." A strain of devilish mischief swelled and he shouted over his shoulder. "Demi's brought you a book, sweetheart."

Reyan was at his side in an instant, but of course she grabbed the book then ignored him completely.

"Thanks!" She beamed at Demi. "I'll take good care of it I promise."

Kainen smiled to see the wholly natural shine in her hazel-grey eyes, such delight at the mere thought of a simple book. He didn't have any fiction in the court library, although he loved reading old histories of Faerie and various accounts of other people's gifts when he could.

"You should look at getting some proper stories in that library of yours," Demi told him.

Although the door to the queen's quarters was open, Taz wasn't at her side. A sign of fragile trust perhaps. Or more likely Demi's time as queen meant she could pulverise anyone who tested her on the spot if she chose and didn't need a guard dog.

Kainen almost flinched when he dragged his gaze away from the queen's quarters and found Reyan staring wickedly back at him.

"He doesn't have time for reading anything other than

ancient histories," she said, as if she knew him inside out already. "Let me guess, fiction is a waste of time when you can conjure any illusion you choose."

He frowned, pained by the blunt but accurate assessment.

"Not a waste of time. More a pointless escape. Why dwell in other people's dreams when I can make my own?"

Reyan snorted, Demi forgotten.

"So you only take interest in what you want to see and don't give a damn about how other people see things? Figures."

They were straying perilously close to an argument and, while Reyan might have forgotten Demi standing there, Kainen hadn't. He pressed a warning hand against her waist, his gaze locked onto hers.

"Sweetheart, you know me too well. But that's hopefully what you like about me."

She couldn't lie to that, but she didn't need to. Instead she flushed bright red, at the hand on her waist or the nickname he couldn't tell.

Demi was already halfway across the hall, a broad smirk on her face.

"I'll leave you two to whatever this is," she said. "Have a good night, but we'll need to discuss things in the morning. There's an issue brewing at one of the other courts I could use your help with. Not too early please."

Her door shut behind her before either of them could answer. Seconds passed. Kainen's fingers still lingering on Reyan's waist tingled, a warning perhaps that she was going to-

"Ouch!" He hissed as she stamped on his foot. "That was unnecessary."

She stalked back into his room and he closed the door before following her into the middle of the floor.

"No more kicking or stamping." He anticipated the opening of her mouth. "No slapping, punching or biting either. No gouging, clawing or spitting."

Her eyes widened then. "Why in the name of Faerie would I spit at you? That's disgusting. I don't know how you were raised, but even in my childhood hell I wasn't dragged up that badly!"

He folded his arms, staring at her. If he backed down now, he had a scary notion she'd take full advantage of it. He was already giving her allowances out of guilt that he'd never allow in anyone else. If even Ciel, his oldest 'friend', had called him a pig, kicked him, stomped on his foot and dismissed him so readily in his own court, he'd have no qualms about pulling rank.

Or retaliating. He grinned.

"But you're fine with the kicking and slapping and clawing?" he asked.

She eyed him for a long moment. "Maybe. If I had to."

The next knock on the door came before he could reply, and Reyan was off across the room like a startled bunny to open it. Kainen noticed the acidic look the woman carrying the tray gave Reyan as she passed.

Meri was his second in command, a stern woman who ran the court in his absence and meted out his more domestic instructions to the staff. Her short black hair looked raked through and the lines around her eyes were deeper.

He bit his lip, realising that his stunt would likely have made things more difficult for those who would have to deal with Blossom.

Then he noticed Reyan, her shoulders rounded as she hunched on the chair he'd summoned, her gaze fixed miserably on the table.

I didn't think how any of this would affect her either.

Guilt swelled as Meri left again without a word, shutting the door behind her.

Kainen sought for some way to repair the damage he'd done, but he couldn't think of a damn thing. Sliding his hand into his pocket so Reyan wouldn't see, he clenched his fist and let the calming tingle of his gift flicker over his palm. He would find some way to make it up to her.

Reyan ate without waiting for him, taking small bites of a burger and staring at her plate. Kainen joined her but his appetite was fading fast, guilt filling his gut until he felt queasy. He dropped his burger onto the plate with a tiny sigh. He could eat later.

Before he could make any attempt to prove he wasn't a complete entitled pig and vanish the tray to the kitchens, Reyan leaned forward and did it. Then without a word, she wriggled beneath a blanket and started reading.

Kainen eased to his feet as quietly as he could. He didn't want to disturb her any more than he already had and strode to the bathroom door, knowing that for him alone it would open to whichever room he wished.

An idea was forming in his head. It wouldn't make up for the mockery and suspicion the court would put Reyan through after what he'd done, but he could give her something nice at least. Something of her own to escape into.

He walked into his study and cast a look back at her as he closed the door behind him.

Yeah, this will be a start at least.

He clicked his fingers, knowing the sound wouldn't reach her now he was elsewhere in the court.

"I need a copy of every *Carrie's Castle* book ever published," he said. "Immediately." Then, more to prove a point to himself than because of her, he added, "please."

CHAPTER FOUR
REYAN

Reyan woke with a start, sitting up in a flurry of bedding that was much softer and a lot greener than she remembered. She eyed the room around her and memory surfaced.

Not a horrible dream then.

She yawned, stretching her arms above her head. The dorms were noisy, both while people slept and while they were awake. Here at least the silence was blissful and she hadn't once reached the edge of the big bed while tossing and turning during the night.

Can't risk getting used to this. Soon as the royals are gone, he'll discard me just as easily back to my 'rightful place'.

Which was as it should be. She had no expectations of getting anything from him and knew he'd only picked her because he didn't want to risk upsetting someone from his court who might develop hopes for something more with him. The way he'd focused on what Demi was saying during the tour, and the hesitation he had around her, all pointed to the court gossips being spot on. He was clearly still infatuated with the young queen.

She swung her legs out of bed and noticed something unexpected on the bedside table. She frowned at the teetering pile of books, all lined up and placed so that she could see the spines clearly from where she sat.

"What in the name of Faerie?" She reached up for the piece of paper tabbed on top of the book tower and read the short script aloud. "Reyan, accept these as the beginning of an apology. They're all yours. Kainen."

She rubbed a hand over her face and eyed the pile of eighteen books. He probably hadn't thought about where she'd store them, the dorms having barely any individual space beyond a chest for clothes at the end of each bed, but it was still an unnervingly sweet gesture.

An apology because he won't ever give me my freedom from the court, not when I'm useful to it instead.

The bitterness was familiar, soothing almost, but she couldn't shake the unsettling truth lying beneath it. Kainen didn't have to do anything for her and yet here were copies of what she assumed was every *Carrie's Castle* book ever published.

She would thank him, take the gift with grace and that would be it. Perhaps someone would agree to store them for her until she found a place of her own in the future. Ciel might; he was her friend as much as Kainen's and had his own room. Perhaps even more so these days.

Although she was dying to sink back into the glorious bed and spend all day reading, she washed up quickly in the opulent rock-walled bathroom and emerged to find food waiting on the table by the sofa. Her armchair was still there and she sank into it to eat. Going to the dorm for a change of clothes could wait until she was full. The dorms might also be empty then and she could avoid all the inevitable questions and veiled snarky remarks.

The door to the bathroom swung open and she almost threw a piece of bread in alarm. Over Kainen's shoulder she could see his study through the doorway and wondered how long he'd slept. She'd read late into the night but he hadn't come in before she fell asleep and now he looked weary.

Did he sleep in his study? Her cheeks flushed. *Of course he did. He was probably just baiting me before for stepping out of line and being rude. And for kicking him. And for stomping on his foot.*

"Demi's asked us to provide a meeting place to discuss whatever she's really here for," he announced, striding across to join her. "After everything that happened, I thought maybe the decks?"

He was asking her opinion, she realised. He sat on the sofa and took a bowl of porridge, filling it with chocolate milk, then jam, then sprinkles. Horrified at the amount of sugar, she gawped until he noticed.

"What?"

She shook her head. "No wonder you're so... you. You're hopped up on sugar all day."

"Don't dismiss it if you haven't tried it, sweetheart." He laughed. "Here, have a mouthful."

He held out the spoon to her, the gloopy brown mess dotted with oozing colour.

"No thanks. It looks disgusting."

"Go on, try it." He pouted, waving the spoon insistently until some splatted onto the table.

She summoned a cloth but leaning forward to wipe up the spill brought her into the spoon danger zone. The moment he could reach, Kainen pressed the spoon against her lips. As she opened them to complain, he tipped the offending food right in.

"You are a complete and utter, entitled, elitist-" She mumbled through her mouthful, glaring at the sparkle of wicked laughter on his face.

The door to the hall opened before she could finish the food or sit back. She turned her head in time to see Demi stride in with Taz right behind her.

Demi looked at Kainen, who was still laughing with the spoon held out, and at Reyan leaning forward so that what was essentially her being fed against her will looked like something intimate.

"Forgive me, but shouldn't you at least knock?" Kainen asked, not sounding bothered in the slightest.

"Queen," Demi said by way of explanation.

Taz grinned. "We wanted to make absolutely sure everything here was as it should be."

With her cheeks burning, Reyan straightened up and finished the mouthful of porridge, which strangely tasted not so bad after all. Not that she'd be admitting that to him.

Kainen dropped the spoon on the table, giving Reyan a look that dared her to comment on his messiness and call him a pig in front of the others. If Demi and Taz's distrust of his motives toward her bothered him, his expert mask of entertained indifference hid it.

"It's fine," she said, because she was sure something somewhere must be fine, so it technically wasn't a lie. "Kainen eats the most disgusting breakfasts so he was forcing me to do things against my will."

A strangled noise escaped Kainen's throat. She held his panicked gaze as she leaned forward again, challenging him right back. She vanished the spoon to the kitchens, the breakfast tray and mess with it, then twisted to face Demi and Taz with a bright smile.

"It didn't taste half bad in the end actually."

Seconds passed, then Demi started to laugh.

"Fair enough," she said. "Let's get this meeting underway then. Also Kainen, Blossom is demanding you pay her some attention as your honoured guest. I'd probably spend the afternoon with her if I were you, just in case things do 'conveniently work out as they should'. Her words not mine."

Reyan was quick enough to see the reluctance narrowing Kainen's eyes, even though he nodded and got to his feet without any complaint.

"Of course. The weather's meant to be nice in our realm today, so I thought we could go out onto the decks."

Demi shrugged. "Wherever you think is best. It's not something we want overheard though."

As Kainen hesitated, Reyan realised he was uncertain. Not of his court or himself perhaps, but of Demi and what might be asked of him. Queen Tavania had offered him release from her service after the war which he'd taken. It was an honour and a kindness considering she could have kept him and used him to manipulate Demi's side of their joint rule later on.

Kainen was still young in many ways, spoilt and entitled. But Reyan glanced at the *Carrie's Castle* books still on his bedside table. Anyone would think he was trying to do better.

She stood up and took control against her better judgement.

"The decks then," she suggested. "It's bracing but nobody will hear you over the water, and I think it's literally the only place we didn't show you yesterday."

Demi eyed her. "You'll be coming with us, won't you? If you're to be married you two should share everything."

"Yes," Kainen said immediately. "I agree."

Reyan caught his eye. She had no idea what game he was playing now, payback perhaps for her resistant behaviour the day before.

His lips lifted in amusement and he held out a hand to her.

"You might need to learn all my darkest secrets, sweetheart," he purred.

She rolled her eyes. "Give me strength."

But she took the hand all the same, because what else could she do? Somehow, taking it by choice felt less defeating than waiting for him to inevitably force or compel her.

They left the room and Kainen seemed willing to let her lead the way, his hand still a pressure around hers. As they diverted through the corridors, she noticed a man coming toward them.

Ciel watched them pass, bowing low enough that his sandy hair fell forward to cover his eyes. But as he straightened up, Reyan caught the flick of his gaze to her hand in Kainen's. He smiled as they passed, but when she twisted back the smile was gone.

She pulled a reluctant face behind the backs of the others, guessing Ciel was annoyed that neither of them had shared the plan or their supposed relationship with him. He was Kainen's oldest friend but she also got on well with him. If she had to trust anyone at court, she would probably have risked trusting Ciel.

"Here we are," Kainen announced as he threw open a large wooden door. "The decks."

Reyan blinked against the bright dazzle of daylight filtering in and stood aside as Demi and Taz ventured through the doorway first. The roar of water dashing down against rocks and rushing between the crevice of the two great mountains filled the air, dancing around the brisk scent of moss and freshness.

She'd seen the decks a few times before, but they were off-limits to the court unless Kainen said otherwise. Sometimes she wondered if it was one of his private spots for hook-ups, but other times she figured he simply didn't like to share. The staff constantly grumbled about wanting one of the outside spaces as a place to relax after work, but as far as she could tell, nobody had mentioned it officially.

She went to follow the others through and tried to slip her hand free of Kainen's but he clung on.

"You might want to hold tight to me," he teased. "The rocks are slippery."

"Oh really?" She bit back. "The only way you can get a girl to hold your hand these days is to force her, is it? Or frighten her with false dangers?"

It came out harsher than she intended, but his eyes sparked with dark playfulness instead of anger.

"Maybe. Or maybe I'm afraid I'll slip and fall, and you're my anchor in the storm."

Reyan rolled her eyes. "Pig. Let go."

"No."

"Fine." She smiled sweetly back at him. "Try to keep up then."

She couldn't harness her ability to merge into the shadows but she was still a performer with or without their help, a dancer who had the ability to move with fluid ease. Even him pulling on her hand didn't unbalance her as she skipped and hopped down the rocky steps of the mountain side like a goat, aware of him stumbling behind to keep up. She wouldn't go anywhere near fast enough to let him fall, but she wanted this snatch of freedom, to have control, to scare him just a little.

He tried to release her hand but this time she clung on. She even heard a tiny yelp of fear as she dragged him past Demi and Taz toward a floating wooden deck tied between the two mountains and being buffeted by the dashing river.

Only when her feet hit the wood did she tumble to a halt, her cheeks flushed and her skin tingling with exhilaration. She turned to face Kainen, guessing there would be some warning, or a punishment.

His cheeks were pink too, but instead of glaring at her he was laughing.

"Rebellious thing aren't you, sweetheart?" he huffed, out of breath.

She shrugged, still alive with adrenaline as Demi and Taz reached them.

"This is definitely something," Taz remarked.

Reyan glanced around at the decks. The wooden sides of the platform were high enough to stop too much water splashing over, and the ornate green lounge chairs, tables and place settings were hammered into place. Even the wild bushes growing around the edges were fixed sturdy. But all the while, the deck rocked and swayed with the water rushing underneath, a sense of natural danger amid the opulence.

Reyan loved it. Clearly, Kainen loved it too. His smile had none of the wickedness that his usual mask showed, his dark eyes bright with something reminiscent to happiness.

He's a different kind of handsome when he forgets he's a lord in charge of manipulating things.

She shook the thought from her head as Kainen summoned cushions and blankets for the wooden chairs and everyone took seats around the low wooden table. While Demi reached into a worn satchel hanging at her side and Taz fussed around with a rucksack, Kainen leaned close to Reyan's ear.

"Relax, you're meant to look like you belong here," he whispered.

She glared at him, but if he really wanted her to play the part, at least she'd be more comfortable. She pulled her feet up onto the chair, mucky boots and all, tucking them underneath her. This brought her into perilously close proximity to her feet sliding under his leg, but she could hold herself in place. Otherwise she might end up breaking the 'no kicking' rule. She thought about summoning her blanket and the next *Carrie's Castle* book while the rest of them discussed court secrets, but it might look a bit too comfortable, even for Kainen's laidback manners. Still, the thought of it made her smile enough to look somewhat at home beside him.

"So, what really brings you here?" Kainen asked. "Given the reluctance when Blossom was introduced, I'm guessing my intended bride wasn't originally your idea. At least, now I'm hoping it wasn't."

Taz raised an eyebrow. "You think you're too good for my sister?"

Reyan frowned but Demi's wry snorting noise drew everyone's attention.

"Oh please, you think everyone is too good for your sister," she shot back. "You hate her so don't start. We have to be friends if this is to work, even you two."

Taz slouched in his seat, giving her a disgruntled look of obedience. How Kainen managed to keep the smirk off his face Reyan had no idea, but manage it somehow he did.

"We've had reports that the nether is growing weaker." Demi began. "The brethren of the Nether Court are worried. They've asked us to visit and discuss, but we're not sure how far they can be trusted or what they expect us to do to fix it."

Kainen's amusement was gone now, his expression grim as he rubbed a hand over his mouth.

"The Nether Court and its brethren have always been secretive," he admitted. "All courts think they're the best, there's no hiding that, but they believe being artful in the very fabric of Faerie holds them in higher regard than mere Fae. If you thought the Forgotten were elitist, you've never met the brethren."

"We met one," Demi said darkly.

Kainen winced. "Yes, unfortunately. My cousin Marten is very much like what you'll have to deal with. Many of the brethren don't concern themselves with Fae versus fairy either. They see that as internal squabbling. No, they've always been concerned more with the human world versus the Faerie realms. Their court is the oldest and the most secretive."

"Which is why we're here," Taz said.

Kainen frowned. "Apart from my cousin, I don't have much else to offer, and I'm guessing you can summon him at will now, Demi."

"I can. It's not him we need. When we travel to the Nether Court, they're going to ask us to assist them with something, a beast deep beneath their court which few have been able to survive. They say there's a way to charm it enough to lull it into another deep sleep, but nobody knows what that is."

"And they expect us to do the lulling?" Kainen asked. "Why not send in FDPs?"

Demi sighed. "It needs to be secret. We're still rebuilding Faerie as best we can and trying to bring the outer realms into the fold. If we let people know that the nether is weakening, those who don't understand will panic and opportunists will take advantage."

Taz leaned back against his seat, his expression becoming serious.

"Putting it bluntly, we're hoping dealing with the nether beastie will stop it disrupting the nether and weakening veils everywhere, but we need more information and they're unlikely to be straight with us willingly."

Reyan wasn't sure what they were asking and she didn't know them well enough to read them. But Kainen's face she could read, and it didn't bode well given that he was now grimacing in her direction.

"You need someone to go in unseen," he said, speaking to Demi even though his gaze was now fixed on Reyan.

Realisation dawned and a brief flicker of excitement filled her as she thought about actually leaving the court for somewhere other than her father's house.

"You need me to go in shadow form and spy on them?" she asked.

"You don't have to agree," Demi insisted. "This isn't something we'd expect you to do unless you were willing, and Kainen should know better now than to force you to do anything."

Reyan gulped and spluttered. Kainen patted her on the back, but the subtle rub between her shoulder blades afterwards was more like a plea. He had forced her to be his pretend bride already. He could easily force her to go on Demi's mission, to spy on the Nether Court for them. She looked at him, waiting for the command.

"I wouldn't force you to do this if you chose not to," he said, surprising her. "I know you can move through shadows unseen, and travel through them to safety easily enough if you have to, but it's your choice."

Reyan bit her lip. Choices. She'd always wanted choices, the freedom to choose for herself. Now here one was and she had no idea what to do.

"It would be a short trip to their court," Demi added. "We'll go for the meeting by realm-skipping, and all you'd need to do is slip away and wander a bit, then report back anything you think we need to hear. Chances are we won't hear anything of use, but you never know. It would be good to have an idea of the layout too if possible, but the danger to you would be minimal."

Taz sighed. "The danger is never minimal, but what she means is they're likely to go straight for her first so you should be okay."

Demi started to laugh at the sheer resignation in his tone, a boyfriend who was more than familiar with being dragged into absolute mayhem for the girl he loved. Reyan had heard their stories and even seen one of them unfold. To be part of the great stories of Faerie wasn't really her goal, but perhaps if she helped them now, it might be a good mark toward her earning her freedom one day. The alternative was lingering in the court without Kainen's protection if Blossom decided to attack her for being 'chosen' by him, or going through her old haunts to the whispering and shunning from people who used to smile at her.

"I'll help," she decided. "I don't know how much I can do, but I'll try."

Demi grinned, leaning back so that she was nestled under Taz's arm and against the back of their shared cushions. After a beat of awkwardness, Reyan realised Demi seemed to be waiting for something, assessing her. She sat beside Kainen, but there was no relaxed easiness between them, no hint of affectionate touching. She let her feet slide a few inches until her toes touched his leg. It was the closest she would go affection-wise, but she raised her eyebrows at him next.

"You didn't order drinks or anything, did you?" she asked, her tone dry. "Never mind, I'll do it."

There, a sign of affection and an excuse to stop doing it in one swift move. She made to stand up, but Kainen shook his head.

"You're right, I forgot, sweetheart. I'll do it."

She froze as he reached out and pulled her feet back toward him so that they were nestled completely under his leg. Despite the gentle anchoring the movement added to her position, she had to force herself not to pull away.

When she didn't protest, he smiled lazily at her and clicked his fingers. Demi flinched at the action, almost sending her satchel flying off her lap.

Reyan frowned but she understood why. She knew that Demi had been tortured at Kainen's hand during the war, almost completely against his will. She also understood the subtle tightening of Taz's arm around Demi's shoulders, a reflex to comfort as though he was well-practiced at doing it by now.

But it was the sudden tension of the boy next to her that saddened Reyan's heart the most. Kainen's thigh was tense over her toes as he clenched his jaw. Being forced to play a monster couldn't be good for his soul or his self-esteem, even if he was still an entitled, arrogant arse.

Demi's cheeks were flushed, embarrassment perhaps, but Reyan ignored that. She pushed her fingers over Kainen's thigh and squeezed the hand still in his lap, not meeting his eyes. A mere gesture of kindness and understanding, nothing more. Everyone knew he'd been in love with Demi, and she reckoned given the odd few glances Kainen sent her way when he thought nobody was looking, he still was.

She ignored the subtle tingling in her fingers, guessing it was residual overspill from the glittering black smoke still wreathing his other hand and waiting for his order.

"Bring drinks and snacks to the decks," he said. As he looked down, Reyan forced herself to meet his gaze, to acknowledge the tiny smile meant only for her. "Please."

CHAPTER FIVE
KAINEN

Reyan's hand was still tucked around his. Not a gentle touch either, but her fingers curled tight and firm like she wanted to reassure him.

Kainen gulped against a sudden catch in his throat. He was used to bodily contact from various mutually meaningless people, but the subtle kindness of her touch affected him. It was a simple gesture that Reyan didn't need to give him, especially after everything he'd done, and somehow that flustered him.

He took a small breath.

"So, while we wait, what exactly is the plan?" he asked.

He focused on Demi and Taz, keeping his gaze softened between them. Taz had a protective arm around Demi's hips, and once that would have given Kainen a stab of jealousy. He remembered well the way he'd watched Demi and Taz together during the war, taking fleeting glances of her smiling at the boy she'd rejected him for.

But now there was nothing. No longing, no jealousy. Every time he looked at her expecting it to kick in, there was nothing. Only the weary realisation that they weren't here for him, but for what he could do for them. Like everyone else.

Perhaps that's why I picked Reyan to be my fake bride. She's kind enough not to use me. Or rather she's kind enough to keep me sweet rather than trying to manipulate me while she waits for a way to be free of her father's debts.

"We take a troll to the Nether Court and discuss their issue with them," Demi said. "They say the beast is more like a monster that woke up underneath their court and they think it's what's disrupting the nether."

Kainen frowned. "So, we're going there for a chat or they want us to actually deal with the monster? Do we have any idea what actually woke it in the first place?"

"Not sure on any of it yet," Taz said. "I imagine us dealing with it is what they'll be leading to, but we're only going to discuss it with them for now."

"Nothing will be decided today," Demi added. "We thought if Reyan was able to move around unseen, slip away a while, then we might at least find out if it's some kind of trap."

Reyan straightened up, once again drawing Kainen's attention to his hand still in hers. He wondered if she'd simply forgotten or if this was some part of her decision to play the part. Either way the contact felt nice, comforting, and he stayed as still as possible to draw the moment out a while longer.

"I can do that," she said. "Although I'm not sure what I'd be looking for, and I'd need my gift to be released. The kitchens are usually a good place for gossip, but if you want actual secrets then I'd need to know where to go."

Demi's eyes narrowed and Taz's head tilted to one side. Kainen knew what they were thinking; Reyan's gift should never have been bound in the first place.

"I should have done that when I took over." He struggled against the unnatural words he had to say next. "I'm sorry."

Reyan's tense fingers relaxed in his.

As if she was expecting me to shout at her for mentioning it. He frowned. *Am I really that awful?*

The conversation paused as Meri materialised with a large tray. Kainen gave her a brief smile out of habit, still worried about how his court must see him, but his gaze was focused enough that he saw hers flick down to Reyan's hand in his. The disapproving thinning of her mouth surprised him, but the tray was on the table and she was gone before he could gather himself.

I haven't explained this to her but as a lord surely I shouldn't have to? He frowned. *She would have known Blossom was coming as my intended bride, but she never struck me as a traditionalist in terms of what side we stand on. Maybe she thinks Reyan is using me for advancement like the rest of the court must do.*

"Kainen?"

Reyan's sharp voice and a squeeze of her fingers around his brought his attention back.

"Sorry, what?" he asked, his cheeks flushing.

"Never mind." Reyan rolled her eyes and shook her hand free. "A host is supposed to serve at official meetings, but I'll do it."

He watched as she rolled bottles of cherry bubble juice across the large table for Taz and Demi, deftly sliding a plate of cookies across next.

Kainen flexed his fingers, the skin cold now that Reyan

had let go. He would have to see about sorting the issue of her out as soon as the fake engagement was done.

She'd been kind enough to recognise when Demi had reacted negatively to him using his gift. Demi's reaction was justified, a residual fear over what he'd once had to do to her during the war, and once before that out of misguided arrogance. He wished he could sit down with Demi properly and apologise, but he guessed that opportunity would never come now. She would too well-protected for him to get close to her unless she wished for it, even though now she was sitting here with only Taz beside her.

Kainen almost snorted at the thought. There was no 'only Taz' in this equation. Even when they were little and Taz was often the kicking boy for his sisters and the rest of the elite Fae youth in his mother's court, his skills and quick thinking were impressive.

They suit each other, he realised. *They're lucky to have found each other. I wonder if there's actually someone out there for me too.*

Definitely not Blossom. It had taken all his charm skills not to pull a face at the mere mention of having to spend time with her for the afternoon.

Reyan dropped a bottle of cherry bubble juice in his lap and held out a cookie without looking at him. Her focus was on Demi, so she missed his amused smile as he took the cookie obediently.

"Do we know anything at all beyond what they've requested of you?" she asked.

Her dark eyes sparked with determination, and Kainen

recognised that look. He'd seen her sparring many times in the court training hall and she was ruthless when she had to be. Not the strongest perhaps, but she was deft in her movements and a born strategist. Now she was assessing this request like an assignment.

She'd have made a great FDP. Kainen watched her hold Demi's gaze without a shred of nerves. *But with her shadow-weaving and her smart mouth she belongs here at my court.*

Possessiveness shot through him, followed by a strain of uneasiness. He'd only been this kind of possessive once before and it hadn't done him any good. The fact that Demi was sitting across from them now, chatting to Reyan as a friend, was some small miracle of Faerie after what he'd done.

He caught Taz's gaze shifting to him, but luckily he'd been staring at Reyan as she talked so he wouldn't be on the business end of any of the king consort's threats.

"We think it may have something to do with the Prime Realm," Demi admitted. "We know so little about it though. All of the realms Arcanium links to are documented, but that is known as the origin realm for a reason and it's blocked to us. I don't know who's doing that is but even Old Tara couldn't, or wouldn't, tell me about it."

Reyan frowned. "Who's Old Tara?"

"She's the embodiment of Faerie." Demi glanced at Taz, her mouth quirking ruefully. "She tells me most things as queen, but not that."

"Wait, Faerie is sentient?" Reyan's eyes widened.

Taz muttered something under his breath, but a few moments of silence passed afterward and he didn't make any effort to excuse himself or explain. Kainen realised the two girls were sitting in awkwardness now and for all her power, Demi wasn't sure what she was safe to say. Determined not to lose the fragile easiness they'd managed to build up, Kainen twisted in his seat to face Reyan, taking the heat off Demi and Taz.

"As far as I know, Faerie is living as much as we or the earth or the animals are," he explained. "I'm not sure how it all hangs together, like how much effort Faerie has to put into each person, but I think on the wider scale of Faerie as a whole, sometimes decisions are made that none of us can comprehend."

Taz snorted. "Very eloquent."

Kainen ignored the subtle sinking sensation inside his gut. He didn't expect friendship from the royals after what he'd done, or even kindness, but it still stung to be mocked and dismissed so easily.

Reyan's eyes narrowed. Any of the court who were sworn to it, and therefore to him, would feel any sleight toward him. He didn't expect her body to begin darkening as though the very shadows lingering in the clefts of the rocks around them were cloaking her though.

Taz's eyes widened as she turned to face him, but Kainen grabbed her hand before she could do anything. Her gift was similar to one of his as far as he knew, but where they could both use the shadows to see people's emotions, he couldn't dissipate into actual shadows and weave through them like she could, or manipulate them like extra limbs.

She turned to look at him, her eyes pinching further. She must have sensed the worry waving off him and took a deep breath.

"No need to protect my honour, sweetheart," he said, suddenly not caring if the others heard. "As I'm sure Taz will tell you, I don't really have any."

He smiled to show her he was okay but she glowered back. He summoned a flicker of sparkling black dust on his fingertip and touched it to the centre of her head.

Immediately he could feel that invisible thread between them, his gift giving him access to her mind. He only ever used that gift on those who knew how to keep him out now; it was one of his personal rules in his court, no gifts against those who couldn't equalise the score.

Reyan blinked back at him, then her voice filled his mind.

Sorry. It's this stupid court loyalty you stuck us all with. It makes us possessive even though I still think you're a complete arse.

Even in his head, her tone was scathing, but it made him laugh.

I know, I'm a pain. He couldn't help but agree with her. *Taz and Demi are anchored so they can mind-speak. I'm simply equalising the board. Don't go feral at Taz though, even if he insults me.*

Reyan's nose crinkled in distaste.

Is that an order? I know he's the king consort, but he's got a mighty attitude on him.

Kainen felt a flicker of delight spark in him. He'd never

met anyone who had a less than glowing reaction to the once-Prince of Faerie. Even his sister had entertained secret childhood dreams of becoming Taz's chosen princess, although she'd hidden it well with insults and sneering.

Yes, sweetheart, it's an order. We need to be good hosts.

A pause, then her ridiculously over-loud huff echoed through his mind.

Fine.

Given that Taz and Demi were looking at each other without talking, he guessed Demi was having a similar mind-conversation with Taz about his behaviour. Reyan waited until they were once again facing forward, but even so her tone was still ever so slightly clipped as she tried again.

"Do we have any contacts at the Nether Court?" she asked, her gaze flicking to Kainen.

He noted the subtle use of 'we' and bit his lip. She sounded every inch like she was really his future bride, his equal. Something about that, even though it was merely pretence, made him feel stronger.

"None since the war," he admitted. "I wouldn't want to ask the court for extended contacts either, not without activating the gossip mill. When is the meeting?"

Demi pulled a face. "This afternoon. The plan is to skip there once we're done here, or as soon as we can if you have things you need to do." Her face brightened with amusement. "I'm guessing there's not much point in you spending the afternoon with Blossom now though, not if you've agreed to support royal business."

Relieved, Kainen grinned. "I am at the crown's disposal, so if you'd rather I not lead her on, I'm only too willing to obey."

Taz looked like he was fighting an internal battle, his lips twitching as if to smile while his eyes narrowed like he wanted to challenge the sleight on his sister, or more accurately, find a way to bring Kainen's ego down.

"If we have to leave now, I'll need to give a few instructions," Kainen added. "But if you want to return to your room, we'll come for you when finished. Unless you want to wait here?"

Demi shook her head and stood, Taz doing the same. Reyan slid to her feet and leaned forward to vanish the bottles and tray. Kainen opened his mouth to tell her to leave it for the staff, but he guessed that attitude wouldn't get him in her good books.

"I've got this one," he said instead.

Perhaps unnecessarily, because Reyan raised her eyebrows at him and stood watching. An unnatural strain of performance anxiety gripped him, but he vanished the half-eaten plate to the kitchen.

"Do you know where it should have gone?" she asked, her tone dry. "Or did you send it to the 'kitchen' without wondering if it's going to appear on some poor random person's head?"

Kainen rarely went anywhere near the kitchens and had done exactly what she'd said. He pulled a face.

"Of course I-" He couldn't lie, and the lifting of her lips suggested she knew it already. "I'll do better next time."

She only smiled, vanishing the blankets and the

cushions to the wooden boxes they stayed in to keep dry while the decks weren't being used.

"Do we need to bring anything defensive?" she asked. "Weapons, or bribes maybe?"

Demi shook her head. "The less put together we appear the better I think. We play to their ego."

"The Nether Court are secretive at the best of times," Taz added. "When Demi first became queen they refused to acknowledge her and would only deal with my mother. The only reason we have this meeting is because we're going in as FDPs on a high level of secrecy."

"So we're dealing with elitist snobs," Reyan said. "I'm used to those."

She gave Kainen a sideways smirk and his heart leapt.

Not his heart, his relief. His heart had nothing to do with what was happening here, and he needed to make sure he didn't start getting his emotions confused again like he did before. Clearly if he'd truly been in love with Demi, he wouldn't be able to stand here facing her now and feel nothing. Confusing his relief with actual feelings for Reyan would likely get him decapitated or something.

Demi grinned. "Likewise. Royalty, courts, it's all so ridiculous."

Kainen couldn't help laughing, pleased when even Taz started smiling along with them. He gave Reyan his best nervous face.

"You'll all be voting me out next," he suggested.

She stuck her tongue out at him. "We won't, most of the court actually likes you."

Surprised, Kainen couldn't control his smile and

completely forgot their pretence, the others hovering nearby and anything else that wasn't the young woman shining back at him with her devilish smile and dancing smoky eyes.

Okay, you'll be voting me out then, he said into her mind, keeping his tone to a seductive crooning.

He knew she wouldn't fall for it, like she didn't fall for any of his other charms and tricks, but that just made the attempt all the more enjoyable somehow.

Her smile widened. *You're just afraid I'll tell the queen all your court secrets if you annoy me again. It's also rude to mind-speak in company, and how do you know she doesn't have the ability to hear right through us?*

She had a point; nobody knew how deep Demi's gifts and powers ran now.

"I won't argue," he said aloud. "Right now I'm much too intimidated to risk it."

"You and me both," Taz agreed.

"Wow, you two actually agreed on something." Reyan pretended to gasp. "Maybe one day you'll even be friends."

Taz pulled a face and turned toward the stairs, snaring Demi's fingers to drag her with him.

Kainen caught the indignation crossing Reyan's face at the dismissiveness and laughed. Without thinking, he grabbed her hand in his and set off after the others up the steps.

"Friends aren't really a luxury I have, sweetheart," he said, loud enough for Demi and Taz to hear.

Reyan was silent for a moment and he wondered if she

was agreeing with him but too kind to say it.

"Oh I don't know." She gave a little shrug. "You grow on people eventually. Thank you for the books by the way."

As they walked up the steps side by side, neither said nor did anything about his fingers still curled around hers.

Kainen shook his head slightly, awareness of an uneasy familiarity settling tight inside his chest.

Uh-oh.

CHAPTER SIX
REYAN

Kainen seemed quite happy to hold onto her hand, and Reyan wondered if perhaps he secretly liked the pretence of it. He smiled at everyone they passed in the halls as though it was completely normal for her to be walking alongside him.

I won't say anything about it, not yet. She eyed the main hall as they walked across, the crowd buzzing around them. *If I upset him he might stop me from going to the Nether Court after all.*

So absorbed in thought, she missed Ciel approaching until he was right in front of them. His rangy height put him a head taller than Kainen but he wasn't as broad-shouldered, tanned where Kainen was pale and blond instead of shades of darkness.

"Rey?" Ciel wiped a hand over his goatee with determination scrawled across his face. "Got a minute?"

She glanced at Kainen without thinking, then realised it looked like she was asking his permission. He noticed before she could correct the gesture and bowed low with his eyes never leaving hers.

"Off you go, sweetheart," he said, a wicked smile flitting across his face. "We'll be leaving soon though so no funny business."

She rolled her eyes as he drifted away to talk to

someone else and faced Ciel with awkwardness fluttering inside her chest.

"So." He shoved his hands in his pockets, bouncing on the balls of his feet. "You and Kainen."

Reyan pulled a face. She couldn't see any way out, because Ciel was her friend and deserved the truth, but also Kainen was lord of the court and she couldn't disobey his wishes.

"I'm a bit hurt neither of you bothered to mention it," Ciel added.

She grimaced. "It's new."

"So new there weren't even any rumours?"

She caught his eye and managed a rueful smile. One of Ciel's responsibilities as Kainen's oldest friend was to make sure he knew all the mutterings and rumblings inside the court.

"Is it real?" he asked.

Reyan pinned her lips firm between her teeth, an obvious refusal to answer. Long ago, Ciel had taught her the game of silence = no. It came in handy plenty of times when he needed information but didn't want to put her in danger by having her tell him other people's secrets that she saw or sensed from the shadows.

His expression cleared and tension leaked from his shoulders.

"Okay, that's something at least. Not sure what he's playing at so I won't press you, but I'm glad."

Reyan frowned. "Why? I know my family is all but ruined socially and every other way these days, but am I that bad a choice for a court lord?"

It was a cruel thing to say considering she knew that her family wasn't socially acceptable for being aligned with the elite, let alone a lord of Faerie, and she was all but goading Ciel into having to admit it.

His cheeks tinged pink and his gaze slid away from hers, fixing with resolute determination on the ground.

"Of course you're not, but you need someone who deserves you."

She couldn't help grinning. "And he, your oldest friend, lord of our court, is unworthy of me? How touching."

He chuckled, catching her gaze and smiling softly as he swept a hand through his hair.

"You know what I mean. But I wanted to warn you to be careful. Lady Blossom was adamant she won't let you stand in her way of 'nabbing him' as she put it. Watch your back."

Reyan hesitated before burbling up the instinctive answer. Insulting a princess wouldn't go well for her if anyone overheard, and there were always ears willing and straining to listen.

"She'd assume a court lord doesn't know his own mind?" she feigned confusion. "Bold of her. But I'm sure he'll get bored of me soon enough, that's what the gossips will all be saying, right?"

Ciel didn't deny it, his eyes sparkling with amused agreement.

"A friendly warning, that's all." He shrugged. "Kainen's waiting for you."

She turned to look over her shoulder, aware of Kainen watching them. Whoever he'd been talking to was gone and now he leaned back against the stone banister of the stairs that led up to the accommodation wing, his eyes fixed on them.

On her.

When she dragged her gaze away from him, Ciel was already weaving through the crowd at the other side of the hall. Reyan shook her head, unnerved by the warning, and started up the stairs without waiting for Kainen.

"Saying farewell, sweetheart?" he asked as he followed her and let them into his room. "I'm sure he can contain himself until we get back."

So self-entitled that he's jealous after seconds without attention. She shook her head in disgust. *Perhaps all his good behaviour before was an act for Demi and Taz's benefit.*

"He was warning me that Lady Blossom is out for my blood, which is what friends do. Not that I can do much about it, or anything else for that matter. Also, if I'd said no to this little outing, would you have really accepted my decision?"

He smiled, reclining on the sofa as she slid onto her chair. He had summoned the chair from somewhere, but knowing him he'd probably not thought it through and left some poor old lady to fall flat on her behind mid-sit.

"I said I would honour your decision, didn't I?" he said. "But as it is, if it's alright with you, I'd rather not leave you alone here with Blossom circling anyway."

Reyan snorted. "You're worried about me? What if she takes over your court while we're gone?"

"Ah, that's why the trustworthy Ciel is staying behind

to mind her. He'll flatter her with so much boring charm she'll drop flat like a side character from *Sweetly Slumbering Cynthia*."

"What, until you return to kiss the maid and wake the whole village?" She had to laugh as he pulled a face. "Poor Ciel."

Silence descended for a few moments. It was the perfect time to thank him for the books. But as she summoned her strength to admit she was grateful, she noticed a considered frown creasing his brow.

"What?"

"You and Ciel are close," he said.

She shrugged. "A bit. So what?"

"I thought maybe you were a certain kind of close. He seemed very attentive toward you today. Not often someone would offer a warning to anyone without expecting something in return."

Reyan found herself rising out of her seat without planning a reason why first. She eyed the bathroom door, wondering if she could excuse herself before she snapped at Kainen for interfering.

She'd also been getting inklings that Ciel was taking an interest in her, a suggestive joke, the odd moment where he touched a fraction too long or lingered closer than he had to. She often turned and found him looking, although he'd always give her a friendly smile or a little wave after.

Even if that were all true, Kainen might be lord of the court but he still had no right to pry.

"That's my business," she said. "But don't worry, I won't do anything to ruin your stupid engagement

68

pretence. Besides, it's not like I have a choice when I have to ask your permission for everything anyway. Who'd want a girlfriend that's tied to a court and completely at someone else's mercy?"

She raised her eyebrows when he stood up and took a step closer, rounding the corner of the table so they were face to face. Or rather face to chin, because he was half a head taller. She tilted her head back, refusing to back down even though her pulse was racing.

Why is my pulse racing?

"Pack your stuff," he said. "We're leaving by troll, but these things can always last longer than expected so we should be prepared. Will you need much space?"

"I don't own anything besides myself and some clothes, so no. Oh, and now several books that I won't be able to carry, much less find a home for."

Okay, that wasn't a thank you. That was more of a 'screw you for the lovely and thoughtful gift you gave me'.

Feeling awful, she opened her mouth again to apologise but Kainen's laughter cut her off.

"If you're planning to flee the moment we reach the Nether Court, I'll only summon you back. But if you do somehow manage to evade me, I'll guard your books until you return to fetch them."

She scoffed. "Why do you care if I come back or not?"

His smile turned wicked, devilishness dancing in his dark eyes.

"Because you belong at the Court of Illusions, sweetheart, with your shadows and your snark, and your snap instinct to kick me first and ask questions later. I take it I'm the only one who has this charming effect on you?"

She leaned forward, inches from his face as she glared back at him.

"I'll kick you somewhere else if you're not careful."

He blew a taunting kiss at her. "Ah-ah little rebel, I ordered no kicks, no slaps, no punches."

He had done, and that infuriated her enough to locate exactly the loophole she needed. Even as she grinned up at him, he seemed to realise there must be a reason for her sudden swing in mood.

"You didn't say no kneeing though, did you?"

She swung her knee up toward his groin with all her might, but he anticipated the movement and had a hand on her shoulder, spinning her so her knee only met air. Her back hit against his chest, his arms winding tight around her. She struggled, but apart from kneeing, he'd sewn up every other possible way she could hurt him.

"No more kneeing me," he commanded.

"Let me go," she seethed, her breathing uneven.

"Why? You were behaving so charmingly before and now you want to play nice?"

Even as he toyed with her she refused to back down. There was no fear, no worry about what he was doing. All she wanted was to find some way of beating him, besting him, and he knew it.

"Let. Me. Go."

Before he could answer, no doubt with some other teasing refusal, the hall door swung open. Both of them flinched, knocking against each other as Demi and Taz strode into the room.

"Are you ready?" Demi asked, moments before taking in the scene.

Her expression hardened, no doubt seeing Reyan's flushed cheeks and Kainen's possessive hold on her.

We can't have been loud enough for them to hear. Reyan grimaced. *Did I shout?*

She froze as Kainen's arms relaxed, dropping so that they circled her hips instead of letting her go completely. She tried to summon a smile, something to suggest they'd only been mucking about, but her breath was still heaving.

"You really should knock," Kainen said. "Queen or not."

Then he nestled his head close beside Reyan's and kissed her on the temple. Her insides flapped with mortified fury, but she couldn't quite bring herself to shove him off. She stood there instead with his arms still around her and her emotions a riot, not able to do anything about her red cheeks.

"Are you okay?" Demi's tone was pure ice and fire, the warning rumble before an explosion.

Reyan hesitated. Even though she could easily answer no because she was beyond pissed off right now, she knew Demi would take it the wrong way. Kainen was a total arrogant pain in the behind, but he wasn't a bad person. If she'd shown any ounce of fear, he would have backed down, apologised and given some amused promise never to do it again. She didn't have enough experience of him to be absolutely sure of that, but her instincts knew it all the same.

Was she okay? In the way Demi meant?

"Yeah, why?" She brushed her hands over her burning cheeks. "Oh, I'm tough enough to handle him, don't worry."

She waved a hand over her shoulder and managed to give him a savage poke in the cheek with her fingernail.

Pretty sure he didn't order no poking. Her lips twitched and she shoved the thought aside. *But I can't let him off the hook for this. I can't let him think it's okay.*

Demi and Taz stepped out into the hall, Demi's expression settling enough to show she was reassured enough not to cause a scene.

Reyan waited, determined not to try and follow until Kainen had let go, but he clung on a second longer.

"Anyone would think you wanted to fight me, sweetheart, all pressed up close."

Yep, I've clearly given him the wrong impression.

As he finally loosened his hold, his arms dropping to his sides and leaving a chill brushing over her skin, Reyan spun around and glared back at him.

"Trust me, being anywhere near you is the last thing I want right now."

CHAPTER SEVEN
KAINEN

"Being anywhere near you is the last thing I want."

And orbs alive, the girl couldn't lie.

He wasn't in the habit of grabbing women who weren't interested in being grabbed. Not except for the one incident with Demi where he'd misread the situation, backed himself into a corner and behaved like a complete idiot for a long while afterwards.

He wanted to blame his behaviour to Reyan on panic, but it was her irritable habit of disagreeing with him that provoked him to bite back, something he rarely let himself descend to. He was the lord of the court, always calm and unrufflable, but something about her was needling him which only made the irritation worse.

But Reyan's icy glare in his direction as she left his room told him he'd massively overstepped the line, even though she put on a smile for Demi's benefit. He was surprised she hadn't slapped his face, kicked him or kneed him between the legs. But of course she couldn't because he'd forbidden her from defending herself against him.

Now she sat tense at his side in Demi's rickshaw, her eyes fixed outside the cart. The moment they skipped through the purple grey swirl of the nether and the rickshaw stopped, she was out and looking around at the Nether Court.

The courtyard of brown stone caught the fierce sunlight and muted it into cosy warmth. Several buildings were clustered around the edges of the courtyard, which had a neatly trimmed square of grass in the middle. But above them towered a mountain, and past the buildings at the edge of the court, the land fell away into a steep drop.

Reyan stood spinning back and forth gently. The wind danced her blonde hair around her shoulders as she soaked the new surroundings in with her lips slightly parted in awe.

When was the last time she was outside the court or her father's house? A stab of realisation hit him. *Possibly never, not at any age where she'd remember it clearly.*

The urge to show her the entire world of Faerie flared, but he shoved the thought aside. She wasn't his girlfriend. She could barely stand the sight of him now, and she thought he was a pampered lord with no manners.

Reyan stood obediently while he brushed a thumbprint of his black dust over forehead so he'd be able to communicate his thoughts to hers at a longer distance, but she didn't lift her gaze. Even when he murmured into her mind that her gift was unbound for the duration of their visit, she didn't deign to look once at him.

"Welcome."

A voice drew his attention away from Reyan. Demi and Taz stood close together, and he noticed now that Demi had a small circlet of silver in her hair decorated with holly.

How would our charcoal and silver court colours look with blonde?

The thought slammed into him and he flinched. Reyan's

eyes twitched to his reaction, but now he was the one who didn't dare meet her gaze.

Why am I thinking about Reyan in our court's colours? Stop it, this is madness.

Demi greeted the man cloaked in dark brown with strains of muted purple. The man lowered the cowled hood, revealing a thin face, russet red-brown hair and sharp, shrewd eyes. As he came to a halt in front of them, Kainen noticed one eye was light brown and one eye blue, but the young man looked genuinely relieved to see them.

"I am bid to welcome you to the Nether Court," he said, his voice low and steady. "My name is Sannar."

Sannar dropped to his knees with an ungraceful thud, his wince visible as his legs smacked the hard ground. Demi waved her hand to have him rise, but she looked perplexed at the behaviour.

"I apologise in advance, my queen. Some here may not receive you in the correct manner," Sannar added.

Kainen sensed the animosity radiating from Taz's corner immediately. As queen, Demi could have the Nether Court disbanded if she chose, with the Oak Queen's agreement. But the Nether Court held secrets that descended into the very fabric of Faerie. To anger them would be to risk unleashing chaos, and Demi knew it. Sannar wasn't Lord of the Nether Court either and Kainen didn't recognise him, so chances were the court's lady had sent someone random to welcome them.

Demi smiled wide all the same.

"No worries, and people call me Demi so you might as well do the same. Thank you for welcoming us. My king consort, Taz, and also with us are Kainen, Lord of the Court of Illusions, and Reyan, soon-to-be Lady."

Kainen nodded to Sannar, who eyed him and Reyan before bowing low, once to him and once to her.

Then Sannar turned to Reyan.

"Welcome, Lady. I'm intrigued by your appearance."

Kainen stiffened by the sudden sultry lilt in Sannar's voice. He was barely even an adult, Kainen's age at the most, and stood there with a brown nether brother robe barely able to cover the hems of his jeans cuffed over a grubby pair of boots.

Reyan only laughed and looked down at her jeans and her plain black t-shirt.

"You find me insufficient?" she asked, her tone playful.

She never uses that tone on me. Kainen stared at her. *Then again, perhaps she's wondering if charm here will give her some way of escaping me, or place to hide when she inevitably manages it one day.*

The mere thought was intolerable as Sannar chuckled, taking a step closer.

"I meant your appearance at my court is intriguing, my lady," he said, his body angling toward her. "We were under the impression that the Court of Illusions was to wed a princess, yet you don't fit my memory of any of the royal family."

As Sannar moved to take her hand, perhaps to kiss it, Kainen fought the urge to punch the smug smile off his face.

Reyan raised her eyebrows, her playfulness rippling through the slight hint of shadows massing around her. In that moment, the shadows seemed to sparkle with wicked darkness. Before Sannar could grab her, a slight twitch of her gift had her at Kainen's side with unnatural speed.

Kainen wondered then if she was drawing closer toward him for protection, or just because her gift finally being unbound gave her a chance to use it. As Sannar frowned to find her not where he expected to find her, Kainen's pride roared and he decided he didn't care what her reasons were.

He failed to keep a lid on the delighted smirk crossing his face as Reyan's arm brushed his and her hand slipped around the crook of his elbow. He knew she was only doing it to keep up the pretence, or possibly because the vibe Sannar was giving out had too many elements of dedicated interest toward her, but it was his arm she was holding, not Taz's or Demi's.

In that moment, muddled though the specifics were, he knew one thing for certain.

She's mine.

"Things change," Reyan said. "As it is, I'm only here because he asked me to be. He didn't say anything about having to deal with court things though, so I'm going to stay with the rickshaw until you're done."

Sannar frowned. "I see. We're about business then, which I suppose I appreciate."

As he turned away and set off toward the steps leading up to the building without another word or a look back, Demi pulled a resigned face and set off after him with Taz in tow.

Kainen turned to Reyan, but the absence of any

playfulness on her face brought the smile straight off of his.

"He's not looking," she said. "So don't do whatever you were about to do."

Kainen froze, his mind full of what he'd been about to do to keep up their pretence.

She gave him a knowing look. "Yeah, that. Don't. I'll do what you asked me to, so go play lords and ladies."

Ouch.

He frowned at her, but she refused to back down, her arms folded and her face all scrunchy against the sunlight.

"Okay. Be careful," he said instead.

She nodded. "I will."

"Properly careful. Don't get involved with anything, don't talk or stop to help anyone-"

"Kainen?"

Scary how his name sounded so right from her lips. "Yeah?"

"Go away."

Double ouch.

He did as he was told, a court lord reduced to obedience by one command. He couldn't help risking a look back though when he reached the doors of the building, just a glimpse. Reyan stood talking to Demi's realm-skipper, Trevor. No doubt she would wait until the coast was clear to fade into the shadows and go exploring, but he couldn't help wishing he had her beside him instead. Both to keep her safe, and because if anything was going to happen to him, she'd probably scare them off with her glaring.

He almost got left behind but Sannar was waiting for

him at the far end of the corridor. He'd barely noticed the enormous doorway of earthy rock carved with ancient symbols that led them into the mountain, or the cavernous corridor they walked down. As he entered the room where Demi and Taz were already seated, restlessness swamped around him.

He sank onto a chair at the long table with Taz between himself and Demi, and Sannar sitting opposite them. The wide open window arches overlooked part of the courtyard, but from there he couldn't see the rickshaw or Reyan.

"We're here as requested," Demi began. "What exactly is the problem?"

Sannar clasped his hands on the tabletop and Kainen recognised the dutiful expression covering the young man's face. He knew it well, because he often felt it falling from his own face at the end of every day, the weight of responsibilities and playing a part lifted only temporarily. It took all his effort sometimes, but he was good at playing the part.

Except recently when Reyan's got me goading her in front of the whole court and royalty.

"There's a beast that has long since dwelled beneath our court," Sannar said. "It was there before the court began, sleeping. Legends tell of its ability to consume matter, the nether and the life inside it."

"Let me guess, beastie's woken up," Taz suggested.

Sannar nodded. "We believe so. We think this might be what is causing the weakness in the veil between Faerie and the human realm."

Kainen frowned. "So essentially you have a nether-sucking creature beneath your court. No idea how to send it back to sleep, or get rid of it?"

"There are tales of course, but none that make much sense. We have theories that the Prime Realm banished the creature here to stop it attacking them long ago."

Demi sighed, rubbing a hand over her face.

"We know the basic histories, that most believe the Prime Realm is the place that all life flowed from, the human world, Faerie, all of it. At Arcanium we call it the Origin Realm."

"Nobody has accessed the Prime Realm in living or recorded memory," Sannar added. "There are rumours that gaps to it appear and disappear in the human world more often than in Faerie, but we've got no evidence to support this."

"If skip-ways are appearing at random in the human world, and it starts spreading into Faerie, that could get messy," Kainen said.

Sannar nodded. "This is the fear. We hope that finding a way to lull the beast will restore the peace of the nether between realms and worlds."

"Hope?" Taz asked. "Nothing confirmed?"

Sannar gave him an indignant look. "Nothing is ever confirmed where the nether is involved. It is a shifting nothingness, bearing matter seemingly at random."

Kainen sensed the balance of power shifting and surged forward to re-establish it.

"I guess nether and matter balance each other out." He'd heard that from one of his cousins who joined the

Nether Court long ago. "So if the nether is fading, so will the matter. Or there might be a big splurge and we'd end up with extra realms or catastrophes in the human world?"

Sannar's shoulders relaxed a fraction, apparently appeased by his knowledge.

"Exactly that. The last big surge we have recorded was the eruption of Pompeii in the human world. They have their own issues of course, tsunamis and earthquakes caused by their own climate control, or lack of it, but we reckon that Pompeii was most definitely the nether's doing."

"And do we have any idea what woke the beast up?" Kainen asked.

Sannar eyed him, then Demi, and finally Taz.

"Um, we haven't had anyone new come to court, except for one woman. She took to visiting a lot recently but we haven't seen her for a day or two."

He seemed reluctant to say anymore until Demi gave him a sharp look.

"You still insist on sponsorship here, right? Who sponsored them?"

Sannar grimaced. "Lady Blossom sponsored her entry. I asked my lady, but she said we weren't exactly in a position to refuse the royal family."

Kainen understood the reluctance, but at least Sannar was giving them truth instead of misdirection and trickery to protect a potential enemy.

Demi nodded. "Say no more then. How exactly do we get to this beast, and what do you know of it?"

"We have a door of *metirin* iron in the tunnels beneath

the mountain," Sannar explained. "Nothing so far has been able to get past it without the nether brothers opening the door, but the few that volunteered to go inside recently returned with wild tales of fire, water, earth, voices, and more. We can't risk any more nether brothers going inside."

Demi glanced at Taz, who rolled his eyes and shrugged his shoulders, wordlessly agreeing to whatever plan she was about to suggest.

"So you want FDPs to go in for you," she said.

Sannar nodded. "That's the one, yeah."

CHAPTER EIGHT
REYAN

Reyan watched Kainen walk into the building out of the corner of her eye. She was furious with him still. Not just for goading her into fighting him when she should have been the bigger person and dealt with the whole thing calmly, but also because he'd been showing the tiniest hint of promise at being a generally decent person.

I can't believe he can be kind and vulnerable out on the decks, then a complete arse to me in private.

He enjoyed winding her up, that much was clear. But she couldn't shake the instinct that the Kainen she'd seen out on the decks, the one who'd spoken into her mind, was the real him without the mask he had to keep in front of the court.

But then if he still has a huge crush on Demi, it's probably all pretence to stay on her good side.

She walked the length of the courtyard under the pretence of having a look, then pressed into the shadow of the mountain. The moment she was sure nobody was looking her way, she took a deep breath and folded herself into the shadows themselves.

She'd once tried to explain to someone how she managed to become shadow and disappear completely, but apparently the fact she dissipated her actual body and became mere thought and intent as part of the shadows was hard for others to get their head around.

When her father had traded her to the court in return for money and some level of protection for himself, the old lord, Kainen's father, had bound her gift. No escaping, no ability to flee when she wanted to avoid someone, and nowhere to hide either. The binding was lifted whenever she performed for the court, dancing with the shadows and contorting as an illusion for the benefit of the court's guests, but she'd missed the freedom of it and revelled in having it back.

Skimming through the shadows along the mountain's edge, she hesitated at the entrance to a tunnel, the wide opening sending out a wave of foreboding that made the shadows shiver.

Weird. Something's down there.

She'd learned to trust the shadows and their ability to read the mood of a place or the emotions of a person. They saw the dark sides of all things, both the good and the bad.

They resisted when she shifted through them and into the tunnel, but where light existed shadow had to dwell. In the firelight placed at even intervals along both sides of the tunnel walls, the shadows clustered with an overwhelming aura of uneasiness.

The sensation increased the further down the tunnel Reyan skimmed. She didn't see a soul and risked letting her human body reassemble, becoming a shadowed outline before taking solid form again. With the shadows resisting, it was easier to continue on foot.

Almost immediately the firelight illuminated a wall blocking her from going any further.

Not a wall, a door. She frowned.

The door took up the entire space of the tunnel, she could see the hinges on the right side, but there was a normal person-sized door cut into it on the left.

She crept up to the enormous door and lifted her hand, shivering as the shadows pulled away from it.

Metirin iron. What in the name of Faerie could need a metirin iron door this big?

She reached out for the handle of the smaller door. It might have been a structure left from older times with nothing strange on the other side at all, but the shadows were afraid of something behind the iron and she trusted them.

"What are you doing down here?" A demanding voice filled the tunnel.

Reyan flinched and scraped her palm on the door's lock as she twisted around. A girl was striding toward her, not much older than she was by the look of it, but with an expression of extreme suspicion. Her dark hair was tied back to reveal a ruddy face and rosy cheeks, cheerful looking enough if she'd actually been smiling instead of frowning behind her thin-rimmed glasses.

Before Reyan could find some kind of excuse, the girl stopped a short distance in front of her and uttered a tiny gasp.

"I'm sorry, Lady! Forgive me."

Reyan blinked. "Er... what?"

"I didn't mean any offence," the girl gabbled. "The shadows are thick in the firelight and I didn't recognise you."

Reyan stood in astonishment as the girl glanced over her shoulder then bowed low.

"Your appointment was all over the *Faerie Net* this morning, of course, but it took me a minute to recognise you."

"My appointment? What about the *Faerie Net*?"

Even as she asked, a cold sense of dread trickled through Reyan's limbs right to the bone. Aside from herself and Kainen, everyone at court thought that their engagement was real. A secret, a big shock, a travesty even given her low-born heritage, but they would have believed his word.

"Your appointment to Lady of the Illusion Court of course! Although they didn't use a very flattering picture of you. Oh, I'm sorry, I didn't mean… Um…"

The girl grimaced, the expression immediately twisting into a suspicious frown.

"Forgive me, Lady, but nobody's meant to be down here aside from the nether brothers, and they get really twitchy about that."

Reyan nodded automatically, still baffled about there apparently being something about her on the *Faerie Net*. Which meant it wasn't just their court and royalty they were tricking now but the whole of Faerie.

"Sorry, I got lost."

It was a lame excuse, and the girl didn't look like she believed a word of it.

"If you'll follow me," she said. "We've had to step up security because we had someone recently asking for access to certain parts of our halls. Rumours are also flying about the Forgotten regrouping, so we can't be too careful."

"Rumours?"

The girl nodded. "My dad is a trader on the river and he hears everything worth hearing. If he says the Forgotten are regrouping, there must be a stitch of truth in it from somewhere."

Reyan couldn't fault that logic but Demi had asked her to find out anything useful. Considering the Forgotten had been Demi's enemy in the last war, any rumours about them would count as useful.

"That doesn't sound good," she agreed. "But you said someone was asking for access, do you know who?"

The girl eyed her for several excruciatingly tense seconds.

"I don't, Lady. Sannar would be the best one to ask. If you'll follow me, I'll lead you out."

Reyan didn't bother nodding as the girl was already turning toward the exit with a determined expression. One final glance at the ominous iron wall and door, and Reyan shuddered. Whatever lay beyond was clearly powerful enough to warrant *metirin* iron, and that would no doubt be linked to whatever the Nether Court had called Demi in about.

None of that helped with the whole 'her being outed as a supposed lady on the *Faerie Net*'. She couldn't fathom Kainen remembering to send out any kind of press release about it, especially as the whole thing was a fake. But then perhaps Meri had done it on his behalf as his second-in-command. It was just the kind of thing she would take charge of.

"Here we are," the girl said the moment they reached the sunshine drenching the courtyard.

Reyan blinked against the light as they walked across the grass to Trevor, who stood inspecting something on his rickshaw.

"Thank you…?"

Reyan left the opening there, guessing having someone in the Nether Court thinking positively of her couldn't hurt.

"Oh, I'm Odella, Lady." She smiled then. "I'm not actually sworn or in service though. I just help out because my mum works here."

Reyan wrapped her arms around her middle, still overwhelmed by the honorific.

"Nice to meet you. Thanks for helping me find my way."

"No problem!"

She watched Odella walk away and made a mental note to check the *Faerie Net* and see exactly what kind of unflattering picture they had of her.

"Any luck, Lady?" Trevor asked.

He was glancing around at the courtyard and his expression was suspiciously innocent, but Reyan guessed he had Demi's confidence already and was assessing her as much as she was him.

"Apparently the Forgotten are regrouping, she says. Or her dad who's a trader did."

"Ah. Traders tend to hear everything worth hearing. So do us skippers, and there's definitely mutterings about the Forgotten. Nobody knows specifics either, which means the rumours are secretive enough to be based on truth."

Thinking back to the brief period where the war spilled into their court and onto the wider realms of Faerie, Reyan remembered how scared everyone had been.

"We don't want them back in any way," she muttered.

Trevor grinned. "No we don't. If I can hazard a suggestion though? As much as the Forgotten's ways aren't great, you may want to channel a little more entitlement in how you speak to people if you're going to pass for a lady of a court."

Reyan tensed. She wasn't a lady and she never would be, but nobody else was supposed to know that. Before she could find some way of brazening the situation out, Trevor chuckled.

"It's new to you clearly and given that picture on the *Faerie Net,* you're not naturally one of the high-borns. But then perhaps you don't want your lord thinking you're using him to climb the social ladder if you love him?"

"The whole thing is very new to me, to be honest," she word-tangled. "But the last thing I'm thinking about right now is social advancement."

"Well there we are then. Worth flirting with a little more entitlement in public, unless he's giving you trouble already?"

Reyan grinned then as realisation settled over her.

Demi's got him fishing on all accounts, even on whether Kainen's coercing me somehow. Or perhaps whether I'm tricking him.

She rolled her eyes at the thought of Kainen's deviousness and the panicked look on his face when he'd chosen her as his fake bride in front of the whole court.

Reyan?

His voice echoed in her mind as though she'd thought him into being, and she reminded herself she was still angry with him. He probably wouldn't apologise for infuriating her, and she didn't expect him to, but that didn't mean she had to roll over and let him treat her however he liked.

Ignoring him, she smiled at Trevor.

"Oh, don't worry," she said airily. "Him I can handle."

CHAPTER NINE
KAINEN

The tension crossing the table was getting on Kainen's nerves. He guessed the tapping of Demi's thumb over her fingers meant she was irritated too.

"Facing a beast we know nothing about is not ideal, but we'll agree to help," she said. "It won't be today, but I think we might be able to get some people lined up to go in and have a look."

Sannar frowned. "We had hoped to keep this quiet. I'm sure FDPs are used to discretion, but talk travels fast in Faerie and we want to limit the amount of people traipsing through the court, upsetting our brothers."

"Maybe they need shaking up a bit," Taz muttered.

Demi shot him a weary look as Sannar's expression shuttered.

"That is exactly what we can't have here," he said testily. "Lord Kainen, I'm sure as ruler of a court you can understand the necessity for not exciting things more than needed."

Kainen nodded, keeping his 'soothing ruffled feathers' look on his face. Behind that mask though he was restless, his foot itching to tap an irritated beat on the brown tiled floor.

Reyan? He sent his mind out to her.

If she was safe, maybe that would stop his leg bouncing

in a frustrated rhythm under the table. She was one of his court, sworn to it, and he was responsible for her. Sure, he didn't think twice when he sent people out on errands for him, but this was a stranger's court and she didn't know much about the world outside their home.

"What exactly do you want us to do?" Demi asked. "Put it back to sleep or get rid of it completely?"

Sannar regarded her, assessing.

Reyan? Kainen tried again. *Are you so mad at me you're trying to run away? I'll give you a head-start if you want, sweetheart, but I will catch up with you.*

The fleeting image of her hurt or in danger flashed through his mind, so vivid he worried it was somehow a warning.

No. She'd tell him if she was in danger. She was stubborn, but not stupid. She wouldn't let her anger rule over her safety.

Would she?

No, she was ignoring him and for some reason that irritated the life out of him. She was obstinate, he knew that much, so she had to be ignoring him on purpose. She wanted to mess him about? Fine, he'd pull rank.

Reyan, answer me.

He started to wonder if she'd somehow strayed beyond his reach, the idea that she'd gotten herself into some kind of mortifying trouble swelling. He leaned forward, ready to launch out of his seat and go searching for her.

Fine, how's this for an answer. Her irate voice filled his head louder than he was ready for. *I don't want to play games or have fun with you. I'm not interested in flirting with you, for pretence or otherwise. All I want is my freedom and that's something you'll probably never give me. Now what do you want?*

How could he answer that? He wasn't sure how so he didn't. She didn't reply again either, but the moment Demi and Taz wrapped up their discussion with Sannar, he stood and craned his neck until he could finally see Reyan through the window. She stood waiting by the rickshaw, chatting with Demi's realm-skipper.

He hadn't even heard the end of the conversation with Sannar, something Demi might have guessed already as she gave him a worried glance.

Reyan didn't look at him as they all clambered into the rickshaw, or when they arrived in the Court of Illusions moments later, landing with a smooth glide inside the queen's quarters.

"Well, that went better than I expected." Demi sighed. "We'll need to make a plan, but I think we can at least go in against this nether beast and see what we're up against. That'll be the next step."

Kainen nodded and slid out of the rickshaw. Even when Reyan stood at his side, albeit at a more-than-healthy distance apart, she wouldn't look at him.

"There's definitely something there," she said, focusing on Demi. "I felt it and the shadows fear it. Down one of the tunnels there's a massive door of *metirin* iron, and whatever is causing the feeling is behind that. I didn't get any further because someone found me, but she said that there are rumours of the Forgotten regrouping."

Demi sighed. "That confirms it then. The nether beast,

whatever it is, will be behind that iron."

"With my darling sister waiting in the wings," Taz grumbled.

Kainen caught Reyan's confused look and decided he'd risk Demi's potential wrath to explain.

"Blossom sponsored someone to spend time at the Nether Court," he said. "The only person they had visit, which suggests whoever woke the beast might have something to do with her, and why wake a creature that can gobble up the nether unless you plan to create some chaos?"

Reyan folded her arms over her middle and shrugged.

"Sounds about right to me."

"Do you want to interrogate her?" Taz asked.

Demi shook her head. "Not yet. Best let her think she has the upper hand and play the situation out. As for the Forgotten, I've got no doubt they're out there somewhere plotting away, but until they want to make a move, we focus on the task at hand. Now, I need to think."

Reyan didn't wait to be dismissed. She turned to leave and dodged Kainen as she passed. He trailed after her, his mind awash with potential things he could say to ease her fury with him.

He closed Demi and Taz's bedroom door behind them and opened his mouth to ask her to join him for a talk, but she gave him a furious glare and stormed into his room, slamming the door behind her. His room. She'd effectively shut him out of his own room.

Undeterred, he hovered outside, wondering madly if he should at least knock before barging in after her.

"Kainen!"

He groaned under his breath, his entire body tensing into knots. He recognised the deceptively soft and girlish voice calling for him and he couldn't think of a reason to run off or see anywhere suitable to disappear to.

He turned as Blossom fluttered to a stop in front of him, decked in flowing cotton trousers and a stiff long-sleeved shirt. She tucked a strand of honey-blonde hair behind her ear and smiled up at him.

Brazen through it and think of an excuse out of it.

He dredged up his usual indolent mask, the smile curling lazily over his lips.

"Lady Blossom."

She batted his arm and he fought the urge to shrug her fingers off as she let them linger.

"Blossom will do. After all, we are old friends." She whispered it like it was some big secret. "We go way back to better days, good old times, don't we?"

No. Absolutely not.

He couldn't risk upsetting her, but his mind was too frazzled from worry about the situation with Reyan to word-tangle effectively.

Blossom slid her hand over his forearm, her fingers chilly enough to bite after the warmth of the Nether Court.

"I understand. You can't say anything inflammatory, not with my awful brother's girlfriend swanning about. We all must make sacrifices, but the tide always turns eventually."

Kainen stared back at her, his mind fighting with his willpower. There were rumours about some of Taz's sisters. The eldest of the Oak Queen's children had rejected any link with royalty and moved to one of the big cities to deal in jewels. The second eldest, Belladonna, had openly defected in support of the Forgotten during the war and was currently in Faerie somewhere hiding out. But Blossom and the other younger princesses, they had barely been mentioned.

Blossom and Belladonna were always close.

He kept on smiling, his instincts clanging warning bells inside his head.

"I always do what is right for my court, and my court supports the rule of the two queens," he said.

A practiced enough line that it would sound genuine to some and suspicious to others. Even adding an unspoken 'for now' on the end would change the meaning entirely, so the way he'd phrased it wasn't a lie.

Blossom smiled, her blue eyes dancing with wicked delight, as if they were flirting around some kind of intimate secret. She brushed her hair back from her face, even though it didn't need moving, and leaned closer.

"Say no more. I imagine there's some deal or trickery that ties you to that horrid common girl? We'll find a way out of it. You deserve to marry someone with actual prospects."

Kainen kept his expression from twisting with great effort.

"Settling down is far from my mind at the moment," he said honestly. "I want to enjoy my youth and put all my effort into my court. I don't exactly lack social connections either. But anything is possible in the future. Have my staff been looking after you?"

Blossom nodded, her eyes rolling as she pouted.

"Yes, and your friend Ciel was most helpful. He will be an asset when we- but never mind about him. I'm not bothered about that cow of a queen or that horrid common girl you're toying with. It's you I'm interested in."

Kainen was speechless for once. Not only because she'd been so unerringly blunt about pursuing him, but also because of how she'd referred to Demi.

Calling Reyan a 'horrid common girl' didn't sit right with him either.

She has Belladonna's traditional ideals alright, but that doesn't mean she's any different to the normal elitist Fae.

He would have to raise this to Demi, it was only right to ensure his support was one hundred percent whole. As queen she had his loyalty and his court's, but he also owed her a debt of gratitude if nothing else after what he'd done to her.

But he had to get away from Blossom first.

"I understand," he said, hoping his smile and the suggestive wink would do the talking so he wouldn't have to. "I have a few people I need to deal with now, but I'm sure our paths will cross again."

Blossom frowned as if he'd confused her with the sudden dismissal, but she covered it quickly with a tinkling laugh and another touch to his arm.

"Of course. You're an important person now after all. Don't leave it too long though."

He forced down a shudder and gave her another smile before striding away from the main hall. If he went that way, Blossom would likely follow him. No, he would go to his study the long way and call Ciel to find out if Blossom had let slip anything useful.

Glancing back over his shoulder at the far end, he halted as a flash of blonde caught his attention. Reyan had left his room and was almost down the stairs to the main hall now, so he turned back and hurried after her.

Lingering at the edge of the arch that separated the hall from the top of the stairs, he watched as Reyan entered the crowd, her head held high as people whispered around her.

Until one person stepped out of the mass.

Anger fired through Kainen's chest, his gift buzzing with sinister thoughts as Ciel approached Reyan.

So they're friends, what the hell is wrong with me?

He watched, the anger turning to sharp daggers as Reyan's shoulders lowered and shook ever so slightly. She was laughing. Two seconds in Ciel's company and she was instantly smiling and laughing.

She's so relaxed with him, he marvelled, huffing a pained breath. *She's even letting him nudge her arm and stand close. If I did that, she'd probably snap at me.*

In that moment, thoughts of giving Ciel a taster of the strange pain he was feeling himself fired through Kainen's mind. His mind manipulation gift snapped with encouragement, urging him to do it.

Ciel could never be good enough for her, but then who would be? He frowned, ignoring the pull of his gift urging him to at least go and break them up.

Perhaps that was the problem. Ciel would do the honourable thing for a girl he liked. He'd be patient, let the girl make all the decisions, gauge her reactions, flatter her. And when the time was right, he'd quietly suggest that he could look after her, save her from whatever fate she was incapable of saving herself from, and they would be quiet and happy as much as court Fae could be happy and quiet, and they would go on to have many children who would all be raised quiet and happy too.

But Reyan didn't need anyone saving her.

Except me. She said that she wanted her freedom and that it was something I'd never give her. Well I'll show her. I'll go to her father, buy the debt in full and gift it to her. See how awful she thinks I am then!

Before the fake marriage thing, she'd smile at him in the hall. Everyone smiled at him, bobbed their heads in deference, but somehow when she did it, there was a little devilish twinkle in her eye. It had nothing to do with seduction, more like she found the sight of him amusing, and now he wanted nothing more than to find out why.

Except here she was smiling at Ciel instead. He bit his lip.

Was this how I made Taz feel the rare few times Demi was smiling at me? No wonder he hates me.

But then, Taz was in love with Demi from the very beginning, whereas with Reyan…

Oh orbs alive.

It couldn't be possible. He couldn't be that unlucky. Falling for Demi was one thing, and getting over her was a huge relief. But falling for Reyan when she thought he was an idiot and now no doubt hated him for making her fake a relationship with him, it was madness. And yet there

99

she was, smiling and laughing with Ciel, who was smiling and laughing back.

And all I can think about is drawing up the memory of his eighth birthday and tormenting him with it until he runs far, far away from her.

Kainen realised his feet were moving. He had no idea what he was doing, but Ciel and Reyan turned their heads as he approached.

"We need to discuss earlier," he said, his tone abrupt.

Reyan raised an eyebrow. That was her, 'excuse me, but a please isn't a sin, even if you are an entitled arse of a court lord' face.

Even that slight movement made his mouth twitch. He wanted to lift his hand, smooth his fingertips over the wrinkle on her brow. Maybe pass his thumb over-

"Please," he added, more for his own sake than hers.

He ignored Ciel staring in surprise at the sudden manners, then the subtle narrowing of his eyes.

He's guessed, he must have. Why do I have to keep getting into these emotional messes?

Kainen turned away, expecting Reyan to follow. He didn't dare look back until they reached his room but unlike the past few days of shared space, she wandered to the opening of the balcony.

To see if Ciel is still there? His chest pulsed hot with jealousy. *I need to end this. As soon as Demi and Taz leave, I'll give Reyan her freedom. And money. She can go anywhere she chooses. Anywhere but here. Anywhere but with him. Or the Nether Court.*

"You wanted to discuss stuff?" she asked, her tone flat,

her back to him.

He wanted her to turn around, to go back to the girl who was annoyed with him, shouting at him for dropping his socks everywhere and being a lazy, entitled idiot. But she didn't and he took a deep breath, forcing himself to do the hardest thing he could imagine.

"I'm going to sleep in the study tonight," he said. "If anyone comes in, not that they can but if they do, say I'm working late, or early. I'm sorry I got you into this."

Her body stiffened as he spoke. He tried to reassess his words, searching for what could have upset her, but he was doing the right thing, being a gentleman for once.

"Okay. Is that what you wanted to talk about?"

No emotion in her tone. His heart broke, his chest panging like a savage case of heartburn.

"Demi will likely ask if you can lend your shadow-weaving skills to the next assignment. Not sure what exactly we'll be facing, but it has something to do with a beast under the Nether Court. I'll allow it but only if it's danger-free, and if you agree."

"You're giving me a choice?"

That hurt. Kainen winced, but of course she couldn't see it with her back to him.

"In this court, while you're safe, I may push my luck when I need to. Outside of this court, your safety is my concern but I'd never force you to do anything you weren't comfortable with. I did that once for the sake of the war. Never again, so yes you always have a choice with me."

When she didn't answer immediately, he took a couple of steps toward the bathroom door. He would hole up in his study, sleep there and eat there. Reyan could decide not to help them and he'd honour that. Then as soon as the awful Blossom was gone and Demi and Taz with her, he'd sort Reyan her freedom and anything she needed. Then he'd ask her to leave.

But he couldn't resist one final jab, a parting shot at angering her, at dredging some form of spark from her toward him.

"Perhaps if you're not interested in coming with us, I should take Blossom instead, see what she's good for."

It was a disgusting comment lined with innuendo, and an even worse thought.

Call me a pig. Glare at me. Do something. Anything.

Reyan shrugged. "Maybe you should."

CHAPTER TEN
REYAN

"I should take Blossom instead."

Reyan had no idea why those words taunted her, even after Kainen had shut himself away in his study. She tried opening the bathroom door despite knowing it only worked as a multi-entry door for him, but of course she found the empty bathroom on the other side.

An hour passed before she decided not to hide away anymore. She still called this court home and she'd be damned if Kainen was going to be the reason she hid herself away in his bedroom.

She left the room and walked the familiar corridor to the main hall. The moment she descended the stairs, doubt swelled. People she knew well enough turned to look at her as she passed. A few managed fake smiles, perhaps thinking ahead of their own social advancement when she became a lady, but many she might have called casual friends turned their heads and scurried on their way.

It was Kainen's fault but she couldn't even bring herself to be angry about it. Also, until he released her from this ridiculous pretence, she couldn't exactly go and help with her normal routine or chores because she might get called away halfway through. The thought of picking up and dropping a task to play at being a court lady was a worse embarrassment somehow than not helping at all.

The main hall pool glinted in the light coming through

from the new sky-holes, but a quick glance at the balcony to the queen's quarters suggested there was no hope of catching Demi's eye and being invited up. She could knock of course, but she didn't have much reason until Kainen came to get her for the next assignment.

"Rey!"

She'd never been so glad to hear a familiar voice. She turned and smiled as Ciel jogged up toward her. As Kainen's oldest friend and unofficial court spy, he commanded a great deal of respect. The moment he joined her, the whispering crowd seemed to return to their normal level of noise and go about their business.

"Regretting your decision to play Faerie-tale princess?" he asked, grinning.

She rolled her eyes. "I'm no princess, and I'm also no lady. But regrets are a luxury and I've next to no way of affording anything, let alone luxuries."

His face dipped into a frown. "I've made a big effort of not asking you or Kainen, but what exactly does he have over you?"

Reyan froze at the abrupt questioning. Nobody had ever told her she couldn't discuss the terms of the debt that kept her tied to the court, but it wasn't something she wanted publicised. She eyed Ciel's earnest face and knew he of all people could be trusted not to blab secrets. She glanced around for potential prying ears and leaned in close.

"My father had some issues after I was born and my mother left us. He ran up debts and sank the whole family fortune. He owed the old lord a lot of money, so instead of causing trouble, he gave me to them instead."

She ignored the disapproving press of Ciel's lips and the pity massing in his blue eyes. She'd seen it all before.

"The terms are that I belong to the court as long as they keep funding my father. If he claims me back, or tries to dictate anything to do with me, the deal is off. If the court decides to reject my service at any time, for any reason, his payments stop."

She forced herself to hold her head high and meet Ciel's gaze as he reached out a hand. She folded her arms across her chest and twisted slightly to avoid the contact.

"That's awful." He kept his voice low at least, even if his pity wasn't veiled. "And Kainen hasn't released you?"

She shook her head. "He can't unless he buys me fully from my father first and frees me, and my father doesn't have any reason to agree to that considering he's living comfortably on the deal already."

Ciel rubbed his mouth. "What kind of payment would your father accept?"

"Why are you so interested all of a sudden?" she asked.

He sighed. Again he reached out, but seemed to think better of it as she took a hesitant, wary step back.

"I'm worried Kainen might buy the debt from him fully and use it, perhaps even force you to marry him. What else would this ridiculous engagement farce be about? I know he hates the idea of a union with the royal family."

Reyan snorted. "Would you want to marry her, royal or not?"

A rueful look passed over his face and he shoved his hands in his pockets.

"Okay that's fair, but I've seen the way Kainen looks at

you."

Of course he had, because Kainen was a great actor. He had to be if he could convince his entire court he was in love with a destitute sworn member who had no wealth and no standing in Fae society. The engagement also very sneakily hid his feelings for Demi too, enabling him to reassure her that she could allow him close without fearing his crush would become a problem again.

"His feeling are his business." She shrugged. "I have very little say in most things, unless I can find a way to buy the debt myself and my father will never give it to me direct."

Ciel frowned deeper. Reyan glanced around but nobody seemed to be paying any attention to them. She even risked a look up at Kainen's bedroom balcony, but there was no sign of him having emerged. Even so, with the previous dirty looks from people and now the weird turn of Ciel's questions, she wanted nothing more than to be back up there. She could sink into another *Carrie's Castle* book and escape the whole thing for a while. Although she couldn't do anything about her growing hunger, too embarrassed to go and ask at the kitchens and not able to summon anything with a click her fingers like Kainen could, not unless it came from the cleaning supply cupboard.

"Has he forced you to do anything you don't want to do?" Ciel's question came completely out of the blue.

"What, Kainen?" she asked. He nodded. "Of course not. You of all people should know he has his issues but he's not a monster."

He didn't look convinced. "There's a rumour going

around that someone came into the room and saw him holding you against your will. Apparently, the queen arrived before he could do anything awful. Then there are all those rumours about how he treated the queen when she was just a fairy."

Reyan started to laugh then, even as the blush fired across her cheeks. Their argument had only been a few hours ago, so news sure did get round fast. Then again, Ciel made it his job to know everything. This was probably his kindly way of finding out what her intentions were with Kainen like vetting some gold-digger, not the other way around.

"No, it's fine."

Irritation flared across his face. "That's fine? You're happy for him to touch you like that?"

"Like what?"

A flash of memory leapt forward, of Kainen holding her tight against him and murmuring into her ear. She'd given as good as she got, or as good as she could with the no attacking stipulations he'd put on her.

But I never once felt scared. Angry yes, but never once have I felt worried about being around him.

"She said he had you pinned and his hands were all over you, and you were telling him to let you go," Ciel insisted.

Reyan bit her lips together, mortified someone had seen that, but also amused by Ciel's fury. The 'she' was also a curiosity. She couldn't remember anyone other than Demi coming in then, but then she thought of the acidic looks Meri had given her recently. She wondered if Kainen's second-in-command was keeping a close eye on her for her sake or for his. His most likely, but at least he had someone who cared.

"Oh, that. I wasn't in any danger, and I know he'd have stopped if I really wanted him to."

The words sounded wrong even as she said them. Ciel seemed to straighten up two more indignant inches until he towered over her.

"If you wanted him to, so what is this, you're interested in him after all? Or perhaps interested in the position more likely?"

People were watching them unashamedly now that his voice had risen, and it was a rarity for him to lose control.

He thinks I'm going to take his place in Kainen's life or something? Maybe he secretly fancies him, who knows.

She let her folded arms drop and gave him her best no-nonsense glare, the one that even had Kainen backing down once or twice.

"Who I'm interested in is none of your business. As for social advancement, I don't give a toss about society or my place in it. Kainen is the lord of this court so he does as he sees fit. But as for my interests, all I want is my freedom."

Her voice filled the entire hall. She was almost sure Kainen would have heard it tucked in his study somewhere, but if he wanted to harangue her about it he could come out of his hole and show himself.

She stormed through the crowd, up the steps and slammed into the bedroom. She couldn't summon food like Kainen did, but apparently he was at least thinking of her because there was a tray of food still hot on the table. She sank into her armchair to devour it.

She shouldn't have lost her temper with Ciel. Even though he was needling her, he was only doing his unofficial job looking after Kainen's interests. She also wasn't in any position to be chatting back to his friends.

I shouldn't have been so snappy with Kainen either. She slammed the empty bowl back onto the tray. *This is his bedroom and because of me he's hiding in his study.*

But there was nothing she could do about that now. When he wanted to speak to her, he would find her. She yawned, covering her mouth with the back of her hand, and eyed the bed he'd conjured up for her.

A misshapen lump rucked up the top of the covers and she pulled them down to find familiar clothes tangled in one big bundle. Her clothes. Kainen had apparently seen fit to summon the entire messy contents of her trunk in the dorms for her, something she'd not even considered.

Relieved she didn't have to face anyone now to go and fetch fresh clothes, she washed in the opulent bathroom and settled down in bed with her book. Tired, her eyelids refused to stay open, but her mind drifted just the waking side of dreams.

He's insufferable really. I never thought about it, but he's always strutting around being charming to people, and yet none of them have seen the real him.

A flash of his arms pinned tight around her waist, his lips brushing her ear.

Even when he's taunting, he's still gentle. I don't think he's the kind of person who wants to be horrible at all, but he's known nothing else all his life.

She wondered what he'd be like if he had people around

him that he could trust and be himself with. No charm or illusion of a court lord, simply Kainen. She smiled into her pillow, guessing he'd still be as fun, still teasing and taunting.

She could imagine sitting on his study desk and laughing with him, enduring that long moment of eye contact that he did so well which could make anyone flustered.

I wonder if he's the kind of person who would curl up and sit still on lazy days, or if he'd insist on finding something active to do.

The image of being curled up beside him flickered, both of them quietly reading with her head on his lap, his fingers idly twining through her hair.

Reyan's eyes snapped open.

The room anticipated necessities according to its occupants, so she hadn't bothered to turn out lights and things when settling down to read, but now her eyes welcomed the darkness the room had plunged her into.

"Oh, no." She whispered to the shadows. "Don't you dare. I do not fancy him."

She could sense the shadows smoothing around her like comforting friends. She settled back down on the pillow with a huff. 'Fancy' was a silly word anyway, a childish word that was nowhere near overpowering enough to match up to lust and not pure enough to embody real love.

When he comes out of that infernal study, I'm going to behave myself. We'll do the assignment, get everything sorted, the royals will go home and everything will return to normal.

Kainen would do his duty to his queen and once that was over, he'd forget all about the fake engagement. He could carry on hiding his crush on Demi, she could go back to being invisible and one day save enough to buy her freedom from the court.

She felt sure that was how it was supposed to be, and she was only upset because it was a cruel and stupid system that left her back where she started with no reward for her efforts.

She most definitely wasn't upset because she fancied him.

CHAPTER ELEVEN
KAINEN

Kainen knew he was being childish.

That still didn't stop him from making a rash decision about Reyan without consulting her first. He met Demi and Taz outside their rooms a while after his not-actually-an-argument with Reyan, mindful to keep his voice down so close to his bedroom door.

"Reyan hasn't technically agreed to this part of the assignment yet," he admitted. "I know you're worried about losing time though, so I'll do my best in her place."

Demi frowned. "She said she doesn't want to go?"

"Not exactly, but she hasn't said a definite yes and I don't like the idea of taking her into danger unless I know exactly what it is first."

He voiced his reservations against his better judgement and expected some smart remark from Taz at least, but was met with raised eyebrows. The quiet surprise on both their faces somehow made him feel worse instead of better.

They think so low of me they assumed I'd find a way to force her. Or they can see that I wouldn't force her, but they're surprised I actually care.

He hadn't told anyone except Meri that he was leaving the court either, but he grudgingly agreed that she could tell Reyan of his absence if the matter happened to come up. Not Ciel or anyone else though, he'd been adamant about that. If she found that weird, she was even better at masking her emotions than he was. Which was also why her showing such disapproval of seeing him and Reyan together seemed strange.

He pushed his thoughts aside as Demi opened her bedroom door and stepped inside.

"We'll go by troll now then, if you're ready?"

She and Taz were still giving him wary looks, but he ignored it and shut her bedroom door behind them. Leaving Reyan behind was for the best, safest for her.

"Always ready," he quipped. "How bad can an ancient slumbering nether beast be anyway?"

"I'm thinking 'us' level bad," Taz scoffed.

As Demi pulled out her orb and called her realm-skipper to pick them up, Kainen risked a tiny smile in Taz's direction.

At least he's talking to me.

The air shivered as Trevor arrived with the rickshaw to skip them back to the Nether Court, but Kainen spared a glance toward the bedroom door before clambering into the back seat.

Reyan would likely be even more furious when she found out he'd gone without her. But perhaps they would be able to see what type of danger the nether beast was, then she could find some way to help them still.

Trevor took off at a run and Kainen watched the nether twist around them momentarily before Demi's room vanished and the courtyard of the Nether Court formed around them. Whereas they'd visited in blistering sunshine earlier, now the air was warm and balmy and the courtyard lit by firelight in the night-time. A distant chiming echoed from somewhere, almost like bells or gentle voices singing, and Kainen wished he'd risked bringing Reyan after all.

Maybe I can find some way to trade for a longer visit here without the added danger element. We must have something the Nether Court want. Our wine maybe. Then she could enjoy herself a bit more.

Putting that thought on his mental 'to do' pile, he clambered out of the rickshaw and turned to see Sannar striding toward them, his nether brother robe partly tucked into the waist of his jeans.

"We'll have to move fairly quickly," Sannar said.

Moments passed before he realised who he was talking to, and Kainen tried not to smirk as Sannar dropped to his knees, his head almost touching them.

Demi rolled her eyes.

"It's fine, you don't have to bow every time I show up. This isn't an official 'me as queen' visit anyway, I'm here as an FDP."

"Don't tell Milo that," Taz muttered.

Kainen remembered Milo from his time at Arcanium, the quiet young man who Demi and Taz had befriended on assignment and dragged back with them. He was now Arcanium's librarian and also the Chief Aide to Demi's royal court.

Demi caught Kainen's eye and pulled a face.

"Milo's taking this whole queen and court thing way more seriously than I am," she explained. "He insists no appearance is 'just an FDP' appearance when you're royal."

Kainen nodded. "Courts are serious. The way Faerie was before the war, courts were actually the only places someone without family could make a name for themselves."

"That's true," Sannar said, then realised he was still kneeling before a queen. "Sorry."

Kainen held his ground as Demi turned to face him.

"Does your court still demand sponsorship?" she asked, arms folding over her chest in pre-emptive defence.

"No, not since I stopped that. I don't think many of the other courts bother either. Maybe a recommendation will help, but I know the Flora and Fauna courts definitely take people on merit now."

Sannar looked up, doubt scrawled across his face, then stood up again.

"We technically do insist on sponsorship, but there's always a way around it. I try to take through as many without a sponsor as I can without... well, without people realising."

'People' meaning his lady. Kainen couldn't help but be impressed that Sannar was essentially flouting his court's rules in the name of good. It was also easier to see him as a person without Reyan here clouding the issue.

Without me clouding the issue because of her.

Demi's grumpy expression settled and she dropped her arms to her sides.

"Well, that's something. I'm not taking any of this lightly," she insisted.

Taz slid an arm around her shoulders. "Of course you're

not. You're unfailingly dedicated to every piece of paper Milo waves under your nose, most of which have very little purpose but look good with your signature on it. Although, your signature is awful."

Sannar's gaze bounced between them with horrified fascination, but Kainen scuffed his feet, eager to get going. Sannar grimaced at the noise and looked over his shoulder.

"Well, welcome all the same," he said, his voice lowering. "But we'll have to be quick because the lady isn't too keen on you being here. She didn't technically say no, but I think she's worried you'll make things worse. Um… sorry."

Demi shrugged. "She doesn't like me because I'm young with human blood, that's fine. A lot of Fae don't. Lead the way and we'll see what we're dealing with, but it won't be fixed in one night anyway."

Sannar nodded and set off toward the shadow of the mountain. Kainen took a steadying breath and raised a protection warding around himself, trusting Taz and Demi to sort themselves.

They were more than capable, he knew that, but as they followed Sannar into the mountain and down a narrow tunnel lit by fire, his thoughts turned back to Reyan. He had no idea if she could protect or defend herself. As far as he was aware, she had no Fae gift either. Her ability to wield and dissipate into shadow was a rare ability, more often something someone was born with than gifted with. But short of her taking part in combat training at court, he had no idea whether she could so much as raise a warding.

She's very good at vanishing socks though.

His lips twitched at the thought. Such a deep thought that he flinched when Demi appeared beside him with Taz welded to her side, his orange wings unfurled ready at his back.

"We should talk at some point," she said quietly. "About now and the future, not the past. The Lady of the Flora Court and the Lady of this one both patronise me. The Lord of the Fauna Court is never concentrating on what I'm saying. I won't even begin to discuss the jokes the Lord of the Revels court makes. Words will only deal with Milo still, although they keep sending me books which Milo then steals."

Kainen read between the lines and smiled. It was a peace offering, something he didn't deserve and had no right to even hope for. But even though Demi was giving it to him freely, his pride needed some convincing.

"You need someone who'll tell you straight," he said.

She nodded. "Pretty much. Taz knows the ins and outs of being in a court but not running one. Milo knows the histories but not the people. Ace is good with the people, but none of us have actually run a court before."

"Whereas I may be new to it, but I've been running parts of it since I was little for my father," Kainen finished. "Ask whatever you need to. Oh, and at the risk of being unpopular, I got caught by Blossom earlier. She wasn't very complimentary of you, and kept going on about 'old friends' and 'better times'."

He caught Taz's eye, unsure whether to continue. His expression was unreadable in the shadowed tunnel, but he didn't spring to defend his sister.

"We're thinking Blossom is working with Belladonna and any remnant of the Forgotten that survived," Demi announced.

She said it so casually and Taz gave her an incredulous look until she stared back at him. Kainen guessed they were having another mind-speak argument. Then Taz sighed.

"They were always close, but you can probably remember that much," he admitted. "Blossom insisted she had nothing to do with the Forgotten or the war, but my mother didn't exactly interrogate her. I think she's afraid of alienating any more kids. Blossom spends most of her time at the Revel Court now though, and they have been thoroughly interrogated."

"Doesn't mean a thing," Demi grumbled.

"No, but we let it play out all the same."

Kainen let them bicker as the tunnel dipped lower and the air grew colder. He sensed the depths growing thicker too, the age leeching from the very rock and shadow around them.

Reyan would be able to read the shadows and know instantly.

Irritated by his failings, he picked up the pace. Demi had asked to talk properly at some point and that was progress enough. Now he just had to beat some kind of ancient beast and he could go back to Reyan and his fake engagement.

Perhaps he could apologise and offer to speak to her father about the debt, that would cheer her up. Although he liked the idea of surprising her with her full freedom better.

She might even consider staying a while.

Sannar stopped in front of a large door of thick metal, the rest of them hovering behind him.

Metirin iron.

Kainen reached out a hand and touched the cold surface. The only known substance that muted gifts and pierced through wardings. He'd held his protection warding around him for the whole walk, an easy thing for someone who'd practiced and used it for years, but now trepidation sent his blood thundering. Any beast that needed to be kept out by a huge iron door wouldn't be the kind they could settle easily.

"This is as far as we feel safe going," Sannar said. "We have that smaller hatch door, but once that's open you'll need to dash through quick and I'll close it behind you. Knock three times on it and I'll open it again."

Demi frowned but summoned a ball of icy blue fire in one hand, holding it aloft. Taz wriggled with his hands behind his back until his wings stretched outwards and the feathers burst into flame. Unable to conjure such options, Kainen wearily pulled one of the lit wooden torches from the wall.

"First sign of trouble, we double back," Demi warned. "No heroics. We're here to see what we're dealing with."

Kainen nodded, although she didn't bother to look at Taz for confirmation.

"Three, two, one." Sannar swung the smaller hatch door open. "Quick!"

Taz darted inside first with Demi right behind him. Kainen followed, his eyes adjusting to the barely lit gloom around them as Sannar slammed the door with a crash behind them.

"We didn't think to ask if there's any plan of the routes down here," Taz muttered.

Even with his voice quiet, the words seemed to echo off the walls that were right beside them.

"Nobody's been this far in living or recorded memory other than the nether brothers going as far as the entrance," Demi reminded him, her words whispering back to them. "There won't be plans. Stay together. Kainen, let your warding merge with ours. If I say back, we run."

He nodded and focused on the edges of his protection, pushing the dome around him out until the strands of magic wove around the combined safety of Demi and Taz's.

That they trusted him enough to let him in, or Demi did at least, was another blessed miracle. But then she never had been the type to leave anyone stranded, not even him.

"Not leave anyone stranded, not even him."

His own thoughts whispered around them. He stumbled to a halt, the other two turning to face him.

"We're definitely not alone." Demi glanced around as if she could see right through the darkness.

A crackle of blue light seared past her, blazing orange like fire sparks before dissipating into the darkness.

"Was that your fire?" Taz asked.

Demi nodded. "My energy gift, and if I saw right, your wings."

"And the whispering might be my mind-reading gift," Kainen added. "A beast that uses our gifts against us?"

They took another couple of steps, their footfalls

echoing even though the walls remained tight either side of them with Taz's wings wisping a brushing sound against the rock.

Looking up, Kainen could make out the ceiling, so close he could jump and touch it, but no natural cause for echoes.

"The nether is basically chaos," Taz murmured.

Demi grimaced. "So the gifts we have, but wielded with no control?"

"Sounds like a standard day at Arcanium," Kainen said without thinking.

Even Taz grinned at that. Another flash ripped past them, ice blue like lightning. Kainen dodged as it seared right through their warding, but knocked his head right into the path of a searing patch of flaming feathers.

"Orbs, are you okay?" Demi asked.

Kainen pressed tentative fingers to his cheek and winced.

"I'll be fine, but if it can get through wardings that easily, especially a queen's combined with a king's and a court lord's..."

He left the ominous suggestion hanging there as a dull thundering noise started up and the tunnel shook. A dark green blur emerged from the darkness, moving fast.

"Did you bring Leo?" Taz asked.

Demi shook her head. "No! He's at home, I checked with Ace before we left the court."

The enormous lizard charged toward them and Kainen dropped his torch. He shoved Demi toward Taz and leapt in the other direction. The thundering pounded closer and he pressed flat against the tunnel wall. A brisk brush of air whipped his hair about, then nothing. No pounding, no air.

"It doesn't seem to hold the attacks for long," Demi said.

She and Taz looked further away than the tunnel should have allowed, but close enough to be visible as she twisted back and forth.

"Can you guys see the atrium as well?" she asked.

"No, just darkness and you," Taz said, his hands clamping onto her shoulders. "Can you feel that?"

"I can hear you, but nothing else. Urgh, sour. Kainen, is this you?"

The sour taste on the tongue. Demi had mentioned it to him before that his compulsion gift tasted sour, like licking an earwax-covered lemon. He'd never ended up asking how she knew what an earwax-covered lemon tasted like.

"I promise you I'm not using any gifts right now," he shouted back. "You're both a lot further away than you were though."

As if the nether beast had heard him, Demi and Taz disappeared, blinking out of existence.

"You've vanished. Can you hear me?"

Nothing. No voices echoed back, and he couldn't even see lines of anything in the dark. He reached behind him and rested his fingers on the wall, something solid the nether apparently couldn't or wouldn't take from him.

He started shuffling along the wall. It would lead him back to the door. If Taz and Demi were in trouble, he could get Sannar and the courts and half of Faerie back here to help. They'd tear down the mountain if they had to.

Before he could go more than a few steps, light blinded

him. Raising one hand to shield his eyes, he blinked enough to make out his father's dark hall from their old house. The moment his father had been carted off to the Forever mountains as a traitor and Kainen had been named Lord of the Illusion Court in his place, he'd had torn the house down and renounced the Mage of Nightmares title. Nobody needed any more nightmares, least of all him.

The familiar scent of dust and silver polish tickled his nose, the chill from the enormous room made almost entirely of black marble seeping into his bones.

A sour taste on his tongue.

The beast is using my own gift against me.

He forced himself to face one of his most shameful memories, the same way he'd forced countless others to face theirs through his gift.

Demi sat in the cage glowering up at him, distrust clear in her eyes.

How did I never see that when it happened? I thought she was fighting back, but she was just fighting. She's petrified.

Shame and guilt-induced rage filled his insides and burned through his gut as darkness swamped around him once more.

Something solid slammed into his chest. He grunted, the breath pummelled out of him as his feet left the floor. The sensation of being pushed through the air filled his head and he reached out to shove at whatever was pushing him. His hands wavered through nothing. A jagged pulse of energy raged where matter should have been, and he sent his gift forward, seeking anything he could find.

Age and malice screamed back at him, a roar of pure chaos that wanted to tear the ordered fabric of Faerie apart. The absence of anything except feeling filled him, as though he'd become nothing except wisps of the nether. But the sensation slipped away again so suddenly that he was almost glad when something, a wall he assumed, slammed against his shoulders. He jolted, his head flying back with a sickening crack.

The pressure against his front disappeared and he hit the ground in a crumpled heap.

As his consciousness slithered away, he heard frantic voices calling his name.

It's okay.

He tried to reassure them, although who 'they' were he couldn't remember now.

It's okay. She's safe at court.

CHAPTER TWELVE
REYAN

Reyan stood at the edge of Kainen's balcony the morning after her altercation with Ciel and sighed to herself yet again. Kainen had been good to his word and remained in the study all night. At least, she assumed he'd been in the study all night. He could move through the court at will without ever once passing through the bedroom to get out, so he could have left it without her knowing. Either way, she hadn't seen him and assumed he was avoiding her.

Maybe it's for the best. I know he's not a bad person, but I can't let anything distract me from getting out of here. Not even dodgy suggestive dreams of a future I'll never have.

Short of asking Demi to somehow free her from the court, which she had no reason to do, Reyan had to rely on Kainen letting her go out of sheer decency.

She walked across the floor and stooped down to pick up yet another discarded sock. Her fingers skimmed cold stone instead of fabric and she frowned.

That's the second time I've done that, thought the shadows were one of his socks needing tidying.

In any other case she'd have assumed the shadows were trying to tell her something, or the court was. But Kainen had been on her mind ever since he'd left the room in a huff.

She waited for- no, *wanted* him to come find her and ask for her decision about the assignment he'd mentioned. She could knock on the bathroom door, guessing that whatever room was behind it for her, he would likely hear it and answer. He could also summon her with a click of his fingers if he chose, yet he hadn't bothered.

Taking a deep breath, she marched over to the bathroom door and rapped three loud knocks on the wood before she could lose her nerve.

He has to tell me what Demi wants from me anyway. This has nothing to do with me and him. Not that there is a me and him. Because there isn't.

Moments trickled away until she realised he either wasn't on the other side or wasn't willing to answer. Restless, she eyed the room for other ideas.

She could try finding Ciel, but that would be excruciating. Especially as she had the unnerving idea that Ciel was beginning to see her more as a potential life-mate and not as his friend.

While waiting for Kainen to surface, she'd slept, eaten from the food that had randomly arrived, bathed, read another *Carrie's Castle* book, and tried to consider some kind of life as Ciel's girlfriend, if he ever decided to come out with it and actually ask her.

Each time she tried visualising it, Kainen popped up in her head. Every romantic scene she envisioned with Ciel, then frustratedly with some imaginary person she conjured up, Kainen materialised with a sarcastic comeback. The thought of him interrupted every imagined kiss. She would have assumed he was using his illusion gift on her but he had no reason to do that.

Someone knocked on the door to the hall and she rushed to answer it, smoothing down her hair as wild thoughts of Kainen coming to fetch her filled her head.

I'll pretend I've barely noticed his absence. No sense losing face over some court lord way out of my league. It's probably a big game to him anyway, passing time until the royals leave and he can go back to mooning over Demi without having to pretend.

She threw open the door, ready to say something quippy like 'oh, it's you.'

"Oh." She blinked at Ciel's hopeful smile. "It's you."

The smile dimmed. "Disappointed? I don't want us to fight anymore, I promise."

She couldn't do anything about the flush on her cheeks, but she shook her head and shrugged her shoulders.

"You're silly, but I agree no more fighting. What's up?"

"I need to talk to you about something, but it's more of a walking thing than a standing in our lord's bedroom doorway thing."

She snickered and closed the door behind her. Kainen could summon her any time he liked, or he could come and find her. A walk would clear her head and do her some good, especially when it came about without her having to beg for it first.

"I heard you might be leaving court again for a bit," Ciel said. "But I thought you would have gone already. Haven't seen him sulking about for a while either. Are you leaving soon?"

"I haven't heard any plans yet but I will being going.

Even if Kai- *he* is a pain in the behind, he said I could have the choice and I want to be able to help Demi."

Ciel shook his head with a soft laugh. "Still amazes me she's our new queen and you call her by her nickname."

"Still amazed she lets me. But she's nice. A good person. I'm glad she's leading us now. One day people won't be allowed to sell their kids into service like my father did with me."

She had secretly hoped that change would have come overnight, backdated so all her problems were done with. But even she knew that it would create a whole host of problems, Fae left without the ability to survive or pay their way when their owners were made to free them, or sent to the furthest reaches of the realms that the queens were still fighting to regain from the remnants of the Forgotten who'd fled into hiding there.

Ciel stopped walking and turned to face her. They stood in the middle of the hallway that led out to the decks. There was nothing out there but also nothing else much in the hall either. With a frown, Reyan stopped beside him.

"I'm going to speak to Kainen later," Ciel announced. "I'm going to tell him that I want to buy your father's debt from him, then go to your father and pay him to free you."

Reyan blinked at him. "I- what? Why?"

"We've become close, Rey. You must know, you must have figured out by now how I feel about you. If you were mine, engaged to me instead, I could protect you."

Her heart started to thud, her blood pounding through her in agonised panic.

"Wait, you're proposing? That's mad, I'm only

eighteen!"

He took her hands and she forced herself not to flinch away as her mind raced.

It could be her ticket out, even though being engaged to him would simply be a different kind of service. He'd have expectations of her, ones she hadn't had any time to process. He had feelings for her, she'd suspected that, but nothing like this.

"I know you're young and I'm only three years older, but I don't think that matters. No doubt you have to finish whatever this mad fake engagement thing is that he's got you doing. But you'd be safe this way."

She could imagine herself being safe with Ciel. He'd care for her, be thoughtful to her.

I can't do it, not when I don't share those types of feelings for him. It'd be one type of chain into another.

"I don't want to take advantage of you," she mumbled, refusing to meet his eyes.

He squeezed her hands. "I know you don't feel for me like that yet. But you could grow to. We get on so well as it is and love can grow from friendship. And you'd be free."

She bit her lip. To be with Ciel, to know she had that safety, that companionship. To be free of the dorms and not have to answer every damn summons Kainen or his staff sent her. Also, not that it mattered to her, Ciel came from a good Fae family, established and stable enough for her freedom to be respected by everyone.

"Say you'll at least think about it," Ciel urged. "If you were mine, I'd always look after you."

If you were mine.

Mine.

His.

The mere thought of being owned again, even by someone kind, had her taking a step back. Before she could pull her hands free, Ciel leaned forward and pressed his mouth to hers.

She froze. He kissed her softly, not seeming to care that she wasn't kissing back. Despite her shock, one thought roared in her head, that he wasn't Kainen.

Orbs alive, what is wrong with me?!

Before she could gather herself and shove him off, he pulled away. His anxious expression had softened, his lips curving up as if he already expected her to say yes.

He might have said something further, although Reyan didn't think she'd be able to answer whatever it was because the sheer panic and wrongness of the whole thing made her feel ill. But before he could speak, a throat cleared.

Reyan flinched back and tore her fingers free of his. Meri stood there with disapproval stamped across her face.

"Word has come through about Kainen," she said. "I thought you should know, considering you're currently his intended."

Reyan couldn't drag her thoughts together quick enough, wrapping her arms around her torso for strength.

"What? Who's intended? What?"

Meri rolled her eyes then, the harsh exterior cracking a sliver.

"He's been taken ill on the assignment."

Reyan froze. "What? What assignment?"

"Orbs alive, do you not pay attention to anything? He left with the queen and king consort last night to do their FDP assignment. He's now sent word back saying that there's a "snag", his wording not mine, and that he's "not too seriously injured", which tells us next to nothing."

He went without me. Why would he go without me, without even giving me a chance to go along? Did Demi decide she didn't need me after all? Is he doing it to be spiteful because I snapped at him?

Except he had given her a chance. She could have gone to find him, could have agreed to go. She could have knocked on Demi's door and asked what the plan was so she could be prepared. It was her choice, he'd told her that much, and she'd refused to put herself forward by doing nothing. By sulking in his room like a maiden waiting to be rescued. Now he was out there somewhere, hurt and probably suffering alone given the past between him and Demi and Taz.

"Where is he?" she asked.

She glanced at Ciel, wondering with rising irritation why he wasn't looking more worried. His attention was on her still despite Kainen, his oldest friend, being injured.

"I'm sure he'll be fine," he said, giving Meri an irritated look. "He's hard-headed with great self-preservation, trust me. You haven't given me an answer."

Reyan's jaw dropped at the disinterest in his tone.

Doesn't he care about the 'snag' part or the fact 'injured' was mentioned?

"Where is he?" she repeated.

131

Meri eyed them both. "He'll need to spend a day or two at the Nether Court while they focus on healing him-"

"Healing him?! How badly hurt is he?"

Meri gave her an odd look, head tilted and eyes narrowed. Reyan had the unnerving suspicion that she was somehow being scanned right through to the bone.

"He didn't say." Meri relented with a sigh. "His only other instruction was to tell you that the block on your gift will stay lifted for your safety, and not to do anything-"

Reyan turned away and stormed back the way she'd come.

"Reyan! Rey!" Ciel's outraged shouting filled her ears but she wasn't stopping to hear any more of his proposal traps.

He went without me. She burst through the door to Kainen's room, slamming it shut because she knew Ciel couldn't get in unless she let him. *He didn't even give me a second chance to decide. Now he's injured, Faerie knows how badly.*

But he'd lifted the block on her gift and she could make use of the fact he'd not given her any specific orders.

The Nether Court was in another realm entirely, and she only knew the theory of its location from old maps and books she'd snuck out of the library about other shadow-weavers. She had no friends to trade or beg a lift from, so she would have to do something ill-advised and dangerous instead.

Calling the shadows around her, she wove into them, letting her being and her body become one with them. Travelling by shadow was how she returned to her father's house in another realm when forced to visit, but she'd never tried to get anywhere else before.

If this works, Kainen will likely be as pissed off with me as I am with him. Good.

CHAPTER THIRTEEN
KAINEN

"I think he's waking up."

The voice rattling around in Kainen's head like a yowling pack of frost cats sounded vaguely familiar. He opened his eyes and blinked against the savage burn of light.

"Hey, you took a real knock," the voice added, soft and feminine.

He turned his head and blinked several times to clear his blurry vision.

"Crashed right into the wall," someone else said, irritatingly, cheerfully male. "Thought your legs would fly off."

Kainen recognised Taz's voice and realised the first must have been Demi's. Memories of the dark void beneath the Nether Court and the malicious entity that dwelled there came swimming back.

He tried to sit up and grunted at the stab of pain radiating from his shoulder right through his head.

"Easy, you're not well enough to get up yet," Demi insisted. "Queen's orders if I have to. You're ill."

Kainen scowled, glad he could at least manage that.

"I don't get ill."

It was true due to luck with genetics and his general inclination to be active. Aside from his sugar fixes, he rarely bothered drinking stimulants like *Beast* or smoking pipes that were popular in most Faerie realms. And as for getting into actual external trouble, aside from the war he was fast enough with his gifts and smooth enough with his charms that he could manage himself.

But the nether beast hadn't cared for his gifts, bouncing them right back at him like light through shadow.

He froze as Demi's face swam above him, tilted sideways and full of worry. She'd tied her tangled hair back but clumps stuck out at all angles and she looked even paler than normal.

"Are you okay though?" she asked. "Head still all there? Do you know who we are?"

Kainen nodded, grimacing as pain pinged through his shoulders.

"Ouch. Yes, you're Queen of Faerie." Taz's wary face appeared beside hers. "And he's the king. He doesn't like me very much."

Taz pulled a face. "You remember what happened?"

"Yeah, the nether beast kicked us halfway across Faerie. I remember it being in my head, using my gift against me, then I was slammed against a wall. There was a lot of pain and passing out. Where's Reyan, is she still at the court?"

Taz and Demi exchanged a look. Panic stabbed in his chest, or that might have been actual physical pain as he tried to sit up again, glowering when Demi pushed him back down.

"She's fine, at the court still that we know of."

He nodded and settled back against his pillows.

"I need to orb Meri." He inched his aching arm toward his hip then stared at them in horror. "Where are my pants?"

Demi's lips twitched and Taz had the decency not to grin too widely.

"You were bleeding and the healer had to check you for bruising and breaks. Your clothes are right there on the chair, but you need to rest."

"I need to orb Meri first," he insisted.

Demi pointed across the room and gave Taz a look. He gawped back at her until she rolled her eyes.

"Well I'm not going to be ferreting around in his pants, am I? Queen."

Taz huffed and disappeared from view. Kainen knew logically he could turn his head and look, but the pain in his shoulder didn't like him moving.

He mumbled thanks as Taz passed him his orb and waited until they left the room to contact Meri.

"I'll keep this quick because you're going to yell at me a lot," he announced the moment her face appeared in front of him, a vision of pearlescent grey confusion. "Consider Reyan's gift containment lifted. She needs to be able to shift for herself. There's been a little snag here and I'll be home in a couple of days when I'm healed."

"Healed? How bad is it?" Meri grumbled.

"Not too badly injured, don't worry. It'll heal, nothing lasting. But keep an eye on Reyan okay? Make sure she has everything she needs. She probably won't feel comfortable asking for things, so make sure there's food in the room as well."

"Well, you certainly have a drama about you," Meri said. "I'll keep things going here and let you know if anything happens, but Lady Blossom is holding a one-woman show for your courtiers so they'll be absorbed for a while longer. Don't do anything stupid."

She disappeared and he let his arm drop with the orb still curled in his fist. Wild thoughts swelled of Blossom using Reyan for target practice, or the court remembering that she was now lady in his stead and trying to attack her. Or worse, request things of her.

Demi and Taz would no doubt go straight back to Arcanium to regroup which left him behind alone to heal, but now that he was on his own his mind couldn't help but wander.

At least Reyan didn't come with us. She'll be mad at me for leaving her behind maybe, but she's safe.

He closed his eyes and tried to get his body to stop aching through sheer power of will. The quicker he healed, the quicker he could go home and smooth things over with her.

Although knowing she hates me only makes me more determined to keep her.

It was madness. She deserved her freedom and he would find a way to give it to her. But he couldn't blame himself for wanting just a little bit longer with her around.

He didn't have the energy to look up as the bedroom door opened, his mind still stuck on thoughts of her and his body too weary to react.

"Well, you're awake and the queen insists you're lucid which is good news."

A female troll appeared with twinkling brown eyes and short black hair tucked behind her bat-like ears. He grunted as she shovelled him up on more pillows until he could see the room without having to move.

"I may not look like a healer but I assure you, I am," she added. "Hallucinations aren't likely but if you have any, let me know. Other than that, you can go back home if you rest overnight. Sannar said he'll be in touch if need be but you're not to hover around on his account, which sounds rude but he doesn't like to be a burden, bless him."

"I'll be fine. I need to get home."

She chuckled. "No, Lord, you need to rest. Your leg broke in two places and took a lot of faffing to heal. Your shoulder was dislocated. There's a bump the size of an orb sticking out of your head. I've done some of my best work, but you need a good night's sleep before going home."

Kainen managed a pained nod and she left him once again with his thoughts. At least he would be able to go home soon. Perhaps he'd let Reyan keep full use of her gifts this time. She might even soften toward him then.

He huffed a pained laugh as doubt filtered through him, glad that the room was mostly in darkness and he could lie down without having to move much. Only the gap in the curtains let in moonlight from outside. Something about the shadows calmed him, as though they were watching over him while she couldn't be.

I might not have her here yelling at me, but that nether beast was the next best thing. It was as immune to my charms as she is.

He smiled, his lips feeling dry and tight. Reyan was the

furthest thing from a beast he could imagine, more like a goddess or an angel.

My secret Lady of Shadows.

"Good thing it's dark in here."

Her voice filled the room and he jumped, letting out a pained yelp. Hallucinations weren't likely, the healer had assured him, but not likely wasn't the same as 'absolutely impossible'.

But she sounded sluggish and raw, like she was exhausted right to the bone. Worry stabbed at him along with a healthy dose of physical pain as he tried to sit up more.

"Are you really here?" he asked.

"Are you in the habit of imagining my voice?" Her responding snap sounded so irritated that he started grinning. "Urgh, you know what, don't answer that."

Definitely her. His heart swelled. *I can't risk upsetting her again, so I can't be too charming or too playful.*

"Are you going to snap at me again if I ask why you're here? Also, why is it a good thing it's dark?"

She huffed in reply and the space around the door took form. His gaze raked over her as shadow became skin and the darkness became blonde hair framing her face.

"I'd have longer to travel through the shadows if it wasn't dark," she explained.

She'd conveniently skipped the explanation of why she'd appeared at all, but Kainen wanted to know. He could be a gentleman, let her off the hook, but she was here for a reason and he very much doubted it was worry for him.

"What brings you here though?"

She shrugged one shoulder, saying nothing. The mere sight of her, so real and solid and whole, set an unnerving tingle in Kainen's chest.

"Answer me."

The command wasn't a compulsion, but he was her lord so she was court-bound to answer him anyway.

"Yes, my lord. Right away, my lord." She rolled her eyes. "Meri told us you were injured, so here I am."

He thought this through for a moment. "But why?"

Hesitation, as if she was trying to find some kind of excuse without lying.

She can't possibly care enough to come here out of her own choice. He frowned. *Can she? She acts like she hates me most of the time, or thinks I'm a ridiculous pig at best.*

"Would you rather Lady Blossom come to nurse you?" she asked, her tone clipped.

He deserved that after his taunt the last time he'd seen her.

She would have to answer him if he made her, but he could tell that tugging on that thread would do more harm than good in the long run.

"Absolutely not." He shook his head. "She'd force a marriage at iron sword-point then off me with the edge of it."

Reyan sniggered. "Now why didn't I think to bring an iron sword to off you with? Would solve all my problems. How are you feeling? What injuries do you have? Are Demi and Taz still here?"

Kainen swam in the volley of questions she threw at

him. He stared at her as best he could in the dim room, wishing now that he'd ruined his eyes and worsened his headache by insisting on having the curtains open, all for the few moments of bliss that came with seeing her clearly. He had the disconcerting notion that she would look absolutely devastating with moonlight shining off her golden hair and dancing with her shadows. But she'd asked him a question and talking to her in the dark was much better than being without her.

"I'll heal. My leg broke in two places-" He hesitated when she gasped. "My shoulder got dislocated. My head has a bump the size of an orb sticking out."

Glad he was prone to the occasional bout of dramaticism which apparently didn't count as outright lying if it was done naturally, he could at least lay the head wound on thick enough to worry her a bit. Apparently enough that she moved closer and perched on the edge of his bed, peering down at him.

"Hi," he whispered, smiling soft.

He could blame the head injury if she thought he was somehow trying to- but no, she was smiling back, her shoulders lowering as worry ebbed from her face.

"Hi. What do you need to heal?"

She does care at least a bit. The gleeful realisation thundered like hoofbeats through his chest. *But I can't get too close and scare her off.*

"They have good healers here so all is mended," he said. "But the residual fixes will take a while to recover from. I can skip back home tomorrow if I rest a bit more. How did you get here?"

"You lifted my gift ban," she said with a wicked smile. "So I shadow-travelled. It's further than I usually go, but it turns out to be fairly pleasant, although I don't think I could do it again for a bit."

Worry spiked in Kainen's chest at the mere thought.

"You shouldn't have come."

She frowned, sitting upright in an instant. "Why not?"

"You've never shadowed that far before. You could have lost your strength halfway and ended up anywhere."

Even though he was uncharacteristically furious at the mere thought of her getting into trouble, he wanted to hug her more than anything else. Being able to hold her, to have her sleep safe next to him, was a dream he'd been playing in his head for more hours over the past day or so than he wanted to admit.

"I don't need them to find me a bed here or anything," she said, still irritable with him. "I'll sit a while until I feel better and make my way back."

"You will not. Look at you, you're half asleep already. You'd never make it. I order you to stay here until I'm ready to leave."

She glared back at him, her grey eyes sparkling and her mouth pressed thin.

"I'm not sleeping in your bed."

The overwhelming urge to laugh bubbled up inside him, but he choked it down with all his might.

"They won't have any other prepared for you."

"Then I'll sleep on the floor."

Sheer practiced willpower kept his lips from twitching.

"In that state? It's stone, hard and cold. You're telling

me you seriously prefer a stone floor to a warm, respectably wide bed with amazingly plump bedding, just because I'm in it?"

He was tricking her and nowhere close to playing fair now. Of course she couldn't say she'd prefer the floor, because who would? She would have to answer that no, a bed was of course preferable to a stone floor, and therefore get in his with him.

She stood with her arms folded and gave him her most dismissive look, the one that wrinkled her nose.

"Yes. Considering you're trying to trick me even now into doing what you want, I'd rather sleep in the freezing cold without blankets on a bone-crunching, muscle-setting floor than sleep in the same bed as you."

Ouch.

Kainen couldn't find any words for several moments. None. Not a single word, let alone any good ones. He could reason away that it was because she was stubborn and wanted to win the argument, not because she hated him, but it still hurt. Either way, the thought of her on the floor in the cold was intolerable.

"Then I'll sleep on the floor and you-"

"No." She shook her head. "You're injured and if you sleep on the floor, you'll take forever to recover and we'll never get back. You can give me a spare pillow and a blanket though, if you have them. Please."

That final word was so drenched in awkward politeness he seesawed back to the desire to laugh. He could make her of course, force her to sleep in the bed by command, but he wouldn't do that to her. Even in his darker days of the past he'd never have sunk anywhere near that low.

Not that I haven't done equally despicable things in different ways. He pushed the thought aside.

"What if I make you promises?" he asked.

That got her attention, one side of her head tilting in consideration. He knew what he should promise her, and exactly what she would ask of him: her freedom. And he'd been planning to give it to her anyway, to encourage her away from him so his heart could heal. He'd spent time away from Demi and felt nothing romantic for her now. He could do the same with Reyan.

But she rushed all the way here on a gift she rarely uses. Because she was worried about me? Does she actually care?

"What kind of promises?" she asked.

He hesitated. He should offer the freedom. It wasn't exactly his to give, yet, but he'd planned to get it from her father and gift it to her. But he needed her to ask him for it first. He needed her to prove that she wanted to get away from him, to end the mad longing in his heart by proving she didn't want to stay for him. Not that her behaviour hadn't shown him exactly that already, but he wanted her to say it one final time.

"What do you want?" he asked.

She eyed him, her lips quirked in a considered frown. Right then to end the agony of not being able to reach out for her, he would have given her anything. Everything. Himself, his court, possibly even his life.

It was the injury, it had to be. There was no normal reason for him to feel so rattled and heartsick over someone.

"Take some time to think about it," he suggested. "With any luck, you'll take so long it'll be morning before we know it. Then I'll skip us back to the court and the issue will be irrelevant."

Her face twisted then. She bit her lip, her gaze drifting down to the bed.

Panic flared. He'd left her alone at the court with Lady Blossom and several court members who wouldn't appreciate being passed over as a potential court lord's bride.

"Is everything okay?" he asked. "Did something happen?"

If anyone dared harm a single hair on her head, or said anything that made her sad...

"Ciel proposed." She rubbed her thumb over bottom lip with a grimace. "I think."

He took a sharp breath, cold air filling his nostrils. He took another. And another. None of them did anything to quell the sudden possessive rage burning in his chest. His court were allowed to choose whoever they saw fit of course, they weren't lords of a court coerced into royal matches, but Ciel proposing to Reyan was madness.

Then again, he'd seen them laughing and smiling together. Reyan had been so relaxed with Ciel in a way she'd never been with him.

What am I expecting? Agony started spreading through him, a different kind of pain to his healing limbs. *That she's going to suddenly say it's me she wants? Ciel is a good person. Self-serving maybe, but he's as honourable as Fae can get where women are concerned. At least he'd look after her, be faithful.*

"You think he proposed?" he clarified, treading carefully. "As in actually asked you to marry him?"

She nodded. "He definitely did."

"What did you say?"

He waited for the inevitable answer. It was as good a sign of closure as he was going to get.

He would congratulate her, offer to try and obtain her freedom as her wedding gift from him, then ask her to leave so he could go to the toilet. He could make it that long before the ridiculous burn in his eyes got any sharper.

"I ran away," she announced, not quite meeting his eyes.

He shifted on the bed, trying to judge the distance to the bathroom door in comparison to his pain barrier.

"Congratulations. Listen, I really need to- you what?"

"I ran away. It seemed like the sensible thing to do at the time. Wait, you assumed I accepted?!"

They stared at each other, Kainen one step away from bewildered tears and Reyan possibly one step away from angry ones, he couldn't tell in the darkness.

What a mess. I need to let her go. Even if she says no to Ciel, she deserves so much better than all of us.

"Are you sure?" he asked through gritted teeth. "He's a nice boy. Good family. Good for you, boring and staid enough to adhere to your whole no sock rule thing. He'd probably keep you safe enough."

There, he'd done it. He would return to the court and start the process of freeing her from his half of the debt, then they'd be rid of each other.

He only hoped in the dark room she couldn't see the tears now leaking down his cheeks.

CHAPTER FOURTEEN
REYAN

Reyan stared through the darkness as her shadows caught the waves of emotion pouring out of Kainen. Heart pounding, she fought the realisation that perhaps he actually cared for her, despite knowing that he was still in love with Demi.

It had to be the head injury, she decided. No doubt he'd retract the whole setting her free thing as soon as he got better and they returned to the court.

So why does that make me feel relieved instead of angry?

The door to the room swung open before Reyan could fathom any of her feelings, let alone Kainen's.

"Only me." Demi strode in with Taz behind her. "Well, us- Oh, what are you doing here?"

Reyan leapt up from the bed, convinced she'd be told off for trespassing, but Kainen's startled yelp of pain turned her head back to him.

"Reyan was worried about me, so she shadow-travelled all the way here." Kainen answered for her.

He caught her eye and managed a watery smile as he discreetly wiped his eyes on the pillow. She glared back at him, not even sure why except that the queen of Faerie wasn't supposed to be bursting into bedrooms and finding her in bed with court lords.

"Well, fair enough." Demi shrugged. "Perhaps it's better you're both here. Clearly the nether beastie isn't something we want to mess with, but we will need to go back in."

"What exactly is it?" Reyan asked.

Focus on the problems you can solve and work out, not confusing men you can't.

Taz pinned both hands behind his neck with a groan.

"We're not sure. It used all our gifts against us but there wasn't a single 'thing' in there. No sense of movement in the air or sound of footsteps rushing by or anything. Just flashes of our gifts being reflected."

Reyan replied without thinking. "Like a darkness mirror."

"Good way of putting it actually," Kainen said. "But we'll need to know more before we send anyone down there."

Demi nodded, leaning back against the doorframe with a hefty sigh. Even though her black curls were a wild tangle and her face looked weary and dull, she still had an air of regal beauty about her.

I can see why Kainen is so taken with her.

Reyan sagged, exhausted from using her gift so much after so long. She wanted to sit back on the bed but decided against it, not wanting to get too familiar.

"I could go down now and see if the shadows can sense anything out," she offered.

Demi opened her mouth, but it was Kainen's voice that answered, his tone as unyielding as *metirin* iron.

"Absolutely not happening. Not on your own and

149

definitely not until we know more about what it is. Your shadows might be able to sense it, but it will use them against you."

"Agreed," Demi added. "Nobody's to go down there until we've rested, healed and decided a plan. We're going back to Arcanium for a bit now to regroup, but Sannar has agreed to do some investigating of old court documents under the radar."

"Don't tell Milo there's old court documents here." Taz grinned. "He'll be using Kainen's illness as a cover to steal them all."

Kainen chuckled. His throat sounded dry and Reyan reached over to pass him some water from the bedside table.

"Thanks." He smiled at her and her insides crunched. "I'll be healed enough to go home tomorrow apparently."

Demi nodded, glancing at Reyan. "And you? Can you shadow back okay?"

"She'll be staying here tonight," Kainen insisted. "I'll get us both back tomorrow."

"And is she okay with that?" Taz asked, his tone flat with disbelief.

Reyan froze as everyone turned to look at her. With her cheeks burning, she realised that she could answer honestly, but she might have to explain why staying the night with Kainen freaked her out so much, and nobody was meant to know their engagement was fake.

"It's fine," she insisted. "I'll make sure he doesn't get slaughtered by anyone else in the night or anything."

Demi snorted but said nothing and even Taz smirked at

that. Kainen's grin might have been the widest of all of them, which set a wholly irritating flutter in her gut.

"You say the sweetest things. I told Meri to make sure you were safe while I was gone and had what you needed, but I can probably summon stuff easy enough now if you want anything."

"Well this seems like a lot of personal growth," Demi said, a slight tinge of amusement in her voice. "

Kainen looked at her, really looked at her, his gaze softening as he managed a soft smile.

"It seemed about time. When you have the right motivation, anything's possible."

Reyan stared at him, that smile and the expression of utter rapture on his face as he looked back at Demi.

This is all about her. It's always been about her. For her. It has to be.

Taz pointedly cleared his throat as though he too recognised something meaningful going on, and the spell broke. Demi didn't seem at all ruffled by that moment, but Kainen settled back on his pillows with a look of complete serenity on his face.

Whether he was impressing Demi for his own advancement or he really was still in love with her, Reyan didn't want to know. But she'd seen that look of admiration on many a face before, and she couldn't imagine anyone getting over what was rumoured to be an all-encompassing infatuation quickly.

"Right, we'll be in touch with the next step of the plan," Demi said. "Try to get some sleep."

Reyan opened her mouth to protest, wild thoughts of

begging Demi to realm-skip her back home now filling her head. But the door shut and left her alone with Kainen before she could find the words.

She yanked the now empty water glass out of Kainen's unresisting hands and thumped it back on the bedside table. She couldn't call him out for how he inevitably felt, but she could be angry about other things and falling back on that felt safer somehow.

"You didn't have to forbid me like that," she muttered. "It's not like I can disobey a queen's command. You're infuriating, you know that?"

He smiled. "True. Although I do have so much fun infuriating you."

She huffed. This was better, him needling her instead of being soulful and deep. This version of Kainen she could handle. She could ignore that adoring look he gave Demi and take their situation for what it was; a lord using someone sworn to his court and her possibly benefitting from the arrangement if she was clever enough. She would have to quash the unsettling swoop of disappointment in her chest immediately.

"It might be fun for you, but I can assure you it's torment for me."

He chuckled. "No, it isn't. Torment is loving someone who has no idea. Torment is knowing someone better than you know yourself and still not being able to make them happy. Bickering over socks on the floor is not torment."

But seeing Demi as queen and in love with Taz clearly was for him. He'd not as much as glanced at another woman since the war either, at least not that Reyan had seen around the court, and he'd not exactly been a saint before that.

He's probably letting out frustration by toying with me after seeing Demi so happy with Taz.

Witnessing that had to hurt him, so his flirty, playful behaviour likely meant nothing, all part of the act. Anyone would want to save face in that situation.

So why does knowing that it means nothing to him hurt me so badly?

She couldn't answer that question, couldn't face it, so she fell back on disgruntled insults instead.

"It's easy to say dramatic things, but you're not the one having to pull all the extra weight picking stuff up off the floor because you're a spoilt brat."

She kept her tone sharp and a wry laugh tumbled out of him.

"I guess I've always been a little bit toxic," he agreed. "Perhaps falling for girls who don't want me is my punishment."

Reyan barely heard him, her mind filling her with many recent memories that didn't involve socks.

Like how he put her blanket back after she was done reading in the bedroom.

Or how he'd noticed the book Demi loaned her and bought her the whole set.

How his only instruction when injured was for her to have her gift so she would be safe.

How he'd given up his own room to her, when he could have easily found her a less comfortable one down the hall.

How-

He isn't toxic. He's kind and, okay, he's also a colossal pain in the behind, but still. He's good where it matters.

Reyan stared at Kainen, taking in his sad eyes even as he smiled down at his hands clasped on the blankets. The shadows absorbed his emotions, sending hits of it swirling through her. She couldn't take on someone else's emotions, but she could sense them. Kainen was in serious pain and not all of it was physical.

She forced herself to focus on practical stuff instead and glanced around the room again. Someone had removed his clothes and left them balled up on a nearby chair, or perhaps he'd been able to change himself. From where he was sitting on a pile of pillows, she could make out that his chest was bare beneath the blanket. She saw the tension of the muscles there, and her heart squeezed in anguish at the mere thought of him in pain.

She couldn't face the more unnerving truths right now, too exhausted for emotions. Even her shadows started to hang back, a sure sign her insides were going haywire. She couldn't travel back either even if he allowed it, not in her current state.

"If I do sleep here, will you promise not to read anything into it?" she asked.

Kainen looked up, the soft, sad smile still there.

"Don't worry, I know you don't see me that way and I'm not in the habit of going for girls who don't want me. If I'm being honest, I don't think you see Ciel that way either, but if he's the future you choose, then I hope you'll be happy. You deserve to be happy."

The words were so kind, so unlike the lord everyone

saw and moaned about throughout the court. They liked him simply because he was more lenient than his father but they didn't know him. Not like she now did. He had his faults, but he was more decent than anyone knew, and something had shifted in the last day spent without him.

She'd missed him.

She'd missed the irritating behaviour and the constant teasing.

She'd even missed his stupid nickname for her.

She had no idea why her swelling emotions had to be fixed on someone she couldn't have, but they were there all the same. Because surely that's what the uneasy swishing in her gut was about, and the ridiculous instinct to shadow-travel further than she ever had because someone said he'd been injured. Along with the irritating daydreams that kept popping into her head, all of which he now starred in.

But even if he was fond of her, his heart was clearly still tied up with unrequited feelings for Demi, and Reyan had no intention of being someone's consolation prize. Their engagement was a fake as well and she didn't have the familial connections to be considered socially worthy enough for a court lord even if all the stars aligned and he did actually like her.

She hadn't answered him but he watched her patiently as her mind raced and she started twisting her hands in her lap.

Sleep. I need sleep.

"Give me a second," he said, as if he knew her anxiety was climbing. "I'll shift to the edge and roll so my back is toward you. Then you can put pillows down the middle and we'll take one each to lie on. I vow I won't touch you." A glimmer of his wicked smile edged onto his face. "Not unless you beg me to."

An actual vow. Her pulse raced with astonishment. Vows were binding, and even when he was making himself vulnerable his focus was on trying to make things easier for her, his characteristic playfulness reappearing to ease them back into normality.

Reyan forced her eyes to roll like they normally would at his crass humour, keeping things light as she stood up and kicked off her shoes. She hadn't thought to grab a coat or bag before whirling away on the shadows. She had nothing except her shoes, her t-shirt, her jeans and her underwear. She wasn't even wearing any socks.

Each pained movement Kainen made to readjust his position hurt her too. After he made four or five tiny shuffles, not managing to turn an inch, she clambered onto the bed fully clothed.

"Don't." She shook her head when he looked at her. "You've vowed, so I trust you. Go to sleep where you are and I'll figure out how to curl around you."

Kainen raised his eyebrows but did as he was told, closing his eyes in a mimicry of sleep. Reyan slid onto the edge of the bed. It was as comfortable as he'd made out and the moment her head hit the pillow her eyes fluttered closed with relief.

"Tell me if anything hurts," she mumbled. "Or wake me if I need to go and get a healer."

Kainen chuckled. "Sleep, sweetheart. I'm tougher than

I look."

She decided not to answer that, but the awkward silence filled the room and she had to say something.

"What happened?"

He sighed. "We could have done with you there. I'm sorry I didn't come to get you before we left. I sort of figured you'd be safest staying behind, but now I'm thinking that wasn't my decision to make."

Reyan let him talk, realising that not only did he need to get the whole thing out, but also he was giving her more proof of what kind of person he was. She closed her eyes and let his voice wash over her.

"The nether beast is something I've never even heard or read about before. There was literally nothing except darkness but it still used our gifts against us. My illusion gift, Demi's energy, Taz's wings."

Reyan frowned without opening her eyes, too comfortable on the plushy pillows to react with anything except her voice.

"I can sense something. It's like when you think someone's watching you but you can't see anyone, you ever have that?"

"Sure. Except this thing wasn't happy just watching."

Reyan sent her gift out and investigated the shadows. They were tense even though the air around them was still and calm.

"I can have a look tomorrow morning before we leave, right?" She wasn't sure why she was asking permission but she did it anyway.

Kainen shifted and inhaled sharply. "Ouch. You can go

to the edge of the tunnel, *maybe*, but not inside. Not without Demi there and no going anywhere without me. We'll see in the morning."

"I don't need an escort." She wrinkled her nose in disgust. "Demi said it was part of the nether, which is kind of a balance to the fabric of Faerie. Chaos and order, matter and nothingness. What if the chaos is in the nothingness? The shadows are edgy even though there's nothing going on, and I reckon they could at least read whatever's down there."

Kainen chuckled and groaned.

"Do I need to get the healer?" she asked.

"No, but I'm dying of thirst."

"Oh how dramatic." She sat up with a huff. "Stay right there."

He didn't protest as she forced her aching limbs out of bed and got the pitcher of water and a glass from the desk at the other end of the room. She drew the line at helping him drink it, but took the empty glass as he slumped back.

"Thanks. I want you to promise me though, no running off to investigate on your own." He turned his head and gave her a stern look, no less severe through the night-time darkness. "Make sure either I'm with you or Demi is."

She scrunched under the covers and glared at him across the pillows.

"You're insufferable," she muttered.

He grinned back. "Promise me, sweetheart."

"Or you'll what, lock me back up at court? Take my gifts away again? Banish me?"

"None of those." His grin faded. "No more containing

your gift either, but I would worry myself sick. And considering I'm already sick, that would technically be in contradiction of your court lord's wellbeing, which I believe you can't do, what with being court-sworn and all."

She sighed. "So this is all basically because I'm a member of your court, right?"

He was silent for a long moment and she had to close her eyes to avoid the intensity swimming in his.

He said he hit his head, that's more than enough explanation. We both need sleep and he doesn't have to sit here answering to me. Besides, even if he did like me like that which I doubt he does, there's no denying how he feels about Demi. I can't compete with a queen.

"Yes, sweetheart, because you're a member of my court. Now, go to sleep."

She stuck her tongue out without opening her eyes and listened to his breathing, determined to keep awake until she knew he was asleep. But whether he was easing a bit of his power into her mind to soothe her, or she was simply so exhausted she couldn't keep going, she lost herself to the world of dreams moments later.

CHAPTER FIFTEEN
KAINEN

Kainen hadn't realised how problematic his vow to behave himself would be. Vows were binding so he literally couldn't touch her, but they'd made no mention of her not touching him.

Soon after Reyan fell asleep, he managed to shift onto his back but that movement rolled her body closer to the centre of the bed. Closer to him. Aware he was essentially pants-less and only protected by the covers, he had to be so careful.

He lifted his arms above his head with great, pained difficulty, resting his hands by his ears with his elbows bent outwards. That would stop him accidentally touching her and breaking his promise. He was pretty sure accidents were okay, but a vow was a vow. He'd never been able to fathom how humans could lie and promise and vow, then break them without a single consequence.

And their stories apparently say we're the scary ones.

He noted the shadows curling around Reyan's relaxed form, but they didn't seem to mind him, as if they could tell he meant her no harm.

What he also hadn't counted on was how deeply and restlessly Reyan slept. She fidgeted from side to side, her nose scrunching adorably as she flailed her legs up and down her half of the bed. She hadn't remembered to put any pillows between them either before passing out.

Smiling to himself, Kainen closed his eyes and willed sleep to come. He even managed to quiet his restless mind for a short while, but the moment he could feel himself drifting under, Reyan shifted. She rolled to face him with a grumble, her leg bending and sliding over his thigh.

Faerie save me.

He thought about whispering to wake her up. He was pretty sure if he commanded her to wake up she would have to. But a quick peek proved she looked so tired and so sweet with her head on his chest that he decided against it.

It was probably the closest he'd ever get to holding her, even though he couldn't actually hold her with the promise of no touching hanging over him. So he lay there in various states of discomfort, slipping in and out of sleep until the light tinged behind the curtains.

As if she felt her shadows begin to curl away to darker corners, Reyan mumbled something and nestled closer. Moments later, she fell still and the featherlight flutter of her eyelashes on his bare chest suggested she was waking.

Do I pretend to be asleep or not?

A loud knocking startled Reyan awake before he could decide. She scrambled upright in a flail of limbs and almost tumbled off the bed. One side of her hair was sticking out at odd angles, and she blinked wildly as the door swung open.

"Good morning, Lord. I've brought you so- oh! Lady!"

The girl in the doorway with a tray of food went bright red. Reyan hastily tried to flatten her hair and leapt off the bed. Annoyed at how scandalised they both looked at the very idea of anyone being in bed with him, Kainen glowered across the room.

"The Nether Court is more like the 'Court of Unnecessary Interruptions'," he muttered.

Bad enough Demi and Taz saw fit to march in without even knocking, but now the other courts weren't even bothering to wait to be invited into rooms.

He relented when Reyan gave him a dirty look, her nose wrinkling all cute and irritated. His mind spiralled back to the night before when Demi had given him that look, the forgiveness he'd hoped a thousand times to see on her face. But he felt nothing. Relief, definitely, but nothing emotional. He wasn't sure if that stare had been a test or if she was somehow scanning his soul and his intentions, but in that moment he realised he was free of her, of the past, all of it.

"I wasn't meant to be here," Reyan insisted. "It's fine, I can eat later. It's Odella, right?"

The girl with the tray nodded then bobbed a curtsey as an afterthought, although she looked happy to have been remembered.

"Yes, Lady. Oh, my mum who works here said that Sannar said he found something useful, but that he'd let the queen's aide know, so if you needed another day to rest it's fine. Um, sorry for disturbing you."

She dropped the tray on the long, narrow table next to the doorway and hurried out again, closing the door behind her.

"Faerie knows what they'll all think now," Reyan

muttered.

Kainen grinned as she caught his eye, then she pointedly stared at his arms still raised above his head.

"I wasn't touching, see?" he said. "I've had my arms like this all night, promise. Actually, if we're being proper about it, you've been touching me. It's been a while since a beautiful girl has chosen to drape herself over me though, so I don't mind."

Her cheeks flushed and she stood up to fetch the tray over, sitting on the edge of the bed with it.

"Sorry. I fidget a lot when I sleep. I thought if I was that tired…" she trailed off and he felt bad for teasing her.

"It's fine, don't worry. I'm feeling a bit better though so I can finish healing at home."

She looked at him then, eying him over.

"Wow, I didn't see the bruises last night." She bit her lip. "Did it hurt when I was lying on you?"

He shook his head, not trusting himself to speak. Somehow he figured 'it's the happiest and most frustrated I can ever remember being' wouldn't help with easing the fragile awkwardness between them.

She stood up, one hand reaching forward as if to touch the bruises. He watched her hand hover moments before she snatched it back and he knew he had to get them home. He would send word of thanks to the Nether Court from his study when he got back, but now he needed to leave.

"You should be fine to travel home anyway, right?" she mumbled.

He managed to get to his feet with bearable aches and pains, the healer's efforts nothing short of a miracle, before grunting a reply.

"I should get back as well," she added.

He lifted his head in time to see her already halfway to the door. He couldn't help the words that flew out next.

"To your awaiting proposal?"

She froze. "I- yes. I should set off before it gets dark."

Kainen watched her reach the door, both of them no doubt fully aware it was the first rays of morning and unlikely to get dark for a very long time.

She was perfect. Perfectly adorable. Perfectly stubborn. And he was completely hers, even though she would probably never want to be his.

"Reyan," he said it, quietly, softly.

No compulsion, no command. No request. She could refuse. She had her shadows; she could flee.

She shuddered, her hand already on the door handle.

He watched her, drinking her in as she turned around, her grey eyes wide like prey.

"You can skip back with me, it's much easier," he reminded her.

His heart leapt as she approached and tilted her head up to look at him, her lips ever so slightly parted. The strands of blonde around her cheeks needed brushing, but he resisted the urge to tuck them behind her ears.

"Oh. Yeah. Okay." She sucked in a sharp breath. "Um, don't you usually need to take my hand or something? For the whole skipping thing, I mean."

"I vowed not to touch."

That made her blush. "You can this once if you need to, or if it's absolutely necessary for the whole pretend engagement thing. But no leaping on me, no unrequested hugging, and nothing whatsoever when we're in the same bed."

She stared up at him and he couldn't help the smile tugging his mouth up.

"Are you planning for us to be in the same bed often then, sweetheart?"

It could go either way. She would laugh it off or he would likely be on the end of some extremely foul language. He hadn't ordered her not to poke him either, as their last mini-wrestling match had proven, and he wasn't in any condition to get physical right now. If she was truly angry, she might even consider poking him right through with something sharp and pointy.

"You're such a pig," she muttered.

That might be true, but he still had to clench every muscle he had to keep himself at bay when her cold hand slipped around his and her cheeks turned even redder.

She would need time. She needed to work out what she wanted for herself before anything else. Which meant first she needed her freedom. He couldn't hope that she fancied or even remotely liked him. But she felt something, that much was clear from the way she'd gone from smart-mouthing and kicking him to hesitant glances and awkwardness. Until she figured out what she wanted and told him he wasn't a part of that, he wouldn't risk losing her without a fight.

For now, she needed time and the chance to make her own choices.

"So, tell me something," he said, keeping his tone low,

intimate. "You know I can skip us back without much effort, yet you'd rather run out of that door and risk shadow-travelling all the way home. You hate me that much?"

Even though he was letting her choose, he was still Fae. There wasn't any harm in making himself the best choice he could be for her. The first step to that would be clearing the air between them, and teasing her seemed to work best for that.

Her cheeks flushed red. "I didn't want to assume anything."

"But you do hate me."

"I- no, I don't hate you, even though you're an absolute pain."

Her lips were a mere leaning distance away. He could drop his head and he'd be kissing her. Would she let him?

"I'm trying not to be," he whispered instead.

"I know." She gulped and took a step back.

Too intense, I'm scaring her.

"Come on then," he said with a sigh, breaking the intimate moment.

He grabbed his scuffed clothing from the chair and squeezed her hand. He didn't look at her, even though his skin tingled the moment she squeezed back. A wave of yearning swept through him, an ache so keening that anything he'd ever felt for Demi seemed laughably childish in comparison.

The nether shifted and the moment his room appeared around them, he dropped her hand. He would let her go, let her decide. If she wanted him, she'd come to him. She'd give him some kind of sign.

Or she'll choose Ciel. His blood roared with fury at the thought.

"The royals have gone back to Arcanium, right?" she asked.

He frowned, searched the sense of the court to be safe, then nodded.

"They have, although sadly Blossom seems to be lingering."

Reyan managed a weak smile. "Then you have your court and your marital freedom back, and I have things to sort out."

He watched her rush across the room and out of the door without a look back. Shaking his head, he followed her footsteps and shut the door behind her.

Miss Primness and Manners forgetting to shut a door behind her. Perhaps Ciel is more important to her than I realised.

CHAPTER SIXTEEN
REYAN

Reyan found Ciel in the main hall and hurried to his side, glad the place was mostly deserted.

Her cheeks were flushed and although she'd slept surprisingly well draped over Kainen's chest, she could have done with sleeping an eternity before having to bumble through this next conversation.

Ciel turned to face her when she called his name, but his face didn't break into his usual smile. She slowed to a halt in front of him, doubt surfacing.

"I can't marry you," she said.

Ciel glanced around at the hall, no doubt to check for eavesdroppers. When he faced her again, she almost stepped back at the bitterness in his eyes.

"After you ran out on me I wouldn't have assumed any different." He sniffed. "I think it's a bit ridiculous though that you're slaving away after him."

Reyan froze. "Who?"

"You know who." He rolled his eyes. "I know your engagement is all nonsense, and he's always been fickle, moving from one interest to the next and leaving people in the dust to pick up the pieces. You may not love me, or have feelings for me, but I would have been a sensible choice."

She skipped over the mention of the engagement, not

able to lie and disagree. It was also true that Kainen had proven himself to be fickle with others in the past. But now everything had to be a well-practiced act, and she needed to remember that was all it was for him. An act to avoid marrying Lady Blossom and to hide the fact he was still pining for Demi.

When she didn't answer straight away, Ciel started to laugh.

"You think he's going to be different because of you?" he asked. "You seriously think that perhaps you're the one to fix him?"

She shook her head but the cruel vein of the laughter punctured the small balloon of her growing daydreams. Even when Kainen had offered her his hand only minutes before at the Nether Court, teased her gently and looked for a moment like he might kiss her in that pre-morning gloom, she'd hoped even though she'd told herself not to. Even if he hadn't still had feelings for Demi, that didn't mean he'd forgo all court tradition and marry a low-born like her.

But she couldn't admit that to Ciel of all people.

"What I think doesn't matter," she said. "What I want doesn't either. We're sworn to this court, both of us. We serve it and him. If he orders me to marry him, I'd have to. Hell, if he ordered you to marry him, you'd have to do it. Is that what this is? You're jealous? You should tell him how you feel. He might even return the sentiment."

Ciel's face flickered with rage. "You don't want to taunt me right now. I proposed to you because I am in love with you. I'll even free you from your debt if you marry me!"

169

Reyan looked around as his voice swelled, bouncing off the walls.

"Keep your voice down," she hissed.

"What, scared your beloved lord will hear us? Good! Perhaps if I offer him something extra as well as your father, he'll agree to the match and *make* you marry me."

Reyan staggered back as if he'd slapped her. His fists were clenched at his sides and for the first time in a long time, an overwhelming wave of fear slammed through her.

Ciel's expression softened, but she'd seen the incandescent violence lurking in those flashing blue eyes, unable to wipe the memory of it from her mind.

"Rey, I didn't mean-" he hesitated. "I'm sorry. I rarely ever lose my temper."

A truth, she knew, but most likely because he was adept at controlling it, at manipulating situations around him with the normal charm and trickery of Fae. What life awaited her when she was no longer a desirable thing but part of his life, already owned and therefore expected to fall in line with his wishes?

I can't risk pissing him off. She bit her lip, thinking fast. *I need to speak to Kainen and beg him not to interfere. If I ask nicely, he'll agree to keep me on here under the current debt until I can find a way to buy it myself via someone I trust.*

She took a deep breath. The most important thing now was making sure Ciel didn't do anything rash that ruined her life.

"Emotions are running high at the moment," she said carefully. "I think the queen may have another assignment and I'll agree to help with that, but maybe when I return we can sort this out?"

She tried to put a bit of timidness in her smile, petrified all the while that he'd see through it. Demi might have another assignment considering the nether beast hadn't been dealt with yet, and she would agree to help. It was the only way to make sure Kainen didn't do anything stupidly rash again and get himself killed or irreparably hurt.

But she wouldn't tell Ciel that part either.

His shoulders lowered, his fists finally uncurling.

"Good. That's fine. That gives me time to sort a few things." He frowned then. "I had intended to take my time with you, but he forced my hand."

Reyan nodded and took a step back.

"I only came to find you quickly," she said. "I need to get on with things. But we'll talk later, yeah?"

He nodded, a smile filtering across his lips. It was the congenial smile she recognised, but she would never be able to look at him again without seeing that fearsome danger. Before he could try to embrace her in any way, she turned and set off toward the stairs leading up to Kainen's room. She didn't dare look back, her step quickening as she walked along the hall and threw open the door.

Shutting it behind her, she slumped her back against the wood and let her breath tumble out.

Kainen wasn't inside. No doubt Meri would be plying him with potions and fixes for his lingering injuries, and she guessed if he wasn't in the room then he was in his study already.

She'd give him time to have a wash and relax a while

before approaching him, but until then she would be bedroom-bound given that Ciel couldn't get in without being invited and it was therefore the only safe space in the court for her now. She could take some time to calm down before rushing in and begging Kainen to be on her side, or at least stay out of it if he wasn't willing to help her.

Faerie knows I need someone on my side though. If Ciel gets his way, one of us isn't going to be surviving long.

She picked up her book, intending to curl up on the chair and read for a bit. Turning to find her blanket, she flinched and accidentally sent the book sailing out of her hand.

Demi ducked just in time.

"What are you…" Reyan panicked. "Sorry, but I wasn't expecting a queen to materialise in my… in his... in the…"

She gave up as Demi started laughing.

"Yeah, most people have that reaction to me nowadays. I wanted to talk to you without anyone else interfering."

Reyan indicated to the sofa and hurried across to rescue her book from the floor before sinking into her chair.

"I would offer drinks and things but I don't have the finger-clicky power," she said. "Not to summon food anyway. I have access to the cleaning cupboard and I'm able to vanish things, but that's about it so far. I can go to the kitchens?"

Demi shook her head and glanced around the room. Reyan bit her lip, wondering how many horrid memories the place brought back.

"I'm getting the feeling Kainen's trying really hard to be a good guy," Demi started, tugging on the cuffs of her hooded sweatshirt. "I want to believe it's true, but I figured I'd ask you. Is he treating you okay?"

Reyan frowned. "Of course. He's got his issues same as anyone, like he's a total pain in the behind most of the time. He's messy and entitled. He has the worst taste in breakfast. But he's good deep down. He's looked after the court as best he can and me too. He didn't have to get me books but he did, and he could have easily forced me to play along with whatever he needed me to do."

Which technically he did, but I'm struggling to hold it against him now. Ciel's taunts about him circled in her mind. *Would he stop if I really wanted him to?*

Demi nodded. "Fair enough. He seems very protective of you at least. So, the nether beastie. It's a big mess of nothing that can mirror our gifts and attack us with them."

"I did feel something yesterday, or today, I'm a bit frazzled from all the travelling, but it was like a tension almost. The shadows were uneasy about it."

"Travelling?" Demi cocked her head to one side. "Was that why you weren't with us?"

Reyan flushed. "Um, not exactly. Kainen didn't tell me you were going anywhere, but to be fair to him I didn't ask either. Then Meri comes in saying he'd been injured at the Nether Court so I sort of shadow-travelled there to make sure he was okay."

"You shadow-travelled all the way across realms to the Nether Court to see if he was okay?"

"It sounds a bit extreme but I panicked. I haven't done that before except to go back to my father's once or twice. But yeah, last night I felt something lurking at the court and then I was too worn out to travel back, so Kainen skipped us back a while ago."

Demi nodded and sat silent for a long while. Reyan tried to stay still and be patient but her nerves began to jitter.

"I'd like you to come back to the Nether Court with us soon," she said eventually. "It's only a hunch, but I think if your shadows can sense things, you'll be able to intuit more about what the beast is thinking, or at least what the general vibe and intention is."

"I can do that. Kainen said I could if I had either him or you with me."

Demi snorted. "He's giving you restrictions already?"

"He's lord of the court I'm sworn to so I can't disobey. But I think it comes from a caring place."

"I reckon it does. Do I need to ask his permission then?"

Reyan grinned. The best thing about being Fae was learning to be artful and twist a situation to your benefit.

"I don't know, but if we're assuming not then he can't exactly stop us, can he?"

Demi laughed as she stood up and Reyan did the same.

If I really were going to be the lady of the court, would this count as my first proper audience?

She smirked at the thought.

"I like that line of thinking," Demi said. "I'll let you know when the time comes, but if everything kicks off I may have to randomly appear, so please for my sake, make sure Kainen isn't wandering around without his pants on."

Reyan giggled slightly hysterically at that thought.

"I doubt that's... we..."

She couldn't lie and couldn't admit that they hadn't

even so much as kissed.

Demi raised her eyebrows. "Right, I'll be in touch."

She vanished and Reyan stood in place a while longer with her book still clutched to her chest.

She didn't know anything about the nether beast, or much about the nether in general, but Kainen had a huge library at court. She also had the awkward feeling that she should go and find Kainen, make some kind of clarification of where they stood, but nerves got the better of her. Instead of heading for the door, she caved and headed straight for her bed.

One chapter, then I'll do some actual work.

CHAPTER SEVENTEEN
KAINEN

Kainen sat in his study chair thirty minutes after returning from the Nether Court. Meri bustled around him with tonics and ointments, but he sat with his thoughts batting back and forth.

I can't let her marry him. She said she refused, but she might change her mind. Ciel can be persuasive when he needs to be.

He grunted in acknowledgement as Meri pulled the collar of his shirt back to reach one of the scrapes on his neck and almost strangled him.

But it's her decision, and I can't dictate what she does anymore.

He huffed, rolling a pen back and forth along his desk.

Perhaps some time apart would do us good. Although if she's going to face the nether beast, I can't let her go into danger without me.

That thought didn't appeal to him at all, but the sting of Meri's ointment now on his cut knuckles gave him something slightly less emotionally painful to focus on.

I'll go and see her father, but first I should make sure she's not going from one trap into another.

Before he could make any kind of decisive action, Demi's face materialised in the shiny black surface of his orb as an incoming call.

Meri grabbed his hand, dropped a selection of pills into it and pointed a determined finger at the glass of water she'd set out for him. Then she realm-skipped away to another part of the court.

"Hi, Demi," he said.

Her face expanded out of the orb's surface, projected into the centre of the room as he swigged down the pills.

"Really quick one. I checked in with Reyan and asked her to come to the Nether Court with me. She's sworn to your court though and your intended, so figured I'd do the tiresome dance of 'asking permission'."

Kainen chuckled, imagining Reyan's reaction to that.

"She's her own person. If she's happy to go with you that's fine. But no leaving her on her own, no sending her in unprepared. I haven't even had time to check she can ward herself properly, so make sure she's protected."

Demi grinned. "Are you giving your queen ultimatums?"

"Where she's concerned? Absolutely."

It felt so much better to say such things without having to pretend them. The actual engagement might be a fake, but his feelings were entirely real.

"Got it. She'll be safe with us." She hesitated. "Did you want to come as well?"

Kainen grimaced then, torn. Protecting Reyan the best he could at the Nether Court was tempting, but she would be safe with Demi. Whereas if he didn't act now, Ciel might do something rash.

"I have something I can't avoid to do first, but I'll get Reyan to meet you and I'll be back soon. We can all go together?"

Demi nodded. "Okay. We'll pick you both up in a bit."

"If you tell Trevor to skip into the south platform, that'll ensure your privacy until I get back. I think he'll know where that is. Leads out from the library-"

He froze, realising what he'd said. He'd told her about that exit once before, a long while ago and cryptically. She hadn't listened or hadn't realised.

"The secret route you once tried to tell me about?"

He nodded. So many apologies frothed onto the tip of his tongue, but Demi sighed before he could coordinate one.

"Never mind the past, it's done. Oh, there was someone poking around in our room when we came back to get our stuff though before I forget. Might have just been staff, but I figured I'd let you know. Tall guy, blonde hair."

Kainen stiffened, his hands clenching the edge of the desk.

"Goatee? Blue eyes?"

"That sounds like the one, yeah. I'll let you go. See you in a bit."

She disappeared, her face vanishing and leaving him raging in silence.

Ciel had been snooping around in the queen's quarters. He never helped out with any staff chores, and he wasn't on any of Meri's cleaning or serving rotas.

So why would he be in there at all without me asking him to?

Either way, it was time to take action.

A perverse wave of vindictive eagerness spread through

him at the thought of what he was about to do. A tiny voice inside his head suggested Reyan wouldn't approve of such gleeful behaviour, but he was doing this for her benefit. Mostly.

He snapped his fingers.

"Ciel," he said into the smoke. "My study, *please*."

The recent pleasantries might have been a Reyan addition, but that one was drenched in pure sarcasm.

He was fast beginning to think of his life in pre-Reyan and post-Reyan terms. Even while she was sleeping sweetly on top of him the night before, he'd marvelled at how fast the situation had escalated. He'd gone from appreciating her as a random, albeit good-natured and beautiful, member of his court, to realising that she was a whole different kind of rare.

Ciel materialised in front of him moments later. Kainen scanned his oldest friend's face and had his answer instantly. He almost felt guilty that his heart sung joyfully at the dour scowl on Ciel's face. Almost.

"I hear a proposal was issued," he said.

Ciel's expression tightened, his eyes narrowing and his mouth pressing thin.

"And initially rejected, I'm sure you'll be glad to know."

Kainen raised his eyebrows at that. While the whole of Faerie thought Ciel was his oldest and most trusted friend, Ciel's service was a life-debt similar to Reyan's, orchestrated between their fathers long ago. The only difference between the two was that Ciel wanted to remain at the court. While the friendship was assumed, it wasn't exactly truthful or honoured by either of them. In the pre-war days, the life-debt was so Ciel could spy on Kainen's father for his own family. Now, Kainen realised that Ciel's desire to remain sworn to the court after the war and the condemning of both their fathers was most likely because of Reyan as much as familial pressure.

"No big talk?" Ciel asked. "Come on, Kainen, she rejected me. You're supposed to be gloating. You win."

Kainen leaned back in his seat, faking nonchalance with far too much enthusiasm.

"Win what?"

Ciel rolled his eyes. "Don't do that."

"Do what?"

"Don't be so you. You're always so sickeningly smug and casual when you win things, and that makes it worse. Why her? Why? She was perfectly pleasant and friendly with me until you did your whole fake engagement thing. You could have picked anyone at court."

Kainen frowned. "What makes you think it's a fake?"

Ciel's family were a bunch of traditionalists. Even now the war was over, Kainen raced to find some way the fake engagement could be used against him. The only possible fall-out was from Taz's family if Blossom felt snubbed, but he doubted Demi or the Oak Queen would care enough to reprimand him over it.

"Oh come on." Ciel folded his arms. "I'm your unofficial court spider, winding in all the information on the court webs. Nothing happens that I don't know about, even with you. If you'd been at her on the quiet before the queen arrived, I would have known."

Kainen ignored the flare of fury at the thought of anyone being 'at her' and sighed, leaning forward to put his elbows on his desk. Now that the initial elation of knowing Reyan wasn't marrying anyone else had passed, he wanted to get on with his plan. But if Ciel did truly have feelings for her, kicking him out of the study with zero explanation now that Kainen had what he wanted seemed extra mean somehow.

Since when have I ever been worried about 'mean'? He fought the urge to smirk. *That girl is going to ruin me.*

"Fine, I had to marry Blossom and I panicked. It was a spur of the moment thing. But getting to know Reyan the past few days, I've fallen for her."

"In a few days? Please. I've been her friend, quietly working on her for two years."

"Working on her?" Kainen sent a warning glare across the desk. "She's not a target, she's a person. If you were truly meant for her, you wouldn't have to 'work on her'. She'd want you back."

Ciel's eyes blazed with hatred, his hands landing on the desk as he leaned forward. Kainen kept his power simmering, not willing to risk an actual fight if he could avoid it.

"I've made an effort with her, something you wouldn't understand. I'm still making that effort, and she will come around eventually. You just click your fingers and expect everyone to come running."

Kainen couldn't say anything to that because it was true. Pre-Reyan, he wouldn't have thought twice about clicking his fingers and expecting others to do whatever he demanded of them.

That's not fair. Even during the war, I was beginning to realise the difference between good and bad, and the right to have choices. It's taken me a while but I'm learning to be better.

And no matter how much 'effort' Ciel had put in, if Reyan didn't want him, he should have respected that.

And I'll have to do the same if she doesn't want me.

He met Ciel's gaze, his own expression falling calm and still.

"What were you planning to do about her situation then?" he asked. "I assume you know all about it after all the "effort" you've put in."

The fingered air-quotes were childish, but he couldn't help it. The mere thought of Ciel thinking he could convince or bribe Reyan into a marriage was laughable, but then what would she sacrifice to feel free after a lifetime of being used?

Ciel's cheeks tinged pink. "I do know actually. My family are well off, and although my brother is the head of it, I have access to our funds. I'm sure I could make her father a suitable offer."

Kainen stood before he could check himself, his gift erupting and calling roiling black smoke to wraith his hands. Ciel pushed away from the desk and raised a hand in preparation. He was sworn to the court, unable to injure his lord unless Kainen willed it, but he could still defend himself from attack.

I need to get there first. I can't risk Ciel offering her a chance at freedom as a trade when I'm planning to give it to her for nothing.

"I'll be gone for the day," he said, his jaw tight. "Possibly a couple. Reyan will be elsewhere too. In my absence, Meri is in control." He clicked his fingers. "Meri!"

She appeared instantly. "You bellowed?"

"Yes. I'll be away from the court for a day or two. You're in command, but run everything abnormal or non-domestic past me first."

Meri regarded him for a moment. He knew she was fond of him in a motherly sort of way, perhaps because it was what he needed and that secured her the second-in-command spot with ample control to do as she pleased. She certainly didn't make effort to spend time with him beyond the necessary and they weren't exactly friends. And yet, he trusted her as far as he could trust anyone.

Almost anyone. Unnerving to realise that he'd trust Reyan with his life and his court in a heartbeat.

"Will the lady have any power to command in your absence?" Meri asked, her lips twitching. "It is tradition, but then you might not have those kinds of plans for her."

Kainen stared back at her.

Would it look weird for me to say no?

The court were supposed to think she was his intended equal, the one who would share his court with him when they married. But she wouldn't do anything awful even if she did have to step in for him.

She'd probably only make things better.

Slowly, he nodded. "My court is at her disposal until I return, assuming she's here while I'm not."

Even Ciel blanched at that statement, and Kainen knew it was a dangerous move to make.

Leaving his court at Reyan's disposal meant that she could do as she liked both in it and with it, unless he told her otherwise or stopped her. Technically, she could even buy her own freedom with his money if she wanted. If anything happened to him on whatever the next assignment was, that seemed like a good idea. But then if he died, the court might well become hers. Courts were an oddity in Faerie, often taking on lives and souls of their own. Assuming the court itself accepted Reyan in his place as his officially public future bride, only the queens could undo or override it.

But if she marries Ciel, he might be able to convince her to let him ruin it all.

"Very well, Lord." Meri distracted him from his worries. "When do you leave?"

He grabbed his leather jacket from the back of his chair and threw it on. He wouldn't need any proof of coin for what he was about to do, but he had to get things in motion before Ciel found an excuse or loophole to leave court.

"I will send word," he said. "Reyan may be leaving with the queen and king consort, or she may choose to stay behind." He fixed Meri with a firm look. "Make sure they're all comfortable either way if they're here."

She nodded. "As you wish. In the meantime, might I suggest we prepare a suitable wardrobe for her? As much as I know she'll detest anything flouncy."

"Why not?" Kainen grinned at the thought of presenting Reyan with some ridiculous outfits, and what drama she might inflict to get out of wearing them. "But maybe get a selection and let me present them to her first. Thank you."

Meri nodded and when Kainen returned the gesture, he released her so that she could go about her business. He bid the door to open onto the nearest hallway and she left with a scary amount of purpose in her step.

Probably at the thought of being able to spend a vast amount of the court's money on clothes.

As the door closed behind her, Kainen took a deep breath. Ciel stood in the centre of the room, his face red and seething. Since he'd been summoned, he was trapped until Kainen left the room or released him. Kainen fixed him with the scariest look he could dredge forth.

"Reyan will choose who she wants," he said. "I won't let you bargain a marriage out of her either."

Ciel snorted. "And if she decides she doesn't want either of us?"

"Then we let her go." Kainen's chest tightened at the mere thought. "Stay within the court until I return."

He didn't wait around to hear the inevitable protests brewing on Ciel's tongue. Instead, he translocated through the court to the library, deserted the way he preferred it, and strode through the shadowy aisles. Trailing his fingers along the shelves as he passed, he imagined asking the court to move the dusty old folios further back so that they could have a fiction section at the front for Reyan.

I doubt bribing her to love me with books will do any more good than Ciel bribing her with her freedom.

She had at least thanked him for the *Carrie's Castle* books which was something, although she'd also thrown it back in his face the next time they'd argued. Trotting down the back stairs that led out onto the mountain and his secret realm-skipping location, he grinned at the memory.

Once she had her freedom, she would have time to figure out what she wanted for her future. He could only hope that he at least still had a shot of being in it.

CHAPTER EIGHTEEN
REYAN

Forty-three minutes should have been enough. Reyan had abandoned her book two pages in, too uneasy to settle. She spent most of the remaining time pacing up and down in Kainen's bedroom, reassuring herself that she wasn't chickening out of speaking to him. The court gave her the time whenever she requested it, one of the perks of being sworn-in staff and not a straight-up member, and she counted those minutes down anxiously.

She was giving him space to rest, to freshen up, to do important lord-type things.

Then her patience fizzled out and a surge of bravery sent her flying toward the bathroom door. Even as she put her hand on the handle and swung the door, she remembered that the door only worked to reach multiple rooms for Kainen.

Expecting to see the bathroom on the other side, her jaw dropped.

"Oh."

Kainen's study was dark, but the lamps flickered on a moment later.

Maybe me staying in his bedroom did something. She stared at the empty study. *But if he's not in here or in the bedroom, where's he gone?*

She stepped through the doorway on tentative feet, sure

he was going to pop out of somewhere to make her jump. She took a couple of steps into the centre of the room, when the door snapped smartly shut behind her. She jumped, whirling around, but no sign of Kainen.

"Okay, slightly unnerving." She bit her lip.

One thought that had circled around and around while she was drumming up the courage to come and see him, was that the royals were gone. Demi and Taz weren't staying at court any longer, so once Blossom left she should be moving back to the dorm. She tormented herself with that thought, wondering if that was why Kainen hadn't returned to the room to see her, because he was waiting for her to get out of it first.

"Kainen?" she called out.

It was a silly idea, but if he was somehow hiding to spook her, she'd let him know she was prepared even if she wasn't.

"Reyan?"

She flinched as his face sprung into view, pearly grey and looming out of the large black orb on his desk.

"Um, hi." She raised a hand and rubbed the back of her neck. "I don't know how I got in here."

He gave her a disbelieving look even as he started to smile.

"You don't?"

"I mean, I did technically come in, but I'm not sure why. I mean, I do know why, but I opened the door to the bathroom without thinking, because obviously that multi-door thing only works for you. But it was the study on the other side, so I don't know how it let me in here instead of just opening onto the bathroom like normal. Then the door shut itself behind me!"

She couldn't quite keep the indignation out of her voice as he started to chuckle.

"My court has a mind of its own," he explained. "All courts do apparently. Mine is a lot like you, very fussy about neatness, so doors close themselves behind me quite often. I think it's a passive-aggressive hint that I'm lazy. Although, not sure why it bothers being passive when it could just be aggressive about it like you."

She flushed at the teasing softness in his tone and hoped he couldn't see the redness flaring across her cheeks. Both of their visions would be grey to the other, but she wasn't sure if the shading would change and rat her emotions out.

"As long as it lets me out again," she said, then hesitated.

She had no idea how to bring up Ciel's behaviour. He was still Kainen's friend. He might call her crazy, or insist Ciel wasn't like that. He might not believe her.

"Demi's said you've agreed to help her, and I've agreed with caveats," he announced.

"What caveats?" Thoughts of Ciel flowed out of her head. "I already said I'd help."

He chuckled. "I know, but she orbed me to ask officially. I told her to pick us up, but I don't want you doing anything dangerous, so wait with her until I get back. I'm just running an errand, then I'll be joining you."

Reyan nodded. She still had to ask him about buying her freedom, or at least ensuring he wouldn't let Ciel buy it instead. Her father might choose to sell her, but it wouldn't cancel out the debt with the court unless Kainen agreed, no matter who she belonged to.

"Where are you anyway?" she asked.

His face froze for a moment. "Private court lord business. I'll tell you when I see you. We have no idea what's about to happen with the nether beast though, no guarantees, so I've ensured your safety and that's all I'm telling you right now."

She froze. "You haven't sold my debt on, have you?"

The vision shook suddenly, his face vanishing and undiscernible shades of grey spinning instead. When his head reappeared, she was almost hyperventilating with panic.

"I almost dropped my orb! Of course I haven't, and I wouldn't without your permission. I may be toxic but I'm hopefully not that much of a prick."

She flushed, mortified. "I didn't mean… I have to be worried about it. I have to ask."

She searched his face for signs of whether he was angry at her, but if anything he looked hurt, like she'd given his heart a savage kick.

"I understand," he said, his voice now subdued. "Don't worry about any of it, okay? I take your safety very seriously."

Of course he did. She knew him better than that. Even well before the engagement he'd hired security every year at his own expense when someone kept trying to attack her at the court's yearly revel.

Will he still expect me to perform? What'll happen if someone tries again this year?

She had a sneaking suspicion it was her father who sent the dangers once a year. It was suspicious that they happened like clockwork at the same yearly court revel but never any other time, and it would be very like him to create a problem then insist the debt with the court that funded him and his habits was what kept her safe. Better to believe that than think someone actually did want her hurt, or worse.

She grimaced at Kainen and pushed thoughts of her father aside. Unless someone magically convinced him to free his half of the bargain, she preferred not to think of him at all.

"Sorry."

Kainen shook his head. "Don't apologise for being cautious. Now, are you up for your first assignment?"

A mischievous grin spread across his face and she nodded, her relief tumbling away to leave another sensation. She blinked, staring at his face until she had enough sense of self to nod. She'd always known he was handsome, sinfully so which everyone at court agreed on, but now that he wasn't showing his usual mask of charm, he was unnervingly attractive. So much so that her gut exploded in flutters as he made a show of beckoning her closer.

She inched toward the orb on the desk, bringing the vision of his face right in front of hers.

"Okay sweetheart, listen carefully. Leave the study and go to the library. Right at the back is a fireplace that's always unlit. In the grate are three logs. Press the one at the back and walk through the fireplace. Go down the steps outside, and you'll find a small platform. Wait there and Demi should arrive, then I'll join you and we can all go to the Nether Court together. And tell nobody about the platform or the fireplace."

She grinned then, forgetting her feelings. "I'm the only person you've told?"

"Yep, you're now part of a very exclusive club of two. Oh, except for Demi, and probably Taz now as well. Also, take a coat as it gets windy up there. The last thing we want is my bride getting a cold."

She rolled her eyes. "Okay, love, calm it down."

His eyes widened. She realised what she'd said the moment his mouth lifted and threatened to dislodge his ears, but he spoke before she could recover.

"I *love* my new nickname. Don't you dare take it back."

She'd been about to do just that, but his command stopped the words from leaving her mouth. She glared at him, even though the smooshy romantic part of her was doing backflips inside her chest.

Orbs alive, this is getting well out of hand. Him flirting is one thing but he's not going to be taking any of this seriously. It's not like it's going to mean anything real to him when he's still hung up on Demi.

"Do you have a coat?" he asked.

She shrugged. She didn't but because she barely ever left the court except to go to her father's, it wasn't much of a hardship.

"I'll take that as a no." He frowned. "Oh, hang on. Wait there a minute."

The vision twisted in another blur of grey. When it

straightened out, she could see the roll of a paved path before everything went dark. The vision was still there but in darkness, and sending her shadows through the orb-waves to investigate was one thing she couldn't do.

She waited impatiently, huffing and tutting in case he could still hear her. A few minutes passed before his face reappeared.

"Okay, sweetheart, there should be a coat on its way to you."

He clicked his fingers and a moment later, a sturdy mock-leather coat dropped out of thin air. It landed on the floor and Reyan reached down to pick it up, marvelling at the softness of the grey fake fur around the buttoned-on hood.

"Does it fit?" he asked, anxiousness in his tone.

Reyan frowned, pulling it on. "It does, but what is this, a loan? I've not got anything to give back or trade for it."

He chuckled then, his expression clearing. The coat's hem stopped around Reyan's knees, and she found a leather belt knotted at the back.

"I owe you for putting up with this engagement, and I owe you even more for putting up with me. A pile of books and a coat are nowhere near enough."

The automatic instinct to be modest rose up, to say no of course she couldn't accept such a gift or owe him for his kindness, but Reyan squashed it. She might be sworn to his court but it was embarrassing to pretend, and he had uprooted her life recently.

And somehow taken a huge chunk of my emotions hostage, but the less said about that right now the better.

She gave him a disapproving look even though she couldn't stop her lips curving up.

"That's basically true, so I'll accept. Thank you." She hesitated. "Are you somewhere safe at least?"

He smiled, the amusement turning to something scarily reminiscent to wistful tenderness. It was similar to the expression she often saw on Ciel's face when she caught him staring.

"I'm fine, no danger. I'll tell you all about it when I see you, okay?"

She nodded. "Okay. I'll go and wait for Demi."

She waited, and he looked like he might say something more. After a moment he sighed.

"See you soon, sweetheart."

He disappeared and her mood plummeted. She had no idea where he was, or what he was doing. Not that it was her business to know, but even though he'd told her he was somewhere safe and couldn't lie, she worried.

I'm worried about a boy I'm not even attached to because it's all fake. He's still in love with Demi, or why else would he put this much effort into the whole thing? Does he think it'll somehow make her jealous, or is he really just using me to save face?

Despite her insistence she'd go and wait for Demi, she walked around the desk and sank into his chair. The riot of emotions, the worry for his safety, the anxiousness without him nearby, it all pointed to one thing.

"Oh, Faerie save me," she whispered.

He kept going on about not getting herself in danger, which suggested there was plenty of danger where they were headed. Given the state of him when she shadow-travelled to the Nether Court, the beast that was mentioned didn't intend to give up without a huge fight. He even said he'd put safeguards in place in case anything happened to him.

Her gaze strayed over the desk and landed on his pad and a nearby pen. She half expected him to be a quill person, all show and very little speed, or at least handy with a fountain pen. She eyed the pot of biros and grinned to herself. He'd put fail-safes in place, so she would do the same.

Grabbing the pad and the nearest biro that was mostly unchewed, she began.

Kainen,

I'm about to set off with Demi, but you've worried me with all your talk of safety, so I need to make sure you know some things.

Firstly, I've come to realise (in the last few minutes but I think it's been coming on a while) that I have feelings for you. I don't expect you to return them, don't worry. I know you're fond of me now but it'll be impossible to live here so close to you when you're still in love with someone else.

I can't help the way I feel, so I'm begging you to consider letting me buy my father's debt outright. I'm not sure how I'd pay you, over a lifetime somehow perhaps and I'm willing to hear your terms.

I'm also worried and reluctant to tell you this, but when I turned Ciel down he made me feel really uneasy. I know he's your friend, but even in writing I can't lie. He mentioned buying my debt from you himself, but I'm hoping if all does go well with the assignment and we return, you won't let anyone buy it until I've had a chance to find a way myself.

I mentioned you trying to be a better person but I don't think you need to change anything. Maybe try to pick up after yourself a bit more, but you are a good man. I think you've actually become my favourite person, and all in the space of a few days.

That's it really.

Love, Reyan.

She found an envelope, sealed it and wrote Kainen's name on the front. The study was off limits to normal court staff, but she wasn't sure if Meri or anyone else would come in to clean, so she tucked the letter beneath the top few pages of the pad. When Kainen came to write something, he would find it.

And if they returned, she would either orchestrate a way to retrieve it before he read it and approach him direct about the debt, or she would die of embarrassment anyway.

With the new coat snug around her, she stood up and went to the door, but hesitated with her hand on the door handle and addressed the court itself.

"If you can somehow bring me out near the library, that'd be a huge help, but no worries if not."

Pushing down the handle, she pulled the door open and stepped out into a familiar hall. Kainen's study was right around the corner from the library, so she had no idea whether the court had heard and obeyed her, or simply chucked her out of a normal exit.

It's not the bedroom though, so asking did something.

She grinned to herself and pulled the door shut behind her, guessing it would lock itself.

"Rey!"

She froze, chills rippling over her skin and turning to panicked heat as she heard Ciel's voice.

She forced a gentle smile on her face before facing him. Worse, he had Lady Blossom standing beside him with her arms folded and a cruel smile playing across her lips. Given how close together they were, they were intimate friends already.

Blossom's honey-blonde hair had been pinned back, sharpening her naturally fae features, but her green eyes flashed with malice as she looked Reyan up and down.

"What were you doing in there?" Ciel asked.

Reyan shrugged one shoulder. "Preparation for the assignment I'm going on."

It wasn't exactly a lie, considering the coat was technically preparation for her wait on a cold, windy platform.

Ciel smiled at her like nothing in the world was wrong, but her pulse picked up an anxious pace from the mere proximity to him. Blossom rolled her eyes with a huff and glanced pointedly over her shoulder, so Reyan took that as a convenient excuse to leave them to it.

"I'd better get going," she said, taking a step back.

"Yes, run along," Blossom cooed. "Wouldn't want to risk any mishaps in empty halls, especially with the court so undefended with Kainen off gallivanting."

How does she know he's away from court?

Reyan glanced at Ciel, but he only nodded while

holding her gaze.

"Of course, you can't keep a queen waiting. Nice coat, is it new? He certainly is spoiling you if it is."

"Uh, yeah. Are you on an errand or..?"

She left the query hanging there, freaked out by not only how much they knew but also Blossom's less-than-cryptic threat about empty hallways.

Ciel frowned. She didn't usually question him, but she needed him to leave without her. She couldn't go to the library or he might wonder why and ask. Might even follow her and stick to her like glue.

"I'm on business," he said vaguely. "Although, you probably know much more than I do these days."

Blossom scoffed at that, but Reyan had no intention of acknowledging her. Princess or not, Blossom clearly had a problem with her and twice as much attitude on a normal day.

I might be the future Lady of the Illusion Court in the eyes of everyone else, but I'll be vulnerable when that pretence is over.

She wondered what Ciel and Blossom could have had to say to each other quite so privately, especially as Blossom was rarely seen without an entourage of fussing maids.

"Oh, I don't know about that." She thought frantically and remembered the communal toilet nearby. "Okay, good luck on your business then. I'll see you when I get back."

She set off toward the library and the bathroom.

"Rey?" The suspicion in Ciel's voice brought her to a halt. "Where are you going? The main hall is the other way."

She forced a laugh, turning to face him and walking backward.

"Bathroom. Might as well use this one. See you later, okay?"

He nodded, his gaze still fixed on her.

"We still have to have our chat, don't forget," he insisted.

She nodded. "Absolutely, can't wait. We'll sort out all the misunderstandings."

She twisted around and strode to the bathroom before he could snare her in any more chat, although she didn't miss the smug smile lighting on his face as she fled. Gnawing at her lip, she looked at her reflection in the mirror.

What if he's waiting outside for me when I get out? She took a deep breath. *I'll go to the main hall and give him the slip. Or go to Kainen's room and shut the door before he can get in.*

She inched the bathroom door open and peered out. She couldn't see him through the gap, but that didn't mean he wasn't lurking.

Moments away from creeping out and hoping for the best, she froze as realisation settled around her.

Idiot!

Kainen had lifted the ban on her gifts. So used to being without them around the court, she'd forgotten. Gleefully gathering her gift around her, she melted into the shadows and used them to sneak out of the gap under the door.

Ciel stood leaning against the wall, waiting for her to

come out. No doubt he wanted to see where she actually went, or perhaps startle her for some creepy reason of his own. She couldn't see any sign of Blossom, but that didn't mean the awful woman wasn't lurking somewhere nearby.

At one with the shadows and bodiless, Reyan slid past Ciel and on down the hall. Unable to open the door in her shadow-form, she crept through the gap under the door and materialised as herself on the other side.

The lamps flickered into life around her as she set off up the spiral stone staircase. Why Kainen had chosen to have such a long staircase she couldn't fathom. Her cheeks burned and her breath came in short puffs as she trudged upwards. Perhaps he simply wanted to keep the library for himself, although he wouldn't need anything more than a court-wide instruction to achieve that.

Or perhaps it was a test. Anyone determined enough to climb this torture to get to some old books would likely be someone he'd see as worth getting to know.

Either way, the constant rotation of steps gave her time to come to the unavoidable conclusion: waiting for Kainen wasn't going to happen.

He got hurt the last time he faced the nether beast, and if anything happened to him the whole court would be entirely undefended against the likes of Ciel and Blossom.

It's not like I'm actually meant to be Lady of it either, so if anything happens to me it won't jeopardise as much.

She stepped into the library, wincing at the waft of heat from the crackling fireplace. Kainen had told her to head to the back and find an unlit one, so she dodged through the shelving units.

Stuck searching until she found what she was looking for, because 'at the back' wasn't exactly clear in a room that was more a lumpy round shape than square or rectangular, she entertained herself with wild thoughts.

He could let me have some of these shelves here at the back for fiction if our pretence was real.

She sighed. If it weren't for his crush on Demi, she still wouldn't be first in line to be his. One day he would no doubt find someone who made his feelings for Demi seem childish and unrealistic. When he found that person, he would probably move the whole of Faerie to suit them. But Reyan wasn't from a well-off or influential family. She knew her lineage was an old one, but pure blood was only one respectable aspect, and in the holy trinity of Fae society, money and social standing also mattered just as much.

Demi had been a fairy and from a human family, but there was clearly something special about her. Kainen had seen it. The once-Prince of Faerie had seen it. Even the Oak Queen and an ancient entity on level with a wrath goddess had seen it.

In comparison, Reyan knew she was okay-looking rather than striking and useful rather than powerful.

"Oh thank Faerie," she muttered as she came across an unlit fireplace. "Although knowing my luck, this'll be the wrong one and they've lit the one I need."

She leaned over and pressed the log at the back of the grate. A waft of air brushed her face and she stepped forward.

The dim, flickering gloom of the library vanished,

leaving her facing a set of rocky steps leading down a steep drop, with bright white sky above her and barren grey cliffs all around. Harsh wind blasted into her, biting at her face and blowing her backwards.

She winced at the push and went down a couple of steps, stopping to stay steady while she looked back over her shoulder. She was sure nobody had followed her, but Kainen had told her not to let anyone see the fireplace and she valued that trust.

Further down at the bottom of the rocky steps, she could see the platform and Demi waving up at her. Increasing her pace, she trotted down, arms out to keep her balance. Pinning a nervous smile on her face, she prepared herself to word-tangle and misconstrue her lord's orders to a queen.

CHAPTER NINETEEN
KAINEN

Kainen stared up at the dilapidated grandeur and a wave of fury swept through him. The house was a fine one, but it wasn't the waste of a fine house that upset him.

Reyan's father had kept a huge property and let it go to ruin, but willingly traded off his child for money.

No wonder she was so surprised when I gave her that coat. I bet he never remembers her birthday or sends anything for Yuletide.

The anger grew in Kainen's chest, stabbing and stealing his breath, but he forced the emotions down deep. He had to be clever now, his normal, charming court lord self. No doubt Reyan's father had heard about the engagement through the Fae gossip mill by now, so Kainen had to be every inch the young lord who had more money than sense.

He'd stopped off at a local shop nearby to buy some of Reyan's father's favourite rose liquor, and heard Reyan's voice saying his name. He thought perhaps the mind-speak had lingered, unnerved by the sheer hope that perhaps that meant they were anchoring together like Demi and Taz had. Then he remembered his orb and felt like an absolute fool.

But seeing her restored every wavering emotion he had. Her smile, the little blush, the way she'd tucked her head down when she was embarrassed then blinked up at him, her worry for him. All of it completely slayed him.

He fixed his face into an arrogant smile and strode through the wilting garden. Even the weeds seemed to be withering rather than thriving, but up ahead the door was opening and he could see Reyan's father.

He'd never met the man but had seen him in passing once at court. As he walked up the wooden steps to meet him on the porch, he took in the clean appearance and the subtle whiff of drink.

He'd been expecting a seeded old man, dirty and swilling in filth. But this was no faded individual and Kainen's anger bounced against his ribcage, his gift dying to fly free. He could compel Reyan's father to obey him, or trick him with visions or torment him with nightmares, but he didn't want to resort to that. Not unless Reyan's safety became an issue.

"Your Lordship." Reyan's father bowed his head. "I'm Merrick. I recognise you of course, but I don't think we've been officially introduced. Only on the money slips, ha ha."

Kainen widened his smile and held out the bottle.

"A gift, nothing more."

It was customary to bring a small token gift when visiting unannounced, unless the friendship was a true one or revolved around the daily life of a court, but many a Fae had been tricked by an unassuming gift being cursed or enchanted.

Merrick took it with an eager smile and no hint of hesitation.

"Very kind. Please, be welcome and safe in my home."

Kainen nodded. If the home was somehow owned by someone else who let Merrick live there, that wording would render Kainen vulnerable. But he had no fear for himself. Foolish and risky perhaps, but he wanted to do this personally rather than send someone on his behalf.

"Can I offer you a glass?" Merrick asked.

"Yes, thank you. I have something I wish to discuss with you."

Merrick waved Kainen through the nearest open doorway. Faded grandeur, but serviceable.

It must be easy to keep this place looking respectable when nobody's using it. He eyed the layer of dust on the nearest antique unit. *He appreciates grandeur over his own daughter. Much like our father favoured everything over us unless we were obedient and useful.*

Merrick was back almost immediately with two glasses and the already open bottle of rose liquor. Given the level of the liquid in the bottle, he'd already had a good glug. Kainen tried not to pull a face, especially as he had no intention of drinking any of it.

"Take a seat, please." Merrick sat on an armchair while Kainen took the sofa opposite. "What is it you want to see me about? Or should I say, what has she done? Nothing expensive, I hope!"

Kainen took the proffered glass only so he could clench his hand around something. When Merrick knocked his back and reached for the bottle again, Kainen vanished the liquid, downed air from the empty glass and held it out. As Merrick poured, Kainen dredged up every element of his charm, both natural, practiced and gifted.

"Reyan is doing wonderfully at court," he began. "The time has come for her to step out on her own, and I'd like to facilitate that for her as payment for her service. She will be offered the full safety of the court either way, but I would like to buy her full debt from you."

Merrick's eyes narrowed. Kainen tensed until laughter boomed through the room.

"Oh-ho, she's managed to snare a court lord." Merrick slapped his thigh. "I knew she'd be safe at your court, safer than she would be with me and my money troubles at any rate. I had many offers for her, mostly for her gift, but she was a good looking thing even then."

Kainen tensed his stomach tight, a sear of cramp shooting through him as he did everything he could not to snare this awful man with his gifts and torture him until he was a gibbering mess.

"You would have sold her to someone random if my father hadn't taken her?" he asked.

Merrick heard the edge in his voice, his face sobering in an instant.

"Oh, not like that. Never like that." He hastily downed his third drink and poured another. "But I had no chance of keeping her safe. I like a certain type of lifestyle, and this way everyone won. She got the safety and connections of a court and I could keep my living. But hmm, to let my beautiful daughter go completely, that would pain me a lot."

Kainen smiled, knowing it was more of a grimace.

"It would earn you a lot, you mean." He pushed a tiny element of his compulsion gift into his next words, just for the sheer necessity of not spending any longer with this man than necessary. "Let's talk in truths without the fluff. Name your price."

"I need a lifetime," he said, the compulsion pulling the answer out of him. "A lifetime of enough to live on until my time is done. And unlimited rose liquor. And an invitation to court. I'd... I'd like to see her dance."

Kainen stared in amazement as Merrick's cheeks flushed bright red and another glass of liquor went down the man's throat. He'd lost count now how many Merrick had downed, but apparently the furtive embarrassment was because he'd shown a miniscule amount of affection for his daughter.

"You will be sober when you visit," Kainen said. "You will be nice to her. You'll stop that ridiculous practice of sending threats after her at our revels when she dances. I already know that's your doing. Agree to those conditions and I will give you an allowance for a lifetime. I will give you access to the rose liquor, and I will invite you to court for the revel each year."

So desperate to seal the deal, Merrick spluttered over the liquid in his mouth and choked it down enough to say yes.

"I will honour this new agreement, replacing the old," Kainen said, standing and holding out his hand.

He winced when Merrick swayed, almost not making it to his feet.

"I will honour this new agreement, replacing the old," Merrick repeated. "I'll go and fetch her talisman."

They shook hands, a subtle tingling warmth of magic

sealing the deal. Kainen pulled his hand free and watched Merrick blunder out of the room. Always cautious, he let a protection warding creep around him. It wouldn't be the first time a deal was struck and someone else would be waiting to conveniently stage a 'random' robbery in which one of the dealmakers was removed permanently, rendering the deal irrelevant.

But Merrick hadn't thought that far. He hurried back in with a small dark blue velvet pouch lined with lilac.

"These are your family colours?" Kainen asked, taking the pouch.

Merrick nodded. "Yes, the Roseglade line is very old. I'm glad that Reyan will be continuing it for us, and with a court lord no less!"

Kainen couldn't help a small smile. Merrick had been so desperate to seal the deal for a lifetime, he'd not even thought about protecting the terms. They'd agreed to a lifetime with enough to live on, but not an amount or how it would be paid. Kainen could give him a lifetime of percats in one go, and it might get spent lavishly in a year. Or he might consider enough to live on a very meagre pittance indeed. He'd also not specified a lifetime of liquor, or an unlimited supply. Only 'access' to it. He could buy Merrick a lifetime ticket to the guided tour and that would suffice for the terms of the deal.

I should punish him considering how badly he's treated her. But I won't, for her sake.

He would keep the money the same, regular every week. He would also let the local shop know to send the bill for Merrick's rose liquor to the court, but if they happened to run out of stock, that wasn't his problem. As for an invitation to the court, he would honour it for Reyan. If she chose not to see her father, or chose not to dance, that would be up to her.

He opened the pouch, peering inside. A coin, a nail and a small tooth, all wrapped in a lock of blonde hair.

"Is this really the talisman of her debt and her freedom?" he asked, weaving the strongest compulsion he had into the words. He had to be sure.

Merrick nodded. "Yes. Whoever owns that, owns her."

Kainen shuddered. The terms of a life-debt were well known, so he had no fear for the items themselves. Someone could steal them or smash them to atoms and he would still own her.

I own her. I feel awful. This shouldn't even be a thing, let alone a thing between us.

He straightened up. "Thank you for your time. I will leave you to your day and you'll receive an invitation to our annual revel."

Merrick sank onto the sofa with the liquor bottle in hand. Kainen walked to the doorway with his protection still lingering, but he heard the words clear enough.

"Look after her. She deserves the world, and I can sense your heart is hers."

He turned back but Merrick was staring morosely into the air in front of him. Ignoring the strain of pity, Kainen sped toward the door and down the garden path to the street.

Her father had one thing right. Reyan was the most amazing person he knew. Sure, Demi was queen and fine in her own way, but Reyan had been gentle and kind to him even when he was a complete pig. When she wasn't shouting at him, at least. His lips lifted at the thought.

He had to go and free her now before there was any danger of her misconstruing the ownership and assuming he was going to use it against her.

I'll make it conditional though. She has to use the court as she sees fit until she's ready to leave, so she doesn't struggle starting out. No silly pride. And she has to ask me for anything she needs. I might not be able to give it to her, but I need to be the one she asks.

The silly suggestions made him grin, because of course there wouldn't be any condition on her freedom. In his hands, it was already hers.

He clicked his fingers, summoning his glittering black smoke.

"Meri."

He waited, unable to quell the smile. Even when Meri didn't answer, which usually meant she was yelling at someone, he was still cheerful. But the next person he'd usually call on was Ciel. Schooling his face into slightly less of a wicked grin, he resigned himself to the inevitable.

"Ciel."

Ciel's face loomed before him almost immediately, shadowy in the black smoke as it swelled in front of him.

"I wanted to confirm my change of location to Meri, but she's not there. Has Reyan left?"

Ciel smiled. "She has, as far as I know, although I didn't see her leave. We also had a chat and she promised me that we were going to sort everything out when she got back.

She was very encouraging. Sounded like she's had a complete change of heart."

Kainen fell still.

She wouldn't. Would she? Unless she thinks she has no other option.

"What did you say to get that out of her then?" he asked, his voice taut with warning.

Ciel laughed, a strange noise unlike any laugh Kainen had ever heard. A cold chill trickled across his shoulders.

"I'm in a position to free her and she knows that. You've confined me to the court, but that doesn't stop me reaching out to her father and making a very profitable offer for him."

Kainen looked past the smoke and saw two men already walking up the garden path to Merrick's house. They must have seen him, possibly recognised him if they were friends of Ciel's, but they were still knocking on the door.

Thank Faerie I got there when I did.

"If that's truly what she wants, not what she feels pushed into, then I'll hear it from her." He ignored the worry thundering through him.

"You won't order us to stay away from each other?" Ciel asked, his tone guarded.

Kainen clenched his fist around the orb's keychain, the vision beginning to shudder.

"Not if she decides you're what would make her happy. I will be compelling her to give me an honest answer though. Tell Meri I'll be at the Nether Court." He knew Ciel couldn't avoid that order, and he couldn't resist a final taunt. "Alongside the future Lady of the Court of Illusions with any luck."

If marrying Ciel was really what she thought would make her happy, he would honour it. But he'd go to his death hounding Ciel to the very ends of Faerie if Reyan so much as furrowed her brow for the rest of her life.

He pulled the orb out again and summoned his realm-skipper next.

As for the future Lady of the Court of Illusions, that was up to her. But she would be his to protect until she told him otherwise. And if she ever told him otherwise, he'd go on protecting her in secret all the same.

CHAPTER TWENTY
REYAN

Reyan stood before the enormous iron door with her heart pounding. The shadows shivered nearby, a pure warning sign of what lay beyond even if the massive door wasn't warning enough.

"Whatever's beyond there, it definitely isn't happy," she said.

Demi nodded. "We'll need to move fast. Taz can transmutate and take animals forms at will so he's responsible for your safety. I'll try to press forward and gain ground, but I may have to fall back if I can't get anywhere. Can you explain your shadow-merging to me before we go in?"

Reyan glanced over her shoulder at the long tunnel behind them before facing Demi.

"I can dissolve into shadow. I'm no good at explaining how it works exactly, but I can't see or hear, I can only sense. I can semi-shadow, so like take form to see with or move with and look like shadow, but you can still see an outline if you look close enough."

"Do you think the beastie will be able to sense you still?" Taz asked.

"No way of knowing, but the shadows can sense it already. I'll see what reaction it has to me. With luck, it won't know I'm there and will be focused on you."

He grinned. "Oh fun, I get to be the decoy. We keep this quick though, go in for short visits."

Demi swiped her hair up into a messy ponytail and pulled the zip of her hoodie a bit higher, looking absolutely nothing like a queen of Faerie.

Except her eyes. Reyan gulped to settle her nerves. *There's a queen in those. Maybe there always was.*

She pushed aside the realisation that there probably wasn't any kind of court lady staring out of her own eyes and faced the door.

"When I vanish, in we go," she said.

Taz and Demi nodded, taking her lead without question. She pulled the shadows toward her, unnerved by their reluctance. Normally they flowed like water to join her, but even they were afraid of what lay behind the door.

She cloaked enough of herself to vanish into them and a pang of fear engulfed her. She'd learned young to ride the emotions rather than fight them, but it was difficult to avoid the choking sensation that came from pure fear, even though her body had dissipated and she became one with the shadows.

A roar of ancient chaos streamed toward her, her only available sign that the door had been opened. She streamed toward it, forcing the shadows further toward the riot of tension.

She couldn't see or hear in her current form, but she could sense the beast's attention. Waves of intent swung from nearby to fix on her.

Reyan sent a gentle communication out, focusing on kindness and love. The sensations pulsed inside her, moments before she realised they weren't her own sensations but the beast returning them with nothing else entwined.

The tangled mess of senses curled around her. Fear, anger and frustration, worry. A tinge of panicked love hanging on the edge of a precipice ready to fall.

She pushed out another wave of emotion, putting all her best intentions and thoughts behind it. The sensation cascaded back, rebounding.

She allowed the faintest hint of her normal self to form, enough that she could regain her thoughts and her hearing.

Silence roared, but the beast's attention was fractured now, and she heard distant shouting.

How can Taz and Demi be so far away already?

She couldn't worry about them now, not when they were strong enough to handle themselves.

It's a void, a mirror. Whatever we're putting in spins back out with no order to it.

She sensed the severing a second before it happened. Her human form wrenched into place, drawing a panicked gasp from her lips. Dropping to her hands and knees with a thud, she yelped as the shadows took their opportunity and fled.

A murky stream of light bloomed behind her and she tried to turn toward it, but the sound of a door slamming left her in darkness once more.

She could still sense the beast's attention on her, although it wasn't a beast or the nether itself. It was something infinitely older, and she had no idea what.

Trying to stand made her knee throb so she stayed down

a while longer, crawling backwards in the hope of reaching the door. Demi had said short bursts, or Taz had, she could barely remember in her rising panic to escape. Knowledge of what the thing was would have to be enough for now.

The darkness swarmed around her, constricting tight. She flinched away but it wouldn't let go, as if the void wanted to take her ability to merge into shadow and force her into nothingness.

She choked out a breath but couldn't draw one in again, and her shoulder dropped to the floor with a jarring crash as her arm dissipated.

A flash of flame darted past her, illuminating a wall.

She squinted as the void dissolved her legs into a type of shadow she couldn't wield or feel.

The flames zoomed past again, distracting the void from focusing on her. The hesitation was long enough that she saw the wall again, and this time letters scratched into it with a shaking, uncoordinated hand.

"Ma-" She coughed and tried again. "Ma-la-dor-ac."

The void quivered, a hesitation before it resumed shadowing her into nothing. She winced as she lost feeling in her gut and her hips, but she didn't dare waste time looking down.

"Maladorac," she said it louder.

Her still-useable arm began to tingle as the void stopped again. More flames zipped by and she lifted her head to follow them as they vanished into darkness.

Maybe Demi can cast flames and she's trying to give me time to get myself out.

She lifted her arm and brought her hand to her face, a

soft gasp puffing from her lips.

Glittering black smoke wreathed her fingers. She'd never seen Kainen wield actual flame as a gift before, but the black glittering smoke? That was definitely his.

He'd told her he would meet her at the court and the mere thought of him arriving gave her enough strength.

She lifted her voice in the absence of being able to get up and face the void.

"*Maladorac.*"

She threw her hand toward the void and wished harder than she ever had before that Kainen's power would work for her just this once.

The darkness stole her vision. She could always see outlines even through the darkest of shadows, but this was the void itself. The pure expanse of nothing.

She had no mouth to scream with, as though her shadows had engulfed her without her consent, but fear swam through her in waves.

Worry for Kainen, if he had arrived and somehow sent her his gift to use. For Demi wielding fire for her, or Taz maybe, she couldn't be sure of anything.

A flash flickered in the nothing as though she had eyes to see, a vision forming from the void.

MALADORAC.

She echoed the word in whatever was left of her consciousness and the vision solidified. Instead of fearing, of struggling to retreat, she pushed toward it.

The vision formed into a roiling mass of images. Flashes of dark skies full of enormous bright stars swirled around her. Rolling lands of golden grass and white skies, then lush green forests and silver waters rolling up hills instead of down danced right through her.

The moment a woman appeared, Reyan surged toward her. The image settled, as though the void knew she was trying to pay attention to it. As if it was helping her.

As if it's helping me to understand.

The woman glimmered, her skin, hair and draped clothing sparkling white. Words danced into Reyan's mind from the woman's lips, an ancient tongue she had no hope of understanding.

"Maladorac, eil-seah, eil-seah."

A sense of contentment swaddled around her momentarily before the tangle of chaos roiled once again. The images flashed faster, of villages and cities, of Fae civilisations growing. Emotions of laughter, sadness and spite.

So much spite. She forced herself not to cringe away from the pain of it all. *The void has been absorbing us for ages. It's in pain.*

The woman's words came back to her.

Maladorac, eil-seah, eil-seah. Eil-seah, maladorac.

She had no idea if she was making things better or worse, but the void seemed to lean into the words, surrounding her. The whirl of images danced faster and she continued thinking the words over and over. The spinning void became a blur, the emotions too distorted to feel anything except utter exhaustion.

You've been absorbing us for too long. That's what it means, isn't it? Maladorac is your name, and eil-seah means to rest.

She desperately hoped that was the right assumption, but the spinning reached a dizzying tension.

Eil-seah, maladorac. NOW.

The tension pulsed a moment before it snapped and she thought of screaming. Pain radiated outward and scattered her consciousness so wide she had nothing except vague awareness. And tingling.

So much tingling. The sensation of her soul being draped in soft comfort filled her mind. *At least I still have a mind. I hope Kainen's okay.*

The tingling intensified and she frowned as her toes twitched. Frowned with eyebrows that had formed either side of a face that felt like hers. She focused on her eyes and forced them open to see a dimly lit dark tunnel and a worried face hovering over her. Over his shoulders, she could see the flickering tips of fiery wings.

"It was you," she murmured. "Thank you."

Taz stared at her for a long moment before crouching down beside her.

"That was insane. Like one of those human horror films Ace is obsessed with. Your body disappeared bit by bit, then half of you slammed into the air and started jerking about."

Reyan did the only thing she could do with that assessment of what she'd just experienced. She flailed up onto her elbow, rolled over and vomited onto the floor.

"Orbs alive, sorry. That was totally the wrong thing to say."

Taz seemed to be panicking now, which made Reyan feel a bit stronger. Her nose stung from being sick, but at least she had a nose.

Taz clicked his fingers and a bottle appeared in his hand.

"Here, drink some water. Wait, you don't know if I'm an illusion or something, right?"

Reyan wiped her lips and held her hand out.

"I'll take my chances."

She guzzled down the entire bottle despite feeling like she might end up rejecting it straight after. The shadows crept closer around her and she knew from them what Taz probably wouldn't dare say now.

They'd gathered the parts of her the void had dissipated and reformed her body from shadow. She let them curl around her, holding them close. But when she reached out for the void, to sense that tangled chaos, everything was calm.

"Beastie's asleep," she muttered. "I think it'll stay that way. I need to get my head around it, but I think I know what happened."

Taz took the bottle, vanished it then reached down to grab her arms. She winced as he hauled her up. The shadows might be able to reform the body she'd dissipated, but they wouldn't be able to fix her split knee or her exhaustion.

"Tell Demi everything but you can rest first. Are you sure the beast is down for good?"

He slid an arm around her waist and together they started a slow hopping walk through the darkness.

"Not for good, but for as long as it takes to wake it again. And it's not a beast, it's a void. Like, imagine the nether is your mind and soul, and Faerie is the fabric of your body, like your blood and bones. The void is the nothing in between."

Taz stopped her at the outline of the door and knocked three times.

"But the void has been absorbing us," she continued. "All the hate and war and anguish and the spitefulness of Fae, it became too much so it woke. Or maybe the nether woke it when it crowned two queens, I'm not sure. Or maybe someone woke it to hurt us, or distract us. Orbs, my head hurts."

Taz frowned but at the door not at her. After a few seconds silence, he heaved it open from the inside.

"Thank Faerie she left this unlocked," he muttered. "Sorry, go on."

Reyan let him reclaim her for support and swam in momentary gratitude as steady firelight on the other side of the door greeted them, more shadows rushing to claim her.

"It showed me its pain and how someone calmed it in the past," she mumbled. "Who knows, maybe she was one of the original Prime Realmers." She paused and wrapped her other arm around Taz's shoulder. "Sorry, but I think I'm going to pass out again."

CHAPTER TWENTY ONE
KAINEN

Kainen's rickshaw landed in absolute bedlam. Nether brothers in their cowled robes were rushing about and the ground underfoot was rumbling. The windows of the nearest building rattled in their frames.

He jumped out of the rickshaw with one thought in his head: find Reyan, throw her into the rickshaw and get her to safety.

"Go back to the court," he shouted to his realm-skipper, Surane. "I should be able to get myself home, but be ready when I or Reyan call. She's got all the same permissions I have and I want her protected."

Surane's worried face swam in front of him briefly, but she couldn't disobey an order.

"Yes, Lord. Be safe!"

She was gone before he could say anything back, but scanning the mayhem he saw a flash of black amid the brown and purple. Pushing forward, he stumbled over the quaking grass.

"DEMI," he hollered.

She twisted, saw him and disappeared. A split second of horror passed before she reappeared beside him with her translocation gift.

"It's absolute madness," she shouted. "Taz has gone-"

"Where is she?"

Demi bit her lip. Kainen's Fae connection hissed through his chest, prickling hot across his shoulders.

"Demi, queen or not, if you don't tell me where she is…" He couldn't threaten her, but she recognised the possessive danger in his tone.

"She went inside. Insisted. A while passed, then suddenly the ground is shaking. I'd already been inside and it attacked me, so Taz has gone after her."

Before Kainen could push past her, the ground fell still. The silence roared through his ears and he fixed his eyes on the entrance to the tunnels leading under the ground.

"I'm going in," he said after a few moments passed. "Anything I need to know?"

"You can't. It'll be able to sense you and will hunt you down. The only way Reyan's lasted so long I think is because she's able to shadow-travel. That's assuming…" She pulled a frustrated face. "Look, the only way I got as far as I did was constantly translocating back and trying to press forward again, but I can't go places I haven't been before with it. It can somehow sense where we are but everywhere inside is pitch black. It's swallowing any light we take inside somehow."

"I'll find her. Take this for me and keep it safe." He held out Reyan's talisman pouch. "Any weaknesses we've discovered since it caned me last time?"

"No, none. It's made of nothing. You can't affect it with gifts, can't injure it physically."

Kainen waved the pouch. "Please, when she gets out, give this to her and tell her she's free. I officially rescind her life-debt from my court and gift her that as the talisman of her freedom from her father. She's free, okay? It's important she knows that, and nobody can doubt it coming from you. Oh, and I told Meri that the court is at Reyan's disposal. If anything happens to me, the court is hers."

Demi stared at him, her mouth dropping open. He glared at her, furious at wasting time. The stilling of the land could mean anything and he strode forward.

Sannar raced up to meet them as they started toward the mountain tunnel, his auburn hair a mess and his robe flapping around his legs. Other Nether brothers rushed around the courtyard toting bundles of papers and shouting to each other, but Kainen only had one thing on his mind now.

"I need you to stand behind Reyan if anything happens to me," he added to Demi as she hurried at his side. "If she doesn't want the court, give it to Meri. If Diana absolutely has to have it, then I guess her, but keep a close eye on her. Absolutely under no circumstances is Ciel to get anything other than a slap. Actually, as Reyan's friend, you need to tell her he's toxic, way more so than me. She deserves everything and he's a complete toad."

He ducked into the cool, firelit gloom of the tunnel with Demi and Sannar immediately behind him.

"I will do all that, but you can't go down there," Demi insisted. "It'll kill you."

Kainen didn't falter, hooking left along the path he remembered.

"Why are you letting Taz go down there then?" he bit back.

"Because Taz's gifts are defensive. He can turn the

walls to liquid and seal them behind him, enough to confuse it and slow it down. That won't stop it for more than a few seconds though, but he can become animals too, fit through small spaces."

"Well mine aren't defensive exactly but I need to get her out of there."

Demi rolled her eyes even as she powered along beside him. She wouldn't stop him from going in and he was grateful for that.

I wonder if Reyan and I will ever have the kind of trust in each other like Demi and Taz do. I should have commanded her not to go in without me.

"Is there anything else I should know?" he asked.

The door loomed at the end of the tunnel and he stopped dead. Every second wasted was a second Reyan was in trouble, but he had to go in with his head not his heart or they'd both be in trouble.

"That's what I'm here for," Sannar said, already sounding breathless. "The nether is linked to the flow of origins, most know that, but to look into it any further we'd need to find the ancient language to even begin comprehending the text about the beast itself. All I recognised was something about trinity, or trio, I'm not sure."

"I've sent it to Milo to start interrogating just in case," Demi added.

Kainen nodded and faced the door.

"So get them both out and nothing else right now, got it."

Demi continued alongside him as he set off again,

determination rising.

"Agreed, no heroics. We're at a disadvantage no matter how you look at it, and the beast currently has all the power. But whatever Taz or Reyan did before you arrived, they seriously pissed it off."

Kainen's lips stretched, the smile appearing at the most inappropriate time.

"She's good at that," he said, stopping at the entrance to the pits. "But I'm better. If it's hurt her, I'll destroy it."

Demi managed a nervous smile. "She really has gotten to you, hasn't she?"

"I'm a reformed character, but I guess part of that was down to you and Arcanium. But mostly her." His voice cracked over the words. "I can't lose her, Demi, I can't."

"Then go get her, but be careful. Retreat whenever you have to before pressing on. It's the only way I made it out."

"Also, now probably isn't the time, but you should know one thing." Sannar pulled a reluctant face. "The visitor that was here right before the beast woke up, the one we discussed? I didn't think anything of it as they've been coming here a lot, but I read that there's a way of summoning a void of sorts. I don't know if it has anything-"

He stopped when he realised Kainen and Demi were both glaring at him.

"What does any of this have to do with anything?" Kainen growled.

Sannar grimaced. "Sorry. The visitor came often with a male escort, Lord Miel. He's a close friend of Lady Blossom and Lady Belladonna, and I think she said he's from another court. They wanted to do some research in the archives as well, and our Lady approved it. Maybe they found what I did, a way to summon the beast?"

"Pass it all to Milo," Demi said. "We'll investigate the moment we know the others are safe. Something more than mischief and Fae trickery is going on here, and Faerie's been too quiet for too long, which is never good. Go back up to the courtyard and make sure nobody else comes down here."

Kainen left them to it and turned toward the vast iron door. He didn't have time to worry about Blossom or what had caused the awful mess; only that Reyan was stuck in it. He heard Sannar's feet slapping a rapid rhythm on the ground as he obeyed, but Demi stayed beside him as they approached the door.

A loud thumping echoed through the tunnel, coming from the door.

Kainen threw up a warding as the smaller hatch door rattled violently and Demi took a couple of steps sideways to raise her own protection. He didn't care that even now she didn't trust him enough to share a warding just the two of them, but he did step in front of her all the same, even though as queen her powers probably way outstripped his.

He narrowed his eyes through the darkness, ready to attack if the beast came at him again. Not that he could do anything with his gifts against it either, but perhaps...

The hatch door burst open and clanged against the rest of the iron wall. Kainen squinted as his eyes fought for clarity against the gloom and a misshapen figure came into view.

Two figures appeared entwined together, one of them barely moving.

Kainen dropped his warding and dashed forward.

CHAPTER TWENTY TWO
REYAN

Reyan was vaguely aware of her head lolling against Taz's shoulder and his strength dragging her along. She hadn't exactly passed out, but she couldn't open her eyes and wasn't moving her feet to help either. It seemed unfair considering he'd protected her against the void, so she tried to rouse herself enough to stand.

She thought she could hear shouting, but as her consciousness resurfaced fully, she recognised a territorial snarl.

"Why does she smell like sick? What happened? She looks half dead!"

Taz's support disappeared, leaving her weightless for a moment before something else pressed against her chest. Someone draped her arms over a broad pair of shoulders. A waft of smoke and the tang of grapes filled her nose, dragging a smile to her lips.

Finally, Reyan managed to open her eyes.

She blinked against the soft amber light from the nearby firelight on the walls and squinted until she saw the face hovering above her. She grinned, relief so strong that she forgot all about the awkwardness between them and nestled her cheek against Kainen's chest.

Moments passed and her smile drooped. He wasn't hugging her back, not so much as laying a single finger on her. She frowned, embarrassed but stubbornly not wanting to let go.

"Sorry, is this inappropriate?" she asked.

He huffed somewhere above her head. "Apparently so, but trust me, I don't care about propriety right now. Are you okay?"

"What do you mean 'apparently'?" She lifted her head to see him standing with his arms raised in the air, as if he'd rather look ridiculous than risk brushing against her by choice. "Why are you holding your hands above your head?"

"I made a vow not to touch you last time we were here, and it appears to be physically binding until you release me. Short of holding your hand to realm-skip, I can't touch you even if I try."

"Oh." *Oh.* She grinned, relieved. "That could come in handy I reckon. Perhaps I should keep you like this-"

"*REYAN.*" His furious tone was drenched with anguish.

"Okay, okay. I release you from it, all of it. You can touch me wherever and whenever. Wait, but nowhere-"

She squeaked in alarm as his arms slammed around her waist. He lifted her clean off the ground, holding her so tight to him that she couldn't breathe. She noticed Demi pat him on the back as she passed and push something into the back pocket of his jeans.

Before she could ask about it, especially as Kainen either didn't seem to notice Demi touching him or for some mad reason didn't care anymore, he lowered her feet back to the ground. She stared up at him as he released her enough to grip her chin between his finger and thumb, glaring down at her.

"What have you done to yourself?" he asked, his tone furious.

She sniffed. "It's barely a scratch. But I figured it out! The void. I saw the word scratched on the wall and sent the shadows into it to get its emotions, but then I started getting visions of it like you do. My hand was glittering with the black smoke too. Did you send it?"

He stared down at her. "I don't think so, not that I know of anyway. Unless the court has claimed you enough to share itself with you."

"Oh. Well, it came when I needed it, so maybe the court wanted to give us a helping hand somehow? Anyway, it's not a beast, it's a void, and it fell dormant when I got the right words to soothe it. Nobody but a shadow-weaver could have done that though, not without being able to send the shadows in. Sorry, my brain's a bit scattered. Are you okay? Did you get your errand finished?"

She hadn't actually checked herself over and several parts of her skin felt sensitive and pained. But now that Kainen was holding her, she knew she was going to be fine.

"What are you doing to me," he muttered. "You drive me mad sometimes. I'll have a healer see to you but I need to ask something first. Are you absolutely sure you want to marry him?"

She frowned. "Marry who?"

"Orbs alive, how many proposals have you had that I don't know about?"

"Oh, Ciel?" she waited for him to nod in case she'd

missed a huge life moment somehow. "No, I don't. I'm only eighteen, and I've barely had my own life yet."

She couldn't help the thrill that rippled through her when his shoulders sagged noticeably beneath her arms, with relief she hoped.

"You're sure?" he asked.

"Why even ask? I told him no the moment we got back after you were last injured here, and I've been dodging him ever since. He even tried to corner me outside a bathroom but I managed to avoid him, or at least put him off for a bit."

"You've been dodging- but he said-" His expression darkened even further. "Forget that. Why don't you want to marry him?"

Reyan stared up at him in open-mouthed astonishment. Surely the letter had made it absolutely mind-numbingly clear?

Unless he didn't get back to the court to read the letter. Or hasn't found it yet. Or he read it and feels guilty for being the reason I'm here risking my life.

It would be so like him to realise that his behaviour had encouraged her to have feelings for him then feel guilty because he didn't return them and charge in to save her.

Perhaps he was worried and didn't want to bring up the letter until he knew she wasn't going to make a scene.

"You know why," she said eventually. "I told you why."

Confusion flashed across his face. "You did? When? We've barely had any chance to speak about any of it. Argh, never mind when. Tell me again."

Perhaps he wanted to hear it from her straight, no letter, no potential for trickery. Perhaps he simply wanted to be a gentleman and let her down face-to-face.

"Because I don't love him," she said carefully. "I was flattered sure, but then he did something really scary and I knew he couldn't make me happy. Besides, marrying him would only mean I'd walked from one trap into another." She took a deep breath. "Didn't you get my letter?"

"What letter?" His voice descended into a savage grumble. "And what do you mean something scary? What did he do to you?"

"I left a letter on your desk after we orbed, in your study."

Kainen grimaced. "I haven't been back since we spoke so I won't have seen it. What did it say?"

Oh. Reyan's cheeks burned and her mind swam with dizzying mortification. *I wonder if there's any way of getting it back. He'll be so curious about what it says I could even use it to barter for my freedom maybe.*

It was a silly idea, a letter in exchange for a person. Reyan flinched as Kainen lifted a hand and clicked his fingers.

"Meri, there's a letter on my desk. Can you pass it through?"

No!

Reyan tried to stand unaided, to step back, but she wobbled and Kainen only clutched her tighter so that she was pinned to his chest. She risked a glance at his face and recognised the wicked amusement flickering at the edge of his mouth.

233

"There's something in there you don't want me seeing, isn't there? Was it a 'I hate you and hope you get eaten by locusts' kind of letter?"

Before she could find some way of replying without letting on what the content of the letter actually was, Meri's voice radiated from the black smoke cloaking his fingers.

"No letter."

Reyan frowned, aware that Kainen stood watching the expressions brew and shift on her face, his matching hers.

"Where exactly did you leave it?" he asked.

"I tucked it in the pages of your notepad, an envelope with your name on." She needed to be sure. "Also, please don't actually read it."

"You hear that?" Kainen asked Meri.

Moments passed. It had seemed like a bold idea at the time but now she was mortified.

"Nothing there," Meri said with a huff. "I've checked the entire top, which needs a proper sort through by the way, shaken out the pad, even checked your drawers, which are disgusting."

Kainen had the decency to turn a shamed shade of pink, but Reyan shook her head. It should be a good thing for her that the letter was gone, but if Kainen hadn't been in his office, and Meri hadn't taken it for some weird reason, then who...

She gasped and Kainen dispelled the smoke, cancelling the orb-connection without saying goodbye.

"He saw me coming out of your study," she admitted. "Ciel, I mean. He was with Blossom but really interested in what I was doing in there, then he followed me to the bathroom. I had to give him the slip because he wouldn't leave. Do you think he went in and took it?"

Kainen swore, his black smoke curling in his eyes, glittering with the promise of wrath.

"He does have access," he said, his voice harsh. "I spoke to him on the way here and he didn't tell me a word about any letter, but he could have been in my study when we spoke. He also told me that you'd accepted his proposal, or he said you sounded like you'd changed your mind at least."

Reyan gasped. "What?! No, absolutely not. I never accepted, not once. I might have said we'll talk later, I had things to sort out, vague stuff like that to get rid of him, but I never said I accepted him."

Kainen took a step back even though he kept one arm at her waist to steady her. She finally met his gaze as he reached into the same back pocket Demi had targeted earlier and held up a small dark blue and lilac pouch between them. When she didn't take it, he tugged one of her hands free from around his neck and folded her fingers around the material.

"What is it?" she asked.

He bit his lip, his gaze furtive. He was nervous, which set her anxiety on edge.

"The token of your freedom. That's where I was earlier, or I'd have faced the beast with you. Or void, whatever it was. I bought your entire debt from your father. Now I'm giving it to you, along with the court's side of the debt, as a gift."

She gawped at him. "Why? Why would you do this? What's the condition?"

"No conditions. No terms. No expectations. I should have done it long ago. Should have offered it to you as payment for pretending to be mine to the royals, if not before. Now it's yours."

Reyan peeked into the pouch. A small baby tooth, a nail of *metirin* iron and a copper coin, all wrapped in a short blonde lock of hair.

"So, I can go anywhere?" she asked. "I'm finally free to do whatever I want?"

Oh, but I don't have any money. Never mind, I'll make money. Perhaps I'll contact the performers' guild, or I could even apply to Arcanium, or approach one of the courts for a job.

Kainen smiled, but as she stared up at him in wonder, his eyes were sad.

"You can go anywhere," he confirmed. "With anyone."

"Why are you doing this? You look like you've just lost a fortune. My father, did he take a lot from you? I won't be able to pay you back whatever it is for a long-"

"Don't worry about it. The thing is done. You're free with no debts outstanding. I owe you this much and I've lost nothing that I wasn't willing to lose."

She frowned, still confused. He'd set her free at some unknown personal cost to him, without getting anything in return.

Does he hope Demi might think better of him for doing a kind, self-sacrificing thing?

"What if I'd said that I did agree to marry Ciel?" she

asked, determined to sniff out any loopholes or tricks. "Would you still have set me free?"

She met his eyes, needing to see the truth there. She wasn't ready for the sheer pain radiating from those depths, the anguish that she thought so little of him.

"Of course I would." He tried to smile. "If you've changed your mind about him then I'll wish you well. I might have to threaten him a bit, make sure he treats you right, but you deserve to have whatever you want. Now your debt is paid, and I release you from being sworn to my court. You're free to leave as soon as we get back and you're healed."

He would have been willing to lose an awful lot to set me free. Because he cares.

Kainen didn't cry, not that anyone she knew had ever seen, but he'd shed tears when he was injured and thought she was marrying Ciel. He could have coerced her at any time during their fake engagement, used his illusion power on her to force compliance, but he never had. Even in the days of his father when the court ran much wilder and more savage, he'd never crossed a lot of the lines everyone else did.

This isn't about Demi at all. It's about me. Us.

Kainen was a good man and he somehow had feelings for her. When the emotions had surfaced she couldn't guess, but now that she had her freedom to go anywhere, leaving his court and him behind with it had lost almost all of its appeal.

She couldn't tell him that, not yet. She had her freedom unexpectedly and the last thing she wanted was to be tied to the court straight after, even if it was for good reasons.

This could be some rebound thing for him, and I've barely ever left the court. I have no idea what to do or what I want yet.

She couldn't do anything about the situation until she knew what she wanted, but she could do her best to bring them back to a less serious level.

A new start.

She glowered up at him.

"So are you saying you're throwing me out now? I know I wanted my freedom and I'm relieved it's finally mine, but I have nowhere to go."

He groaned, lifting his chin until his face was pointing to the ceiling of the tunnel.

"Orbs, no, that's not what I meant. You can stay as long as you like. In fact, I insist you stay as long as you like, a condition of your freedom."

She snorted. "You gifted it to me before setting any conditions, so no, you can't add caveats. But you will tell me why you're doing this for me."

The sheer joy of realising that he had feelings for her, real ones that possibly even matched hers, made her invincible. Her body might be suffering and her familial connections might not be any match for a court lord, but her mind sharpened until she could see the potential future paved clear ahead of her, one she would choose herself. Maybe, one day, it might even be a potential future ahead of them.

Okay, so my realisation came in a dingy firelit tunnel in some far-flung court, but at least I'll never forget this moment.

When he didn't answer her, staring down as if memorising her face instead of paying attention to her words, she reinforced her glare.

"Why are you doing this for me?" She jabbed a finger against his chest for good measure. "I insist you tell me."

A small sparkle of liveliness lifted the corners of his mouth as he looked down at her again.

"No."

"Tell me!"

He shook his head. "No, I won't. But I do have something you can help me with, obligation free, if you want. I'd pay you a going rate, but you're your own person now so you can decide."

Reyan frowned. She needed some time to get on her feet, collect some money. Where better than the court she knew like her own, with a boy she trusted and-

"What is it exactly?" she asked.

"The royals are returning." He at least managed a sheepish smile. "It's only for a few days, but there's always the threat of Blossom returning also, although they haven't mentioned anything yet. It would help me out a lot if you pretended to be my future bride for a bit longer."

She stared at him for several moments, the impish gleam in his eyes suggesting this wasn't so much about the royals or Blossom, even if he pretended it was.

Not wanting to give herself away, at least not until she could find and burn that embarrassing letter and tell him how she felt with some semblance of dignity instead, she hid her face in her hands to cover her smile.

"Oh no. For how long?" she mumbled. "And what is this going rate?"

When he didn't answer, she peeked through her fingers. His dark eyes swam with untapped emotion, fondness and something much deeper. She pressed her hands against his chest, pushing back gently. He let her but when her legs wobbled, he looped a firm arm around her waist.

"We'll discuss it back at the court," he said. "I'm assuming you're okay with me taking you back there to rest and recover, even if you choose not to stay long-term?"

"Yes, please. Maybe I can trade something for a room of my own now," she quipped.

He chuckled. "Stay in mine a while longer for the sake of the pretence. The court has to believe it too or the whole thing will have been for nothing. Wagging tongues cast long rumours after all. I can sleep in my study."

She frowned at that. He sounded exhausted, but perhaps they could avoid discussing it and fall into some kind of easy pattern for a while, spend some time feeling each other out.

"What about Ciel?" she asked. "Does he really think I somehow said yes? I thought I was very clear with the no. His response was too, not impressed. He got really angry with me before as well, scary angry. That's the only reason I said we'd talk later, to get rid of him."

Kainen's eyes swirled with something beyond darkness and shadows, a possessive fury that would have frightened her had she not known that she could trust him. Not just with her life, or her safety, but with everything. He was kind and gentle, messy and irritating, misguided on many things definitely, but above all he was good where it mattered.

"You leave him to me," he said. "No doubt he hoped to buy your debt himself and use that to convince you."

She shuddered. "Unlike you, the boy who seems to be going out of your way to look out for me today. Very selfless of you."

"You know, sweetheart, I think that's the nicest thing you've said about me yet."

"Don't get used to it." She flushed, amused. "But if you are in the mood to take me home, I'm not going to complain."

Kainen seemed to have the same idea and the nether brushed her face a moment later, his room forming around them. She breathed a sigh of relief to see it, sagging against him.

He's even offering to give up this room so I can have it, so I'll be comfortable. So I'll stay a while longer with him. But I need to be sure of some things first.

"Does it hurt?" she asked.

He frowned, supporting her across to the sofa and easing her onto it.

"Does what hurt?"

He fussed around getting her blanket for her from the armchair and she watched in bemusement. The lord of the Court of Illusions fussing like a nesting mother hen. Over her.

"When you were sick before, you mentioned it being torture to see someone you love happy without you," she said. "Does it get easier seeing Demi with Taz?"

He frowned at her for several excruciating seconds before his face cleared and he sat on the edge of the sofa next to her.

She tried to visualise leaving him and the court behind, and her emotions were mixed. She wanted to see more of Faerie, to go out and meet people and have some adventures, make some of her own choices. But then she imagined seeing Kainen happy with someone else like Blossom or one of his fawning courtiers. The mere thought of it hurt, her insides crunching the breath out of her.

"I wonder now if I ever truly loved her," Kainen admitted, tucking in the edges of the blanket. "I like her a lot, she's funny and pretty, but somehow seeing her and Taz together here, they fit. I don't think me and her would fit."

"Stop flapping, I'm fine," she said softly, tugging the blanket away from him. "It didn't hurt seeing her with him?"

Kainen shook his head. "No, strangely not at all. Even when they first arrived, when I started this fake engagement thing, I was so surprised to feel absolutely nothing seeing her, talking to her. I kept looking, waiting for some kind of delayed pining, but nothing. It's the first time I've actually felt a sense of freedom. Weird really."

Reyan sagged against the sofa.

Thank Faerie for that.

"Well, that's something," she said diplomatically. "At least you're not still in pain."

"I think I loved the idea of her, but it wasn't real. Real

is finding someone who challenges you, who makes you stronger when you're weak and lets you be strong for them when they need support. Someone you can't imagine daily life without, and you're somehow less yourself when you're without them, even if you can still physically do everything you did before."

Reyan smiled, seeing her own thoughts reflected in his words. He certainly challenged her not to smack him over the head half the time, but he was strong for her and she knew she could support him in return.

Maybe not yet though. I'm free and that's all I've ever wanted. There has to be time to enjoy it before I settle down anywhere.

"Like when there's a patch so dark it has no shadows," she offered, thinking of the void beneath the Nether Court. "You know the light is there, everything is as it should be, but there's that spot of nothingness that taints everything else."

He nodded. "Exactly like that. When you love someone, you'd rather hurt yourself for eternity to save them, and without them there's nothing worth the light touching."

She caught his eye, the intensity of emotions whirling strong enough that her shadows shivered.

Orbs alive, I'm screwed.

She shook her head and huffed to cover the seriousness, her heart pounding all the while. Despite being adamant about wanting to enjoy her freedom, the idea of leaving him behind bothered her.

"That's very dramatic." She gave him a disapproving look. "I know we're the Court of Illusions and all things dark, but sometimes nobody needs to get hurt and everyone gets to see everyone else smile."

He raised his eyebrows, amused. "And how would you fix it so everyone smiles?"

"A revel, of course." She shrugged, the idea delighting her immediately. "A masquerade. Use it to celebrate our triumph with the nether beast, and the royals visiting again, and to distract everyone from our pretences."

"Would you perform?" he asked. "At the masquerade I mean? You've already made an amazing pretend bride."

She snorted. "When you weren't being infuriating maybe. Would you want me to perform? Will I also get protection like I used to?"

"Yes, although I don't think there'll be anyone attacking you any longer." He bit his lip. "I sorted that."

She raised her eyebrows, her thoughts zooming to the pouch in her pocket, the proof of her freedom.

"My father?" She waited for him to nod. "Thought as much. Nobody else would see me as important enough to attack that routinely."

He scowled adorably at that and she couldn't help smiling.

"Either way, you will have all the protection I can give you, I swear it. Now and after whenever you decide to leave us."

"Okay then, I'll perform." She smiled, then realised it sounded like she was agreeing to leave as well. "Not happy to see the back of me finally?"

He lifted his dark eyes to hers, bewildered agony swimming on his face at the mere thought. She wondered how long it had been since he'd started showing his unmasked self to her, since he'd trusted her enough to reveal himself.

"No." He shook his head. "Not happy at all."

She raised her eyebrows. "You realise I haven't actually said I'd leave yet, don't you? I might decide to stay here forever, find a role for myself, settle down, find reasons to smile again. This court could do with some more smiles around."

She faked a smile, all teeth and taut lips.

"There's one," she said, pointing to herself first then to him as he started laughing. "There's two."

"You focus on the smiling then, sweetheart, and I'll have them arrange a masquerade for you."

She thought he'd retreat to his study but he sat beside her, wiggling onto the sofa until she curled her legs up to make room for him.

He clicked his fingers and started issuing orders into the smoke, the requests rolling so fast that Reyan couldn't keep track of all of them.

"You're making me dizzy," she grumbled.

She leaned forward to get up, then seethed in agony as her trousers brushed her knee.

"You're injured. You should have reminded me." He said it so huffily and she had the urge to giggle.

When he clicked his fingers, she thought he would be continuing his list of demands to the staff, but a first aid kit plopped onto his lap a moment later.

"You are not doing this yourself," she insisted.

He nodded. "Pants off or rolled up, your choice,

sweetheart."

The amusement in his voice told her he was teasing, but she conceded and inched up her trouser leg until the bloody mess was finally visible.

Kainen leaned forward with a wipe in hand.

"Ouch. This may sting."

She squeaked in alarm as he hooked her injured leg over his thighs, his hand hovering by her foot.

"What are you doing?"

He didn't answer as her boot came off.

"I can do this myself you know."

She made to grab the wipe from him but he grinned wickedly at her while removing her sock. She shivered as his fingertip grazed the skin of her ankle, but tried to keep her mind from fluttering away.

"Oh no." She struggled to sit up and he held the sock aloft. "We're not starting that again."

He threw the sock.

"Pick it up, now."

He grabbed her other foot to take off the second one.

"Don't you dare!"

Her second boot dropped to the floor and moments later the other sock sailed across the room.

"Pig!"

He rolled his eyes. "They're fine, sweetheart. I tell you what, I'll even tidy them up personally when I go past next."

"I'll believe that when I see it." She landed a kick against his thigh with her good leg. "Ha, I can kick you now. And punch you and slap you and spit at you. Take that."

"Stop kicking and let me sort your knee out."

She pulled a face. "No."

"Orbs alive." He groaned. "You're going to be impossible now you can argue back."

She grinned and swiped the wipe from him, dabbing gingerly at the edges of the knee wound.

"I always argued back. I just have way more freedom to work with now."

He chuckled and succumbed to handing her items when she asked for them until her knee was properly dressed and he went back to sorting out court things.

Reyan watched him, a restful calm settling over her as she yawned wide and snuggled into the sofa cushions.

I'll wait until the masquerade is over. Once we're not pretending for others, we can start to explore what's real for ourselves.

CHAPTER TWENTY THREE
KAINEN

Decking Reyan out in the Illusion Court's colours could have gone one of two ways. She could have refused as was her right, or she could have embraced them. Now, on the afternoon of the masquerade, Kainen still had no idea which option she would choose.

He had sent along a dress in that very theme for her that morning via Meri with a note pinned to it that read:

'A gift for my 'bride' in traditional court colours, and yes, I know I can't tell you what to do now, but I'm hoping you'll wear it and claim me as if I were really yours for pretence's sake at least. I promise the underwear wasn't my idea – Meri insisted.'

It had worked for Taz and Demi during the war, her wearing his court colours not the underwear bit, or so he guessed, and he hoped to borrow a dash of their luck by doing the same.

But since that night after they returned from the Nether Court, after he'd checked her knee, fed her and packed her off to bed to rest, he disappeared to his study and lost himself in masquerade preparations. Now, moments before the revel was due to begin, he was rattling with nerves.

"Lord!"

One of the young men from the kitchens hurried up to him as he walked through the main hall inspecting the decorations. "There aren't enough *pogberry* puffs. Cook asked if we can substitute with half *oia* berry ones?"

Kainen frowned. "*Oia* berry?"

His mind was still looping through the ceremonial tape he'd had to limbo under to get trailing lilac wish-blossoms delivered on time. Wish-blossoms because they were the rarest and most expensive flowers known to Faerie and his court deserved the best. Lilac because he'd researched late into the night to verify the true colours of a certain old family lineage.

"Cook can't order in any more *pogberry*?"

The man looked horrified. "The revel is tonight and the crowds are already gathering, Lord! We thought *oia* berry because it's Reya-, I mean the La-, the *future* lady's favourite."

"It is? Then go! Make oia berry ones. Quick!"

A vague stab of guilt caught him as the man dashed off in a panic, but Kainen wanted this revel to be perfect. He glanced around the main hall and recognised several of the faces now massing into a waiting crowd around the main hall.

He was right about the timing though. I should probably be glad Meri forced me into my outfit before letting me leave the study.

"Kainen, there you are."

He held in the groan with remarkable restraint, turning his head to nod at Blossom as she joined him and slid a firm hand into the crook of his elbow. Paranoid that Reyan would choose the moment to appear and assume the worst, he turned his body to face Blossom and slid himself free as smoothly as he could.

"Here I am," he agreed. "I've been so busy arranging the revel, I've barely had a minute to think."

Blossom nodded, the movement wobbling her impressive creation of hair, jewels and ribbons. Her dress honoured the Illusion court colours, a glittering, sequined swathe of charcoal fabric that slitted more than it covered. Nothing too scandalous for the reputation of his court, but the way she was leaning toward him to show the hint of silver bits underneath the dress suggested she knew exactly which bits dipped where.

She placed her hand on his arm, fingers tightening.

"Such an important role, leading a court. Are you sure your commoner will be able to keep up with the demands? She's hardly born to it. She may have saved the day at the Nether Court by all accounts, but such ancient entities can always be troublesome, or *reawakened,* some might say. She might not be so lucky next time and wouldn't that be a shame?"

Kainen heard the veiled threat there and forced every essence of rage down as far as he could. He knew the political dance all too well, and causing a scene now would only play into Blossom's hand. She saw him and his court as her rightful collateral given that she was meant to be his bride. Whatever links or involvement she had in the beast's awakening, her main purpose was revenge against Reyan. She'd been given the idea she should have him and his court, and now she couldn't understand why it wasn't hers. Next would come a less-veiled threat against Reyan, which would provoke him into verbally protecting her, inciting a fight further down the line.

But he'd been playing the game as long as Blossom had and against much worthier, more devious minds. Instead of reacting, he took a steady breath and fought back with every ounce of Fae malice he could muster.

"She may not be used to it, but her family line is an old one. I don't need to wed her for money or social standing, especially as she's friends with the queen already. So I can choose her based on her personality, which I find the most charming of any girl I've ever met. She's strong, brave and nothing like the pampered socialites with nothing between their ears that see their sole purpose as marrying well. Oh, no offense."

Okay, that one was probably going to cost him big at some point.

He smiled with devilish wickedness as that taunt sank in.

One hundred percent worth it.

Blossom narrowed her eyes in reply but her amused expression remained, mindful of the crowd always watching for any slight hint of drama.

"Charms are boring," she trilled.

He shrugged. "Clearly for both of us, although I did see you cosying up with Ciel a few minutes ago."

"Oh, he's a good boy. He was assisting me with an issue in my suite."

Either a personal one, or one far beneath what he'd

251

consider his responsibility.

Kainen had a sneaking suspicion that they were planning some kind of mutual revenge, but as long as they stayed clear of Reyan, he wouldn't have to invoke the wrath of a whole court against them.

He scanned the crowd and found exactly the distraction he was looking for.

"If you'll excuse me, lots to do. Enjoy the revel."

He bowed his head, more out of mockery than actual social necessity, then hurried over to Meri. The moment she caught his eye, she circled toward him with a disapproving frown. She tugged his rolled-up sleeves down and tweaked the sparkling black lapels of his otherwise charcoal grey jacket, then nodded.

"Good. Reyan should be out any minute now. Or should that be Lady now to the likes of me?"

Kainen's gut exploded into nervous fluttering at the mere mention of her.

"I'd probably just call her 'you' like you do to me," he quipped.

She raised one eyebrow. "You're nervous. Interesting. At least you finally made a sensible decision for once though. Although Faerie knows what the traditionalist bores will say about her. Then again, any reason to kick them out of court is always a plus."

Kainen glanced once again over the lavish collection of extravagantly dressed Fae surrounded by the finest decorations to rival the courts of either queen. He frowned at a mis-placed patch of wish-blossom, then wondered if he should have added lilac to the sparkling silver gems floating in the pool.

"Stop fussing," Meri muttered. "The place looks fantastic."

He nodded. The rocks of the hall had been chiselled into glittering sculptures, the skylights enchanted with fireflies to cast a gentle glow, the water pool fitted with miniature copies of the decks outside so that people could lounge under canopies on the water if they chose. Or close the canopies for privacy, if they so desired it.

No expense had been spared with wish-blossoms exploding from every available surface or the furnishings of charcoal grey with silver fabrics. All of the court's best artwork had been hauled out of protective storage.

Reyan wouldn't care about this finery, but given that Kainen had taken the liberty of including her family colours alongside his own, the statement had been made.

A throat cleared next to him. He ignored it until Meri gave him a savage nudge to the ribs and nodded pointedly to the main staircase.

Kainen looked up and butterflies exploded in his chest.

The charcoal-grey silk dress clung to Reyan's curves, fitted with a flared, layered skirt. Although he was charming when he needed to be and expertly well-dressed when the situation called for it, he knew next to nothing about the intricacies of women's fashion.

Whoever had made the dress didn't have his shortcomings in that area.

The silk writhed with colour, shimmers of court silver mingling with sultry swathes of dark blue and sparkles of lilac.

She's wearing it!

Beyond that, Kainen had no words.

Demi and Taz were due to arrive with a 'party', and any moment they'd materialise in front of him, but his eyes were fixed on Reyan at the top of the steps. He'd never been less prepared to host a function in his life.

Mutters broke out across the assembled court as Reyan started down the staircase.

Kainen glanced down at his charcoal suit lined with silver, wondering if he should have somehow made more of an effort, although the suit oozed secrets and shadows and fitted him like a second skin.

But Reyan, she was magnificent. Her hair was curled back with hints of black gems sparkling in the golden strands, and the dark silk draped over her figure, moving sensuously as she walked. She lifted her head as she reached the bottom and halted.

"This is where you go to her, stupid boy," Meri whispered helpfully. "Claim her before someone else does."

He had no right to claim her except in the name of pretence, at least not yet, but how he wished their pretence was real. He also had the vague idea that calling your court lord 'stupid boy' was probably punishable in some way, but he left Meri's side without a single reprimand.

As he walked toward her, he saw his own nervousness reflected in her eyes. He would be strong for her even though his insides were in knots. He stopped in front of her and held out a hand.

Her shadows wound around her legs and cuffed her

wrists, but he couldn't help smiling as they slid across to cover him as well. She took his hand, holding tight.

A mutual claiming, if only in my dreams.

"Not too bad," he murmured, wondering how he didn't sound like a total, shaking, lovesick wreck.

She shot him a disapproving look that hid her nerves from anyone who didn't know her as deeply as he now did.

"This took two hours and the hairpins are sticking in my skull," she muttered. "Don't test me right now."

Even as she spoke, a small smile flickered just for him, her eyes glimmering with amusement.

"Well, I meant the choice of dress actually," he winked at her. "You on the other hand are breathtaking."

He meant it and she knew it. Her eyes widened but luckily for him, Demi arrived in the midst of the crowd with several people he recognised before Reyan could call him on it.

"Welcome, my queen."

Kainen dropped onto one knee, his court copying him. A voice that sounded a lot like Beryl Eastwick muttered something along the lines of 'A girl could get used to this'. Kainen might have smiled at that, but the silk of Reyan's dress skimmed the back of his hand as she joined him in kneeling and he shivered. He almost missed Demi's insistence that they rise again. He clung onto Reyan's hand, pretending it was to help her to her feet.

"I'm pleased to be back in such merry circumstances," she said, her voice clear for the crowd. "Kainen, I believe you know the rest of my guests."

Kainen nodded, swallowing a catch in his throat. He

255

recognised the Eastwick sisters alongside the Hutchinson twins. He knew Milo too, big and burly-shouldered with a teetering pile of books in his arms. He seriously hoped nobody had mentioned his library, but Milo was probably planning to steal half of it already. And beside Milo was Ace.

Kainen hadn't spoken to Ace since the war, and remembered well the savageness of Ace's brother-like protectiveness over Demi.

Words fled now that he was faced with several people assessing him, judging him most likely based on the past. He flinched when a voice filled the massing silence.

"You're all welcome," Reyan announced. "The performance is due to start very soon, then the revel, so please make yourselves at home. Or the queen's quarters have been readied in case you prefer to watch the show in private from your balcony."

Kainen's chest swelled to the point of pain and he glanced down to find her smirking up at him. Playing her part to the letter.

Not the letter we never found though. I need to insist that she tell me what was in it one day.

He could have used his gift to compel her, but where would be the fun in that?

Running on pure instinct, he summoned a touch of his smoky magic to his lips and bent down to kiss her forehead. She froze as he temporarily connected their minds, but when he straightened up again she didn't protest or try to pull her hand away from his. Whether she was merely surprised by the action, or determined to act for the sake of getting the payment he'd promised her for pretending, he still wasn't sure.

Demi made motions to her friends, indicating they should follow her to the queen's quarters, and the crowd noise began to climb. Kainen forced a smile as the others passed him, amazed when they all nodded and said hello.

Only once they were walking up the stairs did he look at Reyan.

Thank you, he said into her mind. *I should have expected to see old faces, but it's been a while since the war.*

She grinned. *The all-mighty court lord caught off guard? Whatever will the court say? Oh, one of them wants to talk to you.*

Kainen glanced to the side, his insides twisting when he saw Ace waiting for him alone. He squeezed Reyan's hand and let go.

"I'll go and prepare for the performance," she said. Then with a wicked smile, she added, "make sure you don't miss it."

Kainen watched her go, the gentle swish of her dress giving far too many sinful ideas. Then he faced Ace and waited to see if he was in for threats or forgiveness.

"It's a relief to return in friendlier circumstances," Ace said.

Kainen nodded. "It's a relief to welcome everyone without having to hide anything. Whatever you see here will be what is, I can promise you that, or I'll have something to say about it."

Ace smiled then, the reservation draining from his eyes.

"The past is done," he said. "Demi's forgiven you and Taz isn't threatening to have you hung on the wall anymore, so we're good. I'm glad you were able to move on."

Kainen glanced toward the stage, although Reyan was out of sight now. He sighed.

"It's still new to me. I have no idea what I'm doing, and I reckon she thinks I'm a complete idiot most of the time. But this time at least it feels real, although that might be what finally kills me."

Ace chuckled. "Yeah that feels about right. I swear half the time Milo thinks my IQ is below the floor because I can't remember every page in some dusty old book nobody's cared about for centuries, but I wouldn't trade him for all the realms and worlds of Faerie. But don't tell him I said that."

"I won't, although I've had more than enough of secrets, but I promise that at least the illusions tonight are all above board."

Ace glanced over his shoulder. "Demi asked to speak to you actually before the revel. I'm not sure what about, but while the others are getting settled, she said she'd wait in your room."

"Okay..." Kainen frowned. "I'll go see her."

Ace followed him through the crowd and up the stairs, but to Kainen's surprise, when he opened the door to his bedroom, Ace disappeared into the queen's quarters.

"Hi, Kainen." Demi stood by the sofa. "Sorry to commandeer your room but I figured this would be better without the others interrupting. We're also making it top priority to keep you away from Milo as he's refusing to promise not to 'liberate' your books. I accidentally mentioned the fireplace and now he's got visions of ancient tomes being burned alive before he can save them."

Kainen slid into the room and closed the door behind him, leaning his back against it. Demi's tone was light and friendly but he had no guarantee this wasn't some kind of test of his honour. She eyed him for a moment before sitting in Reyan's chair.

"The Nether Court say the beast is calm," she said. "I have to speak to Reyan about what happened, although Taz gave me the basics, but there are still fluctuations in the human world to the prime world."

Kainen wasn't sure what that had to do with him, but he stayed silent as Demi sighed.

"I don't have as many contacts in Fae circles as I'd like, so I want to ask your permission to move through the court without having to be escorted, if that's okay?"

She wants to spy more like, or see how I'm doing things here.

He smiled. "You're the queen, as you've reminded me. You can do as you like."

"I want to be an FDP not on assignment for the next twenty-four hours though, not a queen," she huffed. "I know people will recognise me, but if they see you ferrying me about then it'll just add unnecessary occasion to everything and that makes people nervous."

Kainen held in the responding snort with valiant effort. If she thought she was in for friendly welcome and some honest chat over tea, she was unfortunately in the wrong court. But perhaps he didn't need to admit it right now.

"I get that. Go wherever you like, speak to whoever you want. My court is an open book. I can't promise they'll be fluffy or obedient, but none of my court would harm or insult you without me punishing it."

She nodded and silence fell. She made to stand up but this might be his only chance to ever be alone with her. He had to make the most of it.

"I'm sorry for everything I did. I know I've explained at a distance why, and that it had to happen on the queen's orders, but before that. I'm sorry, and I bitterly regret it now."

Demi's eyebrows lifted in surprise. "I somehow wasn't expecting that."

"Well, it's true. I can't compel you as a queen, or trick you or any of that. At least I don't think I can, and I wouldn't want to. I honestly mean every word."

She nodded. "I know. Thank you. I'd already decided to let that part of the past go, but I really appreciate the gesture. Besides, Taz is probably haunting the room as a fly or other small, winged creature right now, so you wouldn't get far if you had some mad scheme of revenge planned."

Kainen had to laugh at that, the image of Taz as an angry fly buzzing around lodging itself in his brain.

"Nothing we do is truly ever secret, is it?" he sighed. "The whole court knew I'd set Reyan free before I'd even done the necessary amendments to Meri's staff schedule."

"That was a kind thing to do."

Kainen shook his head. "It was the right thing to do."

He still hadn't figured out what to do about Ciel, who was at court but keeping a suspiciously low profile. Nothing had been said about Reyan's supposed change of heart and Kainen hadn't found any letter when he got back to his study. He had to assume Ciel had taken it, and although his blood burned at the mere thought of something so precious being taken from him, mostly he wanted to find out what it said so he could tease her with it.

"You deserve each other," Demi said, drawing his attention back. "I think you'll be worthy of her now."

He snorted. "If I can keep up. She can vanish into shadow and although it's my court and I should be able to find stuff easily here, she's surprisingly stubborn at disappearing when she wants to."

"Courts are funny things," Demi said with a smile. "They're given life by those who live inside them so it may be on her side. Perhaps the court has already claimed Reyan as its mistress even if you haven't. Perhaps it's helping her hide."

He froze. "What do you mean, if I haven't?"

"Oh, come on." Demi rolled her eyes. "The word-tangling, the vagueness? The way she was so awkward around you in the beginning. You didn't want to marry Blossom and panicked, so you pulled the first person you could grab out of the crowd who wouldn't give you too much trouble for it. Not that I blame you. I might have done the same."

Kainen bit his lip, cutting through the verbal fluff. "I don't know about the not too much trouble bit, but I'd claim her for real in a heartbeat if she'd let me. She's had so long being someone else's pawn though that I want her to choose this time. I haven't even said how I feel about her yet."

"You should tell her then give her space to decide. Don't confuse the issue by letting her think you aren't sure, or you don't care enough."

Kainen guessed Demi was being kind, but he knew the situation better than she did. He knew Reyan better.

"I'll have to do what I think is best, but thank you."

Demi frowned, her head tilting to one side as she regarded him. In that moment, he saw a young queen surveying a subject, reserving judgement. He guessed she would be keeping an eye on him and his court, even if she pretended otherwise, but instead of feeling stifled he found the idea oddly comforting.

"Anyway, it'll be time for the revel any moment." He opened the door and stepped through it into the hall. "You're welcome to linger in here if you want the peace, but it's best enjoyed with friends."

"Then I hope you'll join us to watch it."

She smiled as she approached. A real smile, for him, because she would consider him a friend from now on. He couldn't help the bashful look, honoured and feeling beyond lucky at a second chance.

"The decorations are nice," she added, shooing him out of the doorway.

His smile turned wistful then. That had been another stupid idea of his, one that would go unnoticed by everyone but him.

"They're Reyan's family colours alongside mine. Her lineage was an old, traditional one but it fell into ruin not so long ago. I'm not even sure if she knows what her family colours are, but oh well, it was a sappy idea."

Demi patted his arm and opened the door to the queen's quarters. He thought he heard a momentary buzz zip past his ear and couldn't quell the smile that rose up, although he couldn't see past Demi enough to check if Taz was already in the room or not.

"She may surprise you, but if you tell her straight then she'll get the message for sure."

He frowned. He wouldn't be telling Reyan how he felt, not until he was sure that he wasn't influencing her decision one way or the other. But that didn't stop him giving her options in other ways. He revelled in the wicked smile that crept over his face.

"I'll join you for the performance," he said, taking a step toward the main hall. "But I should check in with the performers first."

Demi laughed. "You go do that."

And what better way was there to cement inter-court relations, he thought to himself, *than by obeying his queen and going to wish the girl he loved luck?*

CHAPTER TWENTY FOUR
REYAN

Sinking into her shadows while the rest of the court were giving her a wide berth, Reyan felt the subtle emotional shift around her.

She looked up in time to see everyone bobbing their heads as Kainen strode up the steps to the stage, but he only had focus for her.

As he drew near, she saw the impish darkness twirling over his lips, the playful sparkle that made her insides flutter dwelling in his eyes. In the gloom backstage, his suit whispered to the shadows and she gulped to see him looking like sin with his brown hair swept back.

But she wouldn't back down to him. She was a performer now in her own right, not a member of his court.

Okay, so the other performers showed respect, but that doesn't mean I have to.

She met his gaze as he stopped in front of her, close enough that a deep breath would brush her chest against his.

"Not honouring your patron?" he asked, his tone crooning to the deepest parts of her.

"I'm not sworn to your court any longer," she murmured. "I'm a performer being paid to perform, and you'll respect me as such."

Fizzles sparked over her skin when his lips wisped

against her ear a moment later.

"How true that is." His fingertips caressed the back of her hand as he lifted it to his lips and kissed it. "A reminder then, that I'll be paying you the same as the other performers, plus enough for you to survive until you find the life you want, one you deserve."

Is that some kind of hint? Enough for me to survive, what, away from the court? Is he going to expect me to leave after this?

They hadn't seen each other since the night they returned, and she'd woken to find his bedroom empty. His flirtatiousness now was the same attitude he usually showed as part of his court lord persona, and she had no way of knowing if this was a performance for his court, or a slow easing of her expectations away from any real future with him.

Ciel's words about Kainen being fickle circled her mind, and who knew him better than his oldest friend? Perhaps he'd been swept up in the danger and excitement of their assignment, but now they were back to reality he'd changed his mind.

The mere thought of him wanting her to leave hurt but she shook her head, determined to hold her own. She would have to be doing that either way now that she didn't have the court's protection. If he'd decided his attention had waned, or he only wanted one thing from her, then at least she could now walk away without penalty.

"Performance payment only please." Her tone came out more primly than she intended. "If I'm going to make a life for myself, I'm going to earn it."

He raised his eyebrows and dropped her hand.

"You accepted the role of my 'bride' and as discussed, there will be payment for that also."

He sounded almost annoyed she was challenging him, but she couldn't fathom the switch in his behaviour as he pulled her close so that she couldn't see his face. She stood tense in his arms with her pulse pounding.

"I'm still lord of a court," he whispered. "I'd advise you that it isn't wise to reject fair payment, or we might need to clear the debt some other way."

Okay, confusion or not, that was definitely suggestive.

He whirled away before she could reply, storming past the curtain and down the steps into the crowd. Reyan pressed a hand to her forehead.

Did he want her to take the payment so badly so he could tick her off as a responsibility sorted?

Or did he hope that by setting her free and insisting on it, she'd want to hang around the court a while and prove she had feelings for him?

But if she did, what would he expect from her after that little performance? A convenient arrangement, or something meaningful?

She'd seen the truth of his feelings when he came to find her at the Nether Court, but then they'd both been under stress. He'd been worried about her, but was that down to guilt? He'd avoided her since returning too, which suggested that was definitely a possibility.

Oh orbs, does he expect me to be just some kind of convenient bedmate or pretend bride to be wheeled out whenever it suits him now?

So distracted by the idea, she didn't notice anyone approaching until it was too late.

"Well, you may think you've won."

Reyan forced her irritable groan to stay inside her throat. She failed somewhat and a soft growl came out instead, but she had to hope it was lost in the pre-performance mayhem backstage.

"Lady Blossom." She kept her tone even. "I don't think of him as a prize to be won, if you mean Kainen. He's his own person and can choose whatever and whoever he likes."

Blossom rolled her eyes and leaned closer.

"Everything is a prize to be won, or a battle to be conquered. And we're far from done fighting this one out."

Reyan shrugged. "If you say so. Kainen made his choice but feel free to keep plaguing him. Desperation is very fetching on you."

Blossom snarled, her face contorting with hatred moments before she remembered where she was. The mask of amusement settled once more but didn't reach far enough to cover the malice in her eyes.

"There will come a time where you'll regret making enemies. Everyone will regret it soon once things are back the way they should be."

"Reyan!" Meri bustled past. "You're up."

Blossom gave her one final glare and swept off, the wide folds of her dress swishing aside props and causing absolute carnage to the performance preparations.

Reyan couldn't do anything about Blossom, or Kainen, or how any of them felt, or Kainen's confusing changes in behaviour, but she could choose to be brave now either way. She stepped onto the stage, aware that the applause from the balcony belonging to Demi quickly faded when nobody else in the audience joined in.

Performing is one thing I can do, Kainen or no Kainen.

She sank into the shadows and threw every effort into her performance, dancing, bending and disappearing, reappearing and gliding across the stage.

The court's audience seemed to forget they'd been bitching about her for the past week, gasping when she leapt and tumbled and faded before their very eyes.

Without thinking, she formed herself into heart formations, splitting her shadows to absorb and manipulate the light.

The thought that Kainen might be setting her free because he felt guilty about taking on the debt danced in her head, and he'd never actually said he wanted her to stay at the court for him. Not once had he hinted that he'd ever consider dating her once the pretence of their engagement was over.

My family's ruined anyway, so I probably wouldn't be seen as a fit match for a court lord, even if he did fancy me. Him not fancying Demi doesn't mean he automatically wants me instead.

She worked her mind into knots as much as she contorted her body through the familiar sequences. Blossom's threat about things being 'back the way they should be' worried her. Unsure if it was a personal threat or a subtle admission of Blossom's allegiance to the remnants of the Forgotten, she focused instead on finishing her routine.

Silence reigned for several moments after she finished, but then the applause filled the hall. She took her bow and happened to glance up.

Kainen stood at the very edge of the queen's balcony with everyone else in the queen's entourage still seated around him. The moment he caught her eye, he crooked a finger at her, a summons.

Anxiety pounding at the thought of what he might want her for, she hurried along the edge of the crowd as the next performer began and padded up the stairs. She only made it a few steps before Demi appeared.

"I wanted a quick word," Demi said, already heading into Kainen's bedroom.

There was no sign of Kainen, but Reyan followed Demi inside and shut the door behind her. Demi took the chair that Reyan now thought of her own, so she perched on the sofa, unnerved to recognise the pattern as similar to the first day they met.

"I wanted to ask you what your plans are," Demi announced.

Reyan frowned. "Um, I'm still unsure what my options are, so I don't really know. Why, are you hiring?"

"I wouldn't have thought you'd need a job." Demi gave her a mischievous smile. "Or is the marriage on hold now?"

Reyan bit her lip, not willing to admit the truth, not without Kainen's agreement. After a few moments, Demi laughed and slouched back in the chair.

"At least you're loyal to him. I know there's no actual

intention between you, nothing official anyway. Oh don't worry, you were both very convincing. I would have faked a marriage too at the thought of marrying Blossom."

She pulled a face and Reyan had to laugh, a touch hysterically now the relief was pounding through her. It still didn't solve or clarify anything about Kainen, but at least she wasn't having to hide things from her queen any longer.

"Before I forget, Blossom collared me backstage before I went on," she said. "I don't know if it means anything, but she made a couple of threats then said something like, 'once things go back the way they should be'."

Demi sighed. "Another mini tick in the box then. We think she's still in contact with Belladonna, her sister who defected to the Forgotten during the war."

"Not exactly stunning evidence though."

"No, but Sannar admitted that Blossom's acquaintances have been visiting the Nether Court a lot, asking to do research on various things, and that she might have been there when your void woke up."

Reyan opened her mouth to reiterate her previous point but Demi sank back against the chair, so she kept her silence instead.

"Taz then confirmed that she has always had a summoning gift, which Sannar said is one known way to wake the nether beastie. So, we can't prove anything yet, but she's on our 'one to watch' list."

"So, does this mean the Forgotten are still active?" she asked.

Demi sighed. "I doubt they were ever inactive. Several

of their followers would have slunk away after the Battle of Arcanium, and it's been suspiciously quiet after the Battle of Queens."

"Kainen said similar. There are still traditionalists here at court too, although they hide it well now."

Demi rubbed both hands over her face, her head dropping back against the chair.

"The traditional beliefs will take a generation or more to change, especially in those who benefitted so strongly from it. I wish I could wave a magic wand but gifts can't do much to change the actual minds of people."

She looked over to the beds then the balcony with a grimace, no doubt remembering what had happened to her in the same room before she became queen.

"Minds do change though," Reyan said gently. "They grow. He's changed."

Demi's expression softened and she sat up straighter with a smile.

"There's still hope. So, don't worry too much about Blossom's threats for now, unless she actively moves against you."

Reyan laughed. "Maybe she'll forget all about it and Kainen and I can dissolve our 'engagement' quietly without a fuss sometime soon. How did you know though that we weren't real? Is it a royalty thing?"

Demi gave her a withering look. "Let's say that I've learned to recognise when people are being pig-headed and kidding themselves."

"Excuse me?"

"While you were performing, a man approached Kainen

from a neighbouring balcony. He asked if Kainen was in a position to hire you out, "nudge nudge wink wink", those were his words. Apparently, he'd been asking your father for a while now."

Reyan shuddered. Kainen had given her freedom, but even if he hadn't, she couldn't imagine him agreeing to such a vulgar request.

"What did Kainen say?" she asked.

"He insisted that you were your own person now, and therefore able to decide who you want to hire yourself out to." Demi's lips twitched with wickedness. "Then he wraithed the man in smoke and had him run himself into the nearest wall until he apologised and swore never to so much as go near you without your consent."

Reyan gawped in amazement. She guessed if the man had access to one of the balconies then he had to be fairly important, or the guest of someone important at least. Kainen's behaviour was perfectly acceptable considering she was his supposed bride in the court's eyes, but he and she both knew it was all a fake, so why be quite so violent about it?

Demi chuckled. "You might find that happens to anyone who so much as approaches you, because Kainen is clearly madly in love with you."

Reyan blinked. "He is?"

Love? Surely that can't be true. Maybe he has some feelings, fancies me possibly a bit or is fond of me after what we've gone through, but love?

"Did you notice the colours decorating the hall when we arrived?" Demi asked.

Reyan frowned. "The court colours of charcoal and silver. Oh, and some dark blue and lilac as well. I wondered about that."

"Do you remember the colours of your own family lineage?"

Reyan shook her head even as an image flashed into her mind. A dark blue and lilac pouch. A lock of her hair curled around a nail, a coin and a tooth.

She gasped, her mind racing over the possibilities.

Kainen had set her free at what was no doubt great personal cost to himself.

He'd decorated the main hall not only in the court's colours but also apparently her family's, despite the ruin attached to it.

He'd told her that he felt nothing for Demi anymore, but spoke of the torment of someone who didn't love him back after all the times she put him down and called him names.

He didn't approach me at all after we got back, but Demi says he loves me. She's queen so maybe she can lie, but why would she?

As realisation dawned, Reyan shot off the sofa and started to pace.

"He set me free because he loves me?" she asked, waiting for Demi to nod before charging on. "He'd rather be unhappy on his own if it means see me happy elsewhere, like with Ciel."

Demi nodded again, her amusement filling the room with sparkles of energy that zinged off the wall like tiny fireworks.

"But he never told me how he felt!" Reyan huffed,

irritation climbing. "Because he didn't want me to feel indebted to him, or love him because I owe him."

"Yep, sounds about right. But I have a suggestion that might solve everyone's issues."

Reyan hovered in the middle of the room, uneasy. Suggestions were often obligations with strings attached. When she didn't answer, Demi sighed.

"You're young and you've had zero freedom so far. I'm guessing you want to get out and see stuff before settling down. I know I did, or thought I did. Continue pretending to be his fake bride for now. I'm sure he won't object and it solves the whole 'find him a suitable marriage to unite the courts' thing. But work for me as well."

Reyan stared at her. "What?"

"Work for me. No allegiance to my court, no swearing in. The Lady of the Illusion Court supporting the crowns with trust for some simple assignments. Your shadow skills would come in handy, and I need someone to visit the Nether Court and keep an eye out there. You've already proven yourself helpful to them, so saying you're checking the beast is still asleep would be believable."

Reyan hugged her arms around her middle. Demi was offering her a better solution that she could have possibly imagined. The dreamy part of her wanted Kainen to admit his feelings and ask her to stay. But Demi was right about her being young and needing to stand on her own for a while first.

"Would he let me do that?" she asked.

Demi laughed. "Would he refuse you anything right now? He's petrified you're going to leave and he'll never see you again. This way you're still a part of his court but you get your freedom without strings elsewhere. Win win."

Reyan nodded, her mind racing. She couldn't find any loopholes, which worried her slightly, but she trusted Demi. She trusted Kainen too, and if she wanted to keep their fake engagement going he'd probably see it as a help to him more than to her social advancement.

He's trying to be so noble that he's getting in his own way. What if I'd decided to leave, he'd have let me go without saying anything?

"He wanted me to choose for myself," she muttered, unable to contain her rising irritation. "Or maybe he didn't want to risk me using him for his court connections or a safe place to stay now I'm on my own. As if I would. He could have just told me. In the name of Faerie, he's an idiot!"

As Demi howled with laughter, Reyan stormed toward the hall door. She threw it open and thundered into the queen's quarters, startling all of Demi's friends.

"Where is he?" she demanded.

Everyone was giving her odd looks, but she didn't care.

"If you mean Kainen, he disappeared straight after your performance," the man who'd wanted to talk to Kainen earlier said. "Taz went after him."

He won't be able to hide from me, court lord or not.

She squeezed past Demi and shot off down the hall. It only took a few steps before she was striding back toward his bedroom and across the floor to the bathroom door.

"Okay, court. I know I'm in a mood right now, but I

really need to talk to him. I promise not to smack him, much. Please give me whatever room he's in."

She waited a moment, but something must have happened as muffled voices started echoing from behind the door. One definitely sounded like Kainen but even in her mood, Reyan didn't want to interrupt if he had to do something important.

She waited instead, insides roiling with anxious excitement.

He might not want me. Demi might be wrong. But I need to tell him how I feel all the same. I need to know.

She counted to thirty the moment the voices ceased. Thirty agonising seconds. Then she summoned her gift, dissolved into the shadows and crept underneath the door.

CHAPTER TWENTY FIVE
KAINEN

Kainen powered out of the queen's quarters and into his bedroom the moment he summoned Reyan up to them. Demi wanted to speak to her, and it was none of his business what about.

He stormed through the multi-door to his study before anyone could catch up to him and slammed it behind him.

Reyan's behaviour on the stage before the revel confused him. She'd been all smiles and support in front of the others, but faced with him alone, she'd turned hesitant.

He couldn't do anything about a girl that didn't love him, but he could punish those who had tried to screw her over. And him.

He snapped his fingers. "Ciel."

In moments, his 'oldest friend' appeared in front of him.

"Yes?" It was a snippy tone, no doubt in the hope of riling Kainen into dismissing him again so he could hide what he'd done.

"I've been hearing stories," he said. "Reyan has told me she never intended to marry you, and that you've been trying to scare and intimidate her. I made myself clear. She was to choose."

Ciel snorted. "And she chose you?"

Pain flashed through Kainen's chest, but he ignored it.

Oldest friend, what a joke.

"Not that I know of, but she has my protection either way."

Ciel's eyes widened. "My friends told me that her father had already sold her debt, but the old man wouldn't say who to. It was you, wasn't it?"

"Why are you so surprised?" That hurt too.

"I never thought you'd have the emotional depth to actually make an effort for another. For your family name perhaps, but for a girl with no family title and no society standing? Not even any money?"

Kainen shrugged. "I told you how I feel about her. I'd do anything to keep her safe, so I bought her debt and set her free."

Ciel's jaw dropped, incredulous fury massing across his face.

"You set her free?! What did she bargain with?"

"You assume I asked her for something in return. I didn't. I'm glad I was right about you not deserving her. As it is, she is my main priority, her and my court. And you, Ciel Whitewater, are no longer a part of either option."

Ciel's eyes widened. "You'd banish me from your court? I'm sworn to it and you protect me, and by extension my family."

Kainen pressed his hands into steeples over his desk, holding Ciel's gaze.

"I can't banish you, not without risking you retaliating. But if you're to stay with all the pleasures that life at court offers you, there will be conditions."

"What conditions?"

A sheen of sweat broke on Ciel's brow. He feared his brother, Kainen knew. The sadistic man who had taken over from their outcast father and wanted to have influence in all levels of Faerie life.

"You will swear never to go near Reyan again, not unless she approaches you first for something. You will swear never to do anything that would be against the interests of me, Reyan or my court, or the royalty that we support, or any of our families or friends ever again."

Ciel's lips twitched, pinched thin as he raced through how this would affect him.

Kainen waited, until Ciel finally nodded.

"I swear."

"Good. Now get out."

Ciel disappeared through the door, leaving it swinging in time for someone else to enter through it. Kainen held in the groan, wanting only to be alone with his morose thoughts.

"To what do I owe the appearance?" he asked, his tone short.

Taz stopped in front of his desk, one eyebrow raised.

"Nice. I overheard what you said to Demi earlier."

Kainen guessed he meant earlier in his bedroom and nodded.

"I figured as much. I don't want enemies, unlikely as it may seem. This court takes all my effort and running it alone pinches sometimes. So I won't cause any trouble if that's why you're here."

Taz shook his head. "I'm here to give you a piece of

advice."

"Let me guess, stay away from Demi?"

Kainen knew he was being belligerent, but he couldn't help it. When Taz started laughing, it did nothing to improve his mood.

"No, she's more than capable of handling herself these days. She's right though, we do need to forget the past. I simply wanted to tell you that two halves are often better than one whole."

Kainen blinked back at him. "I… okay? I'm not sure what to take from that, I'll be honest. You mean in terms of the courts? Is there some kind of rift between Demi and your mother?"

"No, it's not about the queens or the realm. Demi and I are individuals that work better together is what I'm saying, rather than us seeing ourselves as being a completely fixed unit."

Kainen stared at him. Had Taz somehow hit his head at some point? Was there going to be some kind of claim of 'inter-court damages to the king consort's sanity' flying his way?

Taz grinned to see him confused and walked back toward the door.

"Figure it out," he suggested, shutting the door to the hall behind him.

Kainen slumped over his desk. Irritating, infuriating man. He had no idea how Demi put up with Taz, but clearly she found something in him to love.

Reyan might have said the same about me if she loved me. How many times has she called me arrogant, or a pig.

Or 'love'.

She'd only called him that once, but the thought of it made his heart ache. He hadn't asked Ciel about the letter either and couldn't bring himself to summon the man back.

No doubt the letter was either full of Reyan saying how he was an arrogant pig, or that she was leaving him after the assignment and begging him to let her go.

He almost didn't notice the subtle darkening around the door until the shadows were creeping across the floor. A leap of excitement that she'd come to see him flared, then the memory of her hesitancy backstage flashed through his mind.

She's changed her mind and come to say goodbye.

"I'm not in the mood," he called out.

The shadows took shape, the darkness filtering into colour until she became whole and visible. And sat herself right in front of him on his desk, the silk of her skirts settling over her legs and his. As she wiggled to get stable, her hips knocked a bunch of papers and he huffed.

"Now who's being messy."

She laughed. "Ouch, why so grouchy?"

"I just had an infuriating conversation that made no sense with the king consort, who has no eloquence whatsoever, so I'm not in the mood for games."

"You?" Reyan smiled. "Not in the mood for games and trickery and deceit? I'm shocked. What did he say?"

"Something about him and Demi being two halves instead of one whole. I think he was just trying to frighten me off."

Reyan raised her eyebrows. "Or he was trying to tell

you something. I can see what he means, he and Demi are both individuals with their own skills and strengths, whereas a person can't be one whole of everything, it's too stressful. Rather than them trying to balance everything on one head, split the load and balance it on two. But why are you not at the masquerade after you spent so much effort planning it?"

When she said it, Taz's advice made some kind of weird philosophical sense, but Kainen was too busy aching from how close she was to listen to it, so he zoned in on the question instead. Perhaps if he answered her, she'd leave him to his sulking.

He shrugged. "Like I said, and again for the third time now, I'm not in the mood."

"Why not though?"

"I spoke to Ciel and said I'd send him away for lying to me about you. I couldn't do it, so I made him swear not to harm or act against any of us. Or ever approach you unless you did it first, but he didn't seem overly bothered. I don't think he was ever my friend, which smarts a bit."

It did, but the biggest pain he felt was because of her. She had finally sought him out and he was determined to do the right thing and let her choose, but the agony of hoping for a maybe that might never come was killing him.

"You have friends," she said softly.

He snorted. "What, you? I don't want you as my friend."

She should have been hurt, or at the very least mildly rejected. But as her shadows crept toward him, she was smiling. She clearly didn't get what she was doing to him, so he pushed away from the desk and sat back in his chair, craving space from the subtle scent of her.

"Everyone's enjoying themselves." She leaned closer. "You could be too."

He glowered at her. "Why aren't you masquerading and enjoying yourself then? After everything you've been through you of all people deserve to."

This is killing me. Why won't she get the hint?

Reyan shrugged airily, swinging her legs back and forth so her heels made an annoying thud against the desk and her bare toes brushed against his calves.

"That's newfound freedom that you gave me, I'll remind you. As it is, I know what I want but I don't know if it's possible."

He looked up at her. "Is the money I gave you not enough for it?"

"I don't even know how much you gave me," she said with a laugh. "Not even sure I have an account for it to go into. But no, it's not a money thing."

"Oh. What do you need then? Other than a pair of shoes clearly, and some sensitivity training."

He would give her whatever she asked for without expecting a single thing in return, or try to get it for her at least, but he couldn't help the wounded attempt to snap at her.

Instead of getting huffy or offended, she let her shadow wrap around his arm. It reached across his body, but moments later she flinched back. She could feel his emotions and his cheeks burned at the thought. Not only was he suffering, but the girl he loved would know his pain. Pity him for it.

Why won't she go away?

"What do you need, Reyan?" he asked again, his voice soft and pained as he begged her to be kind and leave him be.

She smiled and slid off the desk.

"Demi's given me a task to do at the Nether Court," she announced. "That puts us in a bit of a predicament."

"Does it?" He didn't care about predicaments.

She nodded. "Well, assuming you still need me to pretend to be your future lady for a while. But I have a plan. Actually, it's sort of Demi's plan, but it's a good one."

No doubt the plan involved Reyan's freedom. Perhaps she wanted him to give her sponsorship and vouch for her so she could move to the Nether Court and stay there instead. He pushed past the aching in his chest, the sinking inside his gut that begged him to tell her how he felt. He couldn't put that kind of pressure on her.

"And that is?"

She smiled. "I'll honour the agreement and we keep the pretend engagement going while I'm away. Nobody can argue about me obeying a queen's command. But I have something I need to ask. A favour."

He lifted his head then, gazing at her. When she didn't continue, her gaze fixed on him, he shrugged.

"And?"

She bit her lip and he yearned to lift his hand, to stroke her cheek. His family would be horrified to see him pining after anyone, let alone someone without the appropriate social standing.

"I want to stay part of the court, if you'll let me. We keep the fake engagement going, and I'll come back whenever I can but also see more of Faerie for a while on Demi's payroll. She thinks the enemy aren't really gone and my skills could help her work out who and why. Maybe once I've done that I'll be ready to come home again."

His insides halted their plummeting so hard he missed a breath. He gulped and ended up spluttering like an idiot as he ran through her words one last time.

"You want to stay?"

She frowned. "If that's okay. I know I'm not from a great family or anything, but once our agreement is over I can still be useful. Go back to cleaning or whatever. For the moment though Demi wants me to search the Nether Court for more information, keep an eye out. If I find stuff fast I might be back sooner rather than later."

She doesn't want to leave. He stood, surprising both of them. *She wants to continue being my fake bride and call this home, and I'm giving a great impression of myself by sulking in my lair.*

"You'll always have a home here if you want it," he said, not thinking his words through, not caring if he hung himself on them. "I'll escort you to the Nether Court too when you leave, make sure they know to look after you properly."

She snorted, her expression lifting into amused disbelief.

"You don't think I can look after myself?"

He hesitated. She could, he knew that. But she shouldn't have to. He'd have a word with Sannar in private, a friendly chat with a few suggested warnings laced in, just in case.

"Of course you can. But it doesn't hurt to have a court lord on your side. I thought you were here to ask me for sponsorship actually."

"Why would I..." her face fell. "Oh. You thought I wanted to leave for good? Why?"

He shook his head. "We haven't chased you off yet and that's what matters."

He didn't want to admit the reason, but given her sudden refusal to look directly at him she might have guessed why.

"Come on then," he said, holding out his hand, his heart leaping with hope. "We have a revel to host."

She smiled, still darting diffident glances at him, and grasped the outstretched fingers. He led her across to the study door and threw it open onto the corridor nearest the main hall, letting the onslaught of revelry and noise swirl around them.

He held her hand tight, knowing the time would come soon to let her go. She had to have her own adventures after so long in service, he saw that now. Demi saw it too and had handed him the most beautiful olive branch he could ever have hoped for. Reyan would get her freedom and some experience in Faerie, but he would get the chance to do everything in his power while she was away to remind her that she belonged at the Court of Illusions. That she belonged with him.

He grinned.

Then she can realise that I'm helplessly and irrevocably hers in her own time, as it should be.

CHAPTER TWENTY SIX
REYAN

Reyan woke in her own room with a surprising sense of contentment. She stretched in the wide bed and wriggled her toes under the covers. The revel had gone on late into the night and the early morning, but when she walked back to Kainen's room without thinking, he'd stopped her outside his door.

"It's probably not a wise idea for you to continue sharing my room for the moment," he'd said, grinning all the while. "I don't want you assuming I have sinful intentions, not unless you want to invite them. I have however come up with a clever idea to avoid people being nosy about our sleeping arrangements."

He let them inside his bedroom and strode across to the bathroom door. When she was beside him, he'd opened it with a flourish.

Reyan had stepped past him into a large bedroom with a wardrobe and green furnishings that matched those in his room. It had a low wooden table with two puffy armchairs, a bookshelf and another door.

"That bathroom over there will just be a bathroom, no magic door," he added.

Reyan didn't bother investigating the bathroom, spinning around in the centre of the room instead with confusion on her face.

"You added me my own room?"

He nodded. "You'll have to enter and exit through mine, and we can work out a complicated series of knocks if you like. One for the coast is clear, two for 'I'm not wearing any pants'."

"Why would you have to knock to say you're not wearing any pants? Why not just put on some pants quick?"

She'd wanted to hide the sheer bewilderment, to cover how touched she was that he'd thought of her.

Now she woke in her own bed with her own privacy and it was the most delightful feeling. Someone had even moved her pile of *Carrie's Castle* books into the bookcase. They looked small and insignificant with so much empty space around them, but Kainen had said she could call the court her home as long as she wanted.

If I can keep this room, I'm never leaving.

She found her meagre collection of clothing in the wardrobe and slid into leggings and a long shirt. With boots on, she hesitated a while then chose a delicate scarf in the same green shade that decorated their bedrooms to wrap around her neck.

It was as much a statement to him as to herself. She would leave for the Nether Court, but that would be temporary. She'd be coming back.

When she got to the door between her new room and Kainen's, she lifted her hand, a smile tugging at her lips. Remembering the pants debate from the night before, she knocked once. For a moment, she thought he wouldn't answer. Then the door swung open and he smiled at her, his eyes dredged with sleep.

Or at least, she might have taken more notice of his sleep-dredged eyes if he hadn't been standing there bare-chested.

"Oh, did I sleep late?" he asked with a yawn. "Come through. Have you had breakfast?"

She shook her head and he snapped his fingers.

"Breakfast to my room please, for both of us."

She noted the 'please' with approval and decided not to comment on the socks lying by the nearest armchair. Resisting the urge to pick them up, she sank onto the seat instead.

"Demi mentioned saying goodbye," she reminded him.

He nodded, pulling on a t-shirt. She breathed a tiny sigh of relief. Deciding to take the Nether Court assignment was partly because she wanted to see something outside of the court and her father's house. But mostly, her feelings for Kainen were swelling too strongly and too fast, evidenced by the burning cheeks at the innocent act of seeing a bit of extra skin on him.

If we spend some time apart and we still like each other when I get back, then maybe we can see what happens.

"Is the room okay?" he asked.

She smiled. "I mean, it's not the dorms. Nobody screaming at me to hurry up in the bathroom or trying to convince me to trade my chores for necessities. I don't know how I'll cope."

He chuckled and sank onto the sofa, his feet up on the table. She wrinkled her nose but he noticed the look and grinned wider.

"You're nagging me in your head, aren't you."

"Little bit, yeah." She glanced meaningfully at the socks on the floor beside her.

He sighed then, flopping back. "I'm going to miss that. I will try to practice vanishing my socks while you're away. Did Demi give any indication of how long?"

"Not really, just to scope out the tunnels that haven't been investigated. I think she wants me in there before they have a chance to hide everything."

"You have to be careful."

She laughed. "You worried about me?"

It was more of a taunt than anything, but his face turned serious as he nodded.

"Little bit," he echoed.

Uneasiness filled the air between them but she swiped a strand of hair behind her ear and tried to laugh it off.

"The courts are all friends now, so I doubt I have anything to fear from them."

Kainen frowned. "Sannar seemed very interested in you when we first met him. Not that I... you know, but he might try to use you for his own ends."

Is he jealous? She tried not to smile at that.

It was ridiculous to think she might have a court lord interested in her in any way, shape or form, let alone two. Although Sannar wasn't a lord, by all accounts he ran most of the Nether Court single-handed, and Reyan guessed his interest in her wasn't romantic in the slightest. No, he wanted someone who could quell the threat from the void, which she'd done. He might also be interested in trading on any friendship she had with the queen, but she got the impression he was a nice enough person to deal with.

"I thought we agreed I could look after myself?" She sat up as the food materialised in front of them. "I hope the food is as good there as it is here though."

She leaned forward and hovered over the tray.

"Did you plan this?" she asked, pointing to the two bowls of ridiculously sugary cereal.

Kainen grinned. "Nope. I'll pay for a dental visit though if you can prove that was the cause of any issues."

"More likely my sugar levels are going to explode and I'll be grumpy for days after."

He grabbed his bowl, his eyes shining with devilish delight.

"That's perfect, then the Nether Court won't want to convince you to stay."

Reyan rolled her eyes even as her emotions gave a ridiculous flutter inside her chest. The shadows looped over her skin, climbing up from beneath the chairs and quivering in excitable response.

She managed a single spoonful before a shiver in the air deposited Taz and Demi in front of them.

"You really should knock," Kainen huffed.

Demi grinned. "No point. We're literally dropping in to say goodbye and check everything's still agreed."

"I'm ready to go," Reyan said. "I'll try to be as methodical as I can, and I'll orb message you any details I find."

"Great, thanks. We're going home to plan chasing out some of the socials and our attack plan for the Forgotten in case they're massing again. Hopefully we can also work out what the link is to the Prime Realm, if any, and what woke the beastie."

Kainen put his bowl down and tapped his fingers on the back of the chair. Reyan tried not to take any notice of Taz eying the socks beside her, but the urge to vanish them to the laundry kept rising.

"I don't know much about the nether side of things," she admitted. "But I did hear a legend once that the human world and the Faerie realms all originated from one point of magical existence. Maybe that's this Prime Realm and something's going on there that's spilling over?"

Demi grimaced. "Knowing my luck, we'll have two enemies to deal with."

"Positivity, Sparky," Taz teased. "Come on, Milo's probably been buried by the amount of paperwork he's written up while we've been away."

Demi groaned and pressed her hands to her forehead, but she shot Reyan and Kainen a rueful smile. As Taz grabbed Demi's hand and they disappeared again, Kainen sat back with a sigh.

"I suppose I should get you to your assignment," he said.

Reyan nodded. She shovelled a few more mouthfuls of cereal in and went back to her room to get her bag. With the few changes of clothing she owned and half the *Carrie's Castle* books in tow, most of her belongings were spoken for.

She went back through to find Kainen decked in a leather jacket and boots, his arm outstretched toward her.

"Take this," he said.

She caught the nerves in his voice, the shadows tensing around her as she drew close to him. Hanging from his fingers was a sparkle of silver.

"What is it?" she asked. "I don't have anything to trade for stuff, other than favours and I'd rather avoid that if I can help it, at least until I can get myself settled."

Kainen rolled his eyes, irritation flashing across his face.

"It's not a trade or something to owe favours for. All Ladies of the Illusion Court have worn it. It'll act as a status symbol to anyone who might want to challenge you, not that they should dare."

"Because I'm just that scary?" she asked, unnerved.

Accepting the necklace let alone wearing it seemed to signify something much more serious between them. Sure, they were acting their way through the fake relationship, but fears of losing it or breaking it had her mind racing.

"No, because they'll have an entire court at their back. Whether you take this whole thing between us seriously or not, you represent our court now. A sleight against you is also against me and our court, and I won't be taking it easy if anyone opposes you."

A not-so-subtle rivulet of darkness crept into his voice, the reminder that he was born to a court that dealt in secrets and dark corners. Reyan bit her lip and bundled her hair in her hands, holding it high and turning her back to him.

"What if I lose it?" she asked. "Or it breaks?"

She could barely breathe as he stepped close behind her, his fingertips skimming her neck and sending shivers over her skin as he threaded the necklace around.

"I'll buy a new one. It's not what it is, it's what it represents. To all the eyes of Faerie, you're mine until you decide not to be."

Reyan stepped forward the moment the necklace dropped against her skin, her fingertips ghosting over the onyx pendant woven with silver.

"I'll do my best not to disgrace the court then," she said. "Or you."

He grinned. "Do your best to disgrace us a bit, sweetheart. We have a dark and dangerous reputation to uphold after all. Then again, you're so sensible you'll probably find the information for Demi immediately and not have time for any adventures at all."

He looked so happy in that moment she couldn't help laughing. When he held out his hands, she took them and ignored the tingling as her shadows wrapped around their wrists.

"Ready?" he asked.

She nodded. "Ready as I'll ever be. Also, I've always been drawn to the dark and dangerous things, but it's time for me to explore my own."

"Your own dark and dangerous things? Consider me officially intrigued. I want to know all of them."

She stuck her tongue out at him as the black clouds of his power started gathering around them. There would be time for them in the days to come, but for now it was finally *her* time.

She grinned. "You'll have to wait and find out for yourself."

ACKNOWLEDGEMENTS

Huge thank you to every reader who has joined Kainen on his redemption journey!

To those who've shared on social media, done ARC reads or just given me compliments about the book to keep me going, you are AMAZING and I love you all.

To my family and also my writing family as always, your support means everything to me –Debbie Roxburgh, Anna Britton, Sally Doherty, Marisa Noelle, Emma Finlayson-Palmer, Katina Wright, Alison Hunt, Maria Oliver, the amazing ARC readers (who have caught so many printing blips it's not even funny…) writing Twitter, everyone who joins #ukteenchat, the WriteMentor crew, libraries and schools who took a chance on the Arcanium series, shops that are still stocking the books and giving this indie author a chance to reach more readers, and to the readers who will find these books in the future.

THANK YOU!

ABOUT THE AUTHOR

While always convinced that there has to be something out there beyond the everyday, Emma focuses on weaving magic realms with words (the real world can wait a while). The idea of other worlds fascinates her and she's determined to find her own entrance to an alternate realm one day.

Raised in London, she now lives on the UK south coast with her husband and a very lazy black Labrador who occasionally condescends to take her out for a walk.

Aside from creative writing studies, an addiction to cake and spending far too much time procrastinating on social media, Emma is still waiting for the arrival of her unicorn. Or a tank, she's not fussy.

For the latest news and updates, check the website or come say hi on social media:

www.emmaebradley.com
@EmmaEBradley

Printed in Great Britain
by Amazon

32716300R00172